THESE SILENT WOODS

ALSO BY KIMI CUNNINGHAM GRANT

Fallen Mountains

Silver Like Dust

THESE
SILENT
WOODS

A NOVEL

KIMI CUNNINGHAM GRANT

MINOTAUR
BOOKS
NEW YORK

First published in the United States by Minotaur Books, an imprint of
St. Martin's Publishing Group

THESE SILENT WOODS. Copyright © 2021 by Kimi Cunningham Grant. All rights reserved. Printed in the United States of America. For information, address St. Martin's Publishing Group, 120 Broadway, New York, NY 10271.

www.minotaurbooks.com

Designed by Omar Chapa

Library of Congress Cataloging-in-Publication Data

Names: Grant, Kimi Cunningham, author.
Title: These silent woods: a novel / Kimi Cunningham Grant.
Description: First Edition. | New York: Minotaur Books, 2021.
Identifiers: LCCN 2021015903 | ISBN 9781250793393 (hardcover) |
    ISBN 9781250793409 (ebook)
Classification: LCC PS3607.R3629417 T48 2021 | DDC 813/.6—dc23
LC record available at https://lccn.loc.gov/2021015903

Our books may be purchased in bulk for promotional, educational, or business use. Please contact your local bookseller or the Macmillan Corporate and Premium Sales Department at 1-800-221-7945, extension 5442, or by email at MacmillanSpecialMarkets@macmillan.com.

First Edition: 2021

10 9 8 7 6 5 4 3 2 1

For Dad

Like a bird that wanders from its nest
Is a man who wanders from his place.

—PROVERBS 27:8

I am larger, better than I thought,
I did not know I held so much goodness.

—WALT WHITMAN

THESE SILENT WOODS

ONE

Something wrong, I can feel it: a sting pricking the skin and stitching inward.

A dream, maybe. Memory. Both have brought me their share of grief. I force open my eyes, the slightest tinge of gray seeping through the curtains. Not yet day. But light enough that I can make out the silhouette of her curled on the little bed beside mine, blanket tucked to her chin and wrapped tight around her small legs. Finch, sleeping. Safe.

Sleep pulls, a mighty and sinewy force.

But— Outside the cabin, movement. Something scuffling past the window. A struggle. Thump, death cry, distress.

Up now, Cooper. Get up.

I kick the covers off, sit up. Grab the headlamp, strap it to my forehead. I slide the Ruger, already loaded, from under the pillow next to mine.

Finch rolls over and sits up. She rubs her eyes. "What is it?"

"Stay here."

I slip out of the bedroom. In the main room, I grab the shovel that's always resting against the door, its metal handle propped beneath the doorknob. Slide the top lock, unhook the bottom one, the wooden door tight and moaning as I yank it.

Outside, still dark, the sun not up but coming, the woods gray and the trees, looming in shapes: dark sentinels, soldiers. All these years and still everything always comes back to that. War.

I flash the light around the yard, looking. Most likely just an animal, I know that, but last week we woke up and one was gone, a fat Neptune hen that strutted around like she owned the place. Poof, gone. No scat, no prints, nothing. Just a small hole dug under the fence. Well. Fox, coyote, raccoon, fisher: despite my good efforts to safeguard the place, the girls are an easy meal for any of them, and depending on how much time has passed, how long it took me to wake, the whole flock could be wiped out, all four of them, and then we're in real trouble because we've lost our one and only guaranteed source of protein. Which is not a spot we can afford to be in, once January comes and the snow hits.

Something in the coop, I can hear him thrashing. A low growl. I pound on the metal roof the way I do to get the hens out when they're on the eggs and don't want to move. The sound thunders down and the whole structure shudders like the roof's about to cave in. The thing scuttles out just like the hens always do, wobbles quick down the little ramp and into the grass. I shine the headlamp and see the eyes glowing, a menacing yellow-green in the dark. Raccoon. A bird in his mouth, limp. Smart little devils, that's what Aunt

Lincoln always said. And mean. He snarls and shows his teeth and lunges toward me as if to say, Go ahead.

Which I do. I open the gate and take the shovel and knock him good over the head and then again, *smack smack smack,* until he lies still and even though I'm sure every ounce of fight in him is gone, I keep on hitting him. I know there's a meanness in that, striking him all those times, but sometimes a thing inside of me flashes, dark and despicable: it's there, it's part of me, and on occasion it lurches forth and can't be held back. The hen twitches, the raccoon's jaws still tight around her neck. I use the shovel to pull her free and somehow she is still alive so I hit her too, once, on her tiny head, hard enough to knock that little brain of hers right loose and crush the skull. I kneel down and shine the light on her. Finch won't be happy about losing one of our girls. Neither am I, but Finch—she'll take it personally.

"Cooper?"

I startle: her voice in the darkness.

"Told you to stay in the house, sugar."

She has always had a way of moving undetected. Which is what I've taught her. How we live. Most kids, they lumber through the woods, kick up the leaves, chatter and scare everything off but the thrushes. Not Finch. Mostly this is a good thing, with us needing to hunt for food and live in quiet, but sometimes she does it and catches me off guard, like now, out in the yard and the dark, and me thinking I was alone, no audience to observe the dirty work of doling out death.

She stands beside me, her palm on my back. She puts her hand on my jaw and moves my head to shine the light on the chicken. "It's Susanna," she says.

I pull her onto my lap.

"You hit her." She shivers, nothing but her pajamas on and it's December and cold, the yard glistening with frost. She tucks her bare feet onto my knees.

"She was suffering." We have gone over the ethics of the woods. We live it every day and have since she was a baby. You do not kill something just to kill. But also: you relieve suffering when you can. "She would've just lay there and died slowly, so what I did, hitting her, that sped it up is all. Helped her along."

Finch pulls away, kneels down and strokes Susanna's black and white feathers. She's a Barred Rock, a pretty thing as far as chickens go. Me, I'm doing calculations and hoping she was one of the hens that was three years old and didn't lay every day. We like our eggs. Need them. Come winter, with less sunlight and the hens' productivity tapering off, we already won't get enough.

Behind Finch, the woods burn purple red and then the sun pushes up out of the horizon. All the saplings and pines, the sun stretching its arms and everything bright and bathed in light and throwing new shadows, the world coming alive. I squeeze Finch's hand.

"I don't want to eat her," she says, wiping her face with the sleeve of her top.

"Mmm." Deep down I'm pondering a chicken dinner in the Dutch oven, rarest of delicacies. Potatoes, carrots from the root cellar. Oh, the thought of it.

"It wouldn't be right," Finch says.

"No?"

"Cooper."

"If you say so."

"And can we bury her?"

"Sure. Behind the cabin. After breakfast."

She hops up and we stand looking over the two dead animals. "But not the raccoon," Finch says. "I don't want to bury him. He took what wasn't his. He stole."

I want to tell her he was just hungry, but I don't. Sometimes a person knows something, but they just don't want to hear it; I get it. I scoop the raccoon onto the shovel. Fat, heavy thing, but funny looking now, with his flat head. "I'll take him down over the hill. You want to come?"

She shakes her head. I look around, scanning everything. The red hand pump for the well. The clothesline with my blue flannel shirt and two of Finch's, one yellow and one pink. The stack of wood on the porch. The dwarf apple trees, no longer heavy with fruit. Everything normal.

"Put the skillet on to heat, would you?"

She nods and bounds off for the cabin.

I check the outhouse before I leave the yard because it has always been a place that makes me nervous—far from the house, someone hiding in there maybe—and the thing is, two days ago Finch and me were out scouting and saw footprints by one of our hunting blinds. Too big to be Finch's and too small to be mine. Which means someone else has been around, on our land. Well, not ours, technically. But ours in the sense that this parcel of ground is the place we call home. No other sign that we could find, plus they were a good ways off from the cabin, but still. Footprints.

Finch is eight now. Eight years and 316 days. Which makes her 3,234 days old because there were two leap years in there. I wonder sometimes whether parents keep track of their children's days, and I bet they don't. At least not the way I do, a line for each day in my notebook. I remember before I was a parent, overhearing fathers talk at the grocery store or a restaurant, and someone, maybe the waitress or something, would ask the kid how old they were. And usually the kid would answer, if they were old enough. But more than once, I saw the father answer wrong, a year behind or something, like there was a birthday party in there that he'd missed, and the kid or sometimes the mother would correct him. Not me. I've kept track of the days and I am grateful for each one because if there is one thing I have learned in this life, it's that it can all end, fast. I know, too, that it will. End, I mean. One way or another—Finch and me and the chickens in this quiet pocket of woods—our life out here will not go on forever. It's a thing I don't like to think about.

I walk two hundred yards into the woods, to where the ground dips down and the trees quit and the land opens up a bit. I give the raccoon a pitch and he lands next to an autumn olive with a thud and the leaves above shudder and shake free, showering down white like a blessing. Scavengers will find him there soon. Vultures, crows. Maybe coyotes, maybe a bear. We have them all and sometimes the coyotes sing at night.

On the way back to the house I kneel and grab a handful of white clover. Brush the frost off with my thumb. We'll throw it in with the eggs this morning. Good nutrition and Finch likes it.

In the yard the hens are still all riled up from the raccoon, squawking and rustling about their enclosure. They are sensitive creatures, feathers ruffled easily, if you know what I mean. I talk to them soft and low. "Girls, it'll be all right. Cooper's got your back. I came out as soon as I heard the noise. I took care of that mean old critter and he won't be back. Now settle."

We will probably get no eggs today on account of them being stressed, but we have three from the day before, in the red bowl on the counter.

Inside, Finch has the cast-iron skillet on the cookstove, heating up. She sits on the couch reading a book.

"You all right?"

She looks up and there—flash, memory, a seething wound. Cindy, Finch's mother. Like seeing a ghost and I love it and hate it at the same time. Her blond hair and her green eyes, those are Cindy's, no doubt. That in and of itself has always seemed to be some sort of revolt against the probabilities of genetics: my dark hair and brown eyes should've won out. But it's also the way she looks at me, the way she walks, toes pointed out, the way she winds her hair around her pointer finger. All of it, Cindy's. Her expressions, most of all. How Finch could have and be those things when the two of them only knew each other for four months.

"I'm a little mad at you," Finch says. "For what you did in the yard." She looks away.

I pour a teaspoon of canola oil into the skillet. Measure it because we are always rationing, always keeping track. Tomorrow, December 14th, Jake—my buddy from the Army, he owns the place—should be here with supplies. His annual trip and frankly, the highlight of our whole year. But every year at this time, I'm sweating a bit. Thinking about what it would mean for us if he doesn't show up. We'd need to expand our hunting, maybe dig out the traps in the loft of the cabin. Most troubling of all, we'd need to go out and get supplies.

It could happen, him not coming, and I know that; it's always lurking at the edge of my mind, me and Finch at the start of winter without ample food. The snow piling up, the roads unpassable. I pluck an egg from the red bowl. "I'm sorry about Susanna."

"It's just that maybe we could've nursed her back to health. Maybe she would've been all right, if she'd had some time. If you'd given her a chance."

"No, Finch. That raccoon had her by the neck, and it was broke, I saw how it was bent." I turn from the woodstove and look her in the eye. "Maybe it would've taken a while, but she wasn't gonna make it, sugar."

"Well," she says quietly, "I don't see how that makes it right, what you did."

I crack two eggs and drop them into the skillet, edges turning white, hissing, lifting. I sprinkle the white clover and add a dash of salt. "Sometimes what's right isn't all that cut-and-dried, Finch. Hate to say it, but it's true."

She stretches her legs out onto the little green trunk we use as a coffee table and then snaps her book closed. She walks the book over to the bookshelf in the corner and slides it into place—tidy little creature, Finch is, with the books organized by genre—and then spins to look at me. She saunters over, mouth twisting to the side. "But you always say there's a right and wrong, and you have to do what's right," she says, peering into the skillet. She looks up at me. Those penetrating green eyes, wanting an answer.

But. This house with two rooms and four blankets, an old table, a bookcase. We have a kettle, a Dutch oven, a cast-iron skillet. A sink with a little window that looks out over the long dirt road that leads here. Two shelves above the woodstove. A small and insulated world for both of us, and there is a simplicity to it that makes it difficult to explain the complexities of life. The unreliable and often shifting line between right and wrong. The truth is, sometimes Finch probes for answers that I simply cannot give her, not because I don't want to, but because there is too much to explain. She has never known anything but this cabin, the woods that hold it. It's the life I chose for us. Well—it wasn't so much a choice, I guess. It was the only way.

Let it suffice for me to say this: sometimes bad things happen and you're unprepared and you make choices that seem good to you at the time, and then you look back and wish there were things you could undo, but you can't, and that's that.

I flip the egg and the yolk sizzles.

"Jake will be here soon," I say, hoping to divert her attention.

She grins. "I know. Tomorrow."

I look at my watch: a Seiko, doesn't need a battery. Nicest thing I've ever owned, a graduation gift from Aunt Lincoln. Thirty-three hours. Maybe thirty-two if he times it right and misses the traffic. We'll hear the engine, first: a low purr against the whisper of pines. We'll see the truck emerge, the silver hood gleaming in the sun, the branches that hang over the road, lifting like a drawn curtain. He'll pull into the yard, quiet the engine. He'll climb from the truck, use his arm to lift the bad leg, wince as he stands. He'll lean against his cane and grin, that wide smile, his mouth the only part of his face that made it through the blast unscathed.

Finch will run to him. Throw her arms around his waist and nearly knock him over and he'll throw his head back and laugh and carry on about how big she's gotten since he last saw her.

Finch and me will unpack the supplies, load after load. Up the steps, across the porch, into the cabin. We'll have venison stew, open the front of the woodstove, listen to the fire crack and spit. Once Finch can't stay awake any longer, we'll lean into the night and sit in the living room and Jake will ask about our year, and I'll ask about his health, and we'll laugh and for a week everything will feel good, almost.

Jake will be here and we'll be all right.

"You got your gifts all ready?" I ask Finch, although I know she does. They've been ready for weeks.

"Yep. A bone knife, some pressed violets from last spring." She nods toward a pile on the countertop. "And," she adds. "My cardinal." Finch is quite the artist, and her sketch of a cardinal perched on a branch is one of her best pieces yet.

"Good," I say. "What do you say we bury Susanna after breakfast, then we'll split some firewood and stack it out back? Snow will be here before you know it. Less than a month, I bet."

Finch looks up, her eyes brimming with excitement. "My sled."

I split the eggs down the middle and scoop half onto Finch's plate and half onto mine. "Your sled."

Last year, Jake brought one, but we had a light winter, weeks and weeks of sleet and ice but not one good snow.

I grab an apple from the bowl and pull my pocketknife out and slice it down the middle. I set the plates on the table. "Breakfast."

Finch climbs onto her chair. "I'm gonna make a cross for Susanna, to put at her grave."

"There's some twine in the chest."

"I'll need my hatchet. And can I use your pocketknife?"

"If you're careful."

Finch pushes the egg around her plate. "You think this one was hers?"

Finch and her impossible questions. Why does lichen grow on trees in this part of the woods but not in the other parts? Why do chickens have round eyes? Do you think Emily Dickinson was lonely?

We have four chickens. Three, now. Twenty-five percent chance it was Susanna's. "We can say it was hers if you'd like."

Finch nods and scoops a bite of egg onto her fork. "Her last gift to us."

"Thank you, Susanna," I say.

"Thank you, Susanna."

After breakfast we head out back with the same shovel that ended poor Susanna's life, blood still on the bottom of it. I try to wipe it off in the grass but it's already dry. We go about digging a small grave. I place Susanna in gently, with reverence for Finch's sake, then scoop the dirt over her body and pat it down. Finch recites a poem that she has recently committed to memory. This is on account of the bookshelf in the main room of the cabin being chockfull of books. Some are almost two inches thick and thus provide quite a bit of reading. Hans Christian Andersen, Walt Whitman, Ovid. She has read them all. Jake's father was a literature professor, so I guess you could say what we read here at the cabin is rather highbrow. Which for some reason strikes me as funny since that's the last word anyone would ever use to describe the life we live out here, let alone me. Finch reads and rereads and learns and memorizes, and the truth is, she is now quite a wealth of information regarding *American Literature Before 1900,* which is the book she waded into last spring. Two thousand five hundred sixty-four pages and the print is so small it gives me a headache if I read for too long. Anyhow, I suspect it's not normal for most eight-year-olds to be reciting Emily

Dickinson or Anne Bradstreet or Walt Whitman, but that's what Finch has been doing for half a year now.

"'Nothing can happen more beautiful than death,'" Finch says. Whitman. Believe me, I love Whitman, but this is unbearably morbid from the mouth of a little kid. "Susanna, you were brave and beautiful and you gave us eggs."

"Amen."

"Say something, Cooper. Something besides amen."

Finch doesn't remember, but this is not the first time the two of us have stood graveside together, and even though it's a chicken this time, I can't help thinking about it. About her. Cindy, who, if things had turned out different, should've been my wife, who nearly was. I tilt my head to the sky, sun up now, no clouds at all, nothing but blue and the white streak of one jet, inching across the expanse. "Susanna, you were a good chicken, and I'm sorry you had to go like this, and I'm sorry for hitting you with the shovel, but it was better than a long and painful death." I glance at Finch, who has her eyes pressed tight, and who wrinkles her nose at the last part, still doubting my decision. "Amen."

"You could've done a poem," Finch says, squinting in the bright light. She puts her hand up to shield her eyes and look at me. "A poem would be a better way to say goodbye."

I reach out and tousle her hair. "I'm gonna split wood now."

She holds her hand out. "Knife, please," she says, and I slide it out of my back pocket. "I'm gonna start on a cross."

TWO

Eight years out here and aside from a few snoopers, the only real trouble we've had is Scotland. Our neighbor downriver, so he says, though truth be told, my only confirmation is a line of smoke lifting from the treetops on cold days. Shortly after we got here, he came drifting into the yard, quiet as a ghost. Just appeared. It was August, and the leaves were thick on the trees so if I set Finch on her blanket in just the right spot she could be in the shade, and then I'd move her when the sun shifted west across the sky. She was a baby, then, just learning to sit on her own.

"You're not Jake," he said, and he was there, ten feet behind me. I'm telling you: I never saw him coming, never heard a rustle of leaves, a stick breaking, nothing.

Well. I decided right then and there I couldn't be Kenny Morrison anymore. Not sure how I had the presence of mind to realize this, me not having seen another human being besides Finch for over a month and him showing up and startling me so bad I could barely think, but I did. We were living in the tent because at that point Jake still didn't know we were here, and I felt funny about just moving into the cabin without asking. The only books I had were Aunt Lincoln's Bible and her *The Book of North American Birds* and I guess that's what made me think of birds. Birds on the mind. I went with Cooper after the Cooper's hawk. If you know anything at all about birds, you will recall that the Cooper's hawk is a stealthy creature: sometimes it will fly low to the ground and then soar up and over an obstruction to surprise its prey. Anyhow, that's who I've been ever since, to Finch, too. She's never called me anything else.

"This is private property," I said.

"Yeah, but it's not *your* private property, is it?"

The way he said it, cool and sharp. Just looked at me. And when he looked, it was like he could see beyond the outside and into the inside, like he knew about the things that were there that I wished were gone.

"Who the hell are you?"

He spat to the side and tobacco clung to his chin. He wiped his face with his dirty sleeve and said, "Don't appreciate the foul language or the tone. Uncalled for. I'm Scotland, your neighbor. I live that way." He nodded his head in the direction of a cliff south of here, where the river began to bend. When he turned I could see he had an AK-47 strapped across his back. An AK-47!

"You hunting?" I asked him, nodding to the weapon. I figured, I'll play dumb, like I don't recognize what kind of weapon it is, make him think I'm just a stupid camper out here in the woods. But what I was really thinking is, what does he need an automatic weapon for? And why is he here? And what would I do if things turned ugly and the answer, I realized, was anything. I had no limitations, no lines I wouldn't cross because hadn't I already crossed all the lines I could think of? Thing is, once you've crossed, once you've done almost everything you ever said you wouldn't do, you also lose your sense of assurance that you won't do those things again.

He laughed at my question, a growly, throaty laugh, like he was thinking I'm an idiot, and that's exactly what I wanted. "Yeah," he said, his teeth ugly and gray. "Hunting. Bunnies."

I told him I was Cooper and then I pointed to Grace Elizabeth and said, "That's Finch." When I said the word, "Finch," she looked at me, like it really was her name, like she recognized it and it was right. And even though Cindy was the one who'd named her, who'd leafed through a fat book with ten thousand names looking for the right one, I felt Finch was a suitable replacement, given the circumstances.

He gave a little nod. "Cooper's all right, but I think I like American Prodigal."

"What's that?" I asked.

"You heard me, neighbor." He began to laugh.

There was something about him. Something shifty and scrappy and what? The word that came to mind was "otherworldly," something not quite real. Well, the possibility that he wasn't real did cross my mind, because though it hadn't happened since right after I came back from overseas, it *had* happened, me seeing people who weren't really there. But otherworldly wasn't quite right. Strange. Unnerving.

A crow descended from a nearby pine. Small thing, not full-grown, with a red piece of yarn tied to its leg. Hovered near my face, like a gnat or a mosquito. Fluttering its wings, trying to provoke me. I swatted it and Scotland clucked and the thing flew to his shoulder. He pulled a crumb of bread from his shirt pocket and the crow plucked it from his hand, no lie. "This is Crow," he said. "That's his way of letting you know he doesn't like you."

He slid the AK over his head and placed it on the ground. He wasn't that tall, not as tall as me, and he was skinny, but he looked fast and wiry and strong, the veins in his arms thick and pronounced. He was older than me, maybe twenty years, maybe ten. Hard to say because he had the look of someone who lived hard and it showed. On his right arm he had a large tattoo of a girl with blond hair, the details of her face rendered in great detail: eyes, nose, mouth, everything in color. Another face on the other arm, a woman, and then a USMC tattoo farther down, on his forearm. He was military, too.

He kneeled down next to Finch on the blanket and reached out his dirty hand and took his pointer finger and ran it under her chin. "Pretty little thing," he said, and then he turned to me. "'Children are a heritage from the Lord.' Psalm 127:3. Especially girls." He paused and lifted his head to the trees and a breeze swept in, and the leaves, heavy and green, shivered overhead. "The Bible doesn't have that part about girls. I added that myself."

I'll be honest here. I thought about killing him right on the spot. I could keep the AK and we would never see Scotland again. I was vicious with grief then, a rabid beast, with Cindy just gone and Finch and me hunkered down in our little tent and here was someone that didn't belong in the picture, who stood to threaten the tenuous ground on which we stood, and it just about sent me over the edge.

Settle, Kenny. Cooper. Settle.

I told myself if this were at the grocery store, at a coffee shop, if me and Finch were just a father and daughter out for a morning stroll, and a stranger came up and said she was pretty, there would be nothing abnormal about it. Finch was beautiful and people commented on beautiful babies. It meant nothing. *Quit assuming the worst in people. Quit being so paranoid.* I could almost hear Cindy saying it.

Scotland stood and sauntered over to the porch and looked at the wood stacked against the front. I'd been working at it, here and there, chopping firewood. "This isn't near enough," he said.

"What do you mean?"

"You're planning to be here awhile," he said: a fact, not a question. "You're gonna need a whole lot more than what you've got."

"Needed a change of scenery."

Scotland made a noise that was somewhere between a laugh and a grunt, and I interpreted this to mean he didn't buy it. He shielded his eyes and looked at the rooftop, the chimney, assessing every detail. He wandered over to the small orchard and inspected the branches, leaning close and looking at the tiny balls that didn't quite look like apples just yet. "You been here six weeks already."

He'd been watching us. Keeping track. I thought again of the Ruger. Disturbed by the fact that the idea of killing him swam to me so easily, that it felt like a natural solution. *This is what has happened to you,* I thought to myself. *This is who you are now. There was a time when you would cringe at Aunt Lincoln skinning a deer. Blood, muscle, fascia, bone: you couldn't stand the sight of it. You would position yourself to the side and turn your head. Not anymore.*

My mind flickered to Cindy then and I saw her laughing in the dusk, hair in her teeth. When I came home from Kabul, there were times, moments like sun on water that glimmered and burned and I thought, with Cindy, I could be the man I was before. It would take time, but I could get there, with her love, with a certain pace of life, with grace. I could go back to being a person who had to turn their head from death, who would look away.

Scotland bent over his backpack and opened the flap.

I put my hand on the Ruger.

He reached in and what was he grabbing—

I pulled the gun and pointed it because we had not come this far to be gunned down by a lunatic in the woods.

Crow lifted from Scotland's shoulder and squawked, flapping his wings.

"Here," Scotland said, turning to me. He didn't even look at the gun, just right at me, right in my eyes, gaze steady. Not troubled by the gun pointing at him, not afraid, not even surprised. He wasn't smiling but there was a glint in his eye that suggested maybe he was amused. "Here," he said again, his hand outstretched.

It was a flare.

"You ever get in a pinch, set it off. I'll see it. I got a spotting scope," Scotland said.

Which explained how he knew how long we'd been at the cabin. I held the gun on him. Frozen. On the blanket, Finch toppled to the side and began to cry.

Scotland bent and placed the flare on Finch's blanket. He scooped her up and bobbed her up and down gently. She looked at me, her chubby face red. "Put the gun away, Cooper," Scotland said. "It's not neighborly. And I think your daughter wants you."

I held his eyes and he held mine and didn't blink but there was a scar that traveled over his eyebrow, a thin white line on his tan, leathery skin, and it twitched. Still, he didn't look away. I slid the

Ruger back into my pocket. Finch reached for me and I took her and held her close.

"Listen, I understand the gun," Scotland said. "After what you done, I imagine you're feeling a little skittish."

I turned to look at him, tried to catch his eyes again, read. *He knows.*

He was looking at the woods.

"But here's the thing, neighbor. If I wanted rid of you, I could've done it by now. I could've done it the day you got here, June 29th. But that's not what I want. I'd prefer not to have any neighbors at all, but you're here and you've got your reasons, which is why I'm gonna give you the benefit of the doubt for now and call you Cooper. But if that's our arrangement, I want us to be good neighbors. You understand." He spat to the side.

Finch turned to look at Scotland and reached out her fat hand in his direction. Once more he extended his arm and grazed his knuckle under her chin. Up close, I saw it wasn't just dirt that stained his hands. Also blood. Red streaks that laced up past his wrists. Scotland reached again into his backpack. He pulled out a small stack of newspapers. "Some reading material for you," he said, looking at me. He turned and tugged a dead rabbit from a second compartment and pitched it to the ground, then slid his pack onto his shoulders. He clucked for Crow, who darted off ahead of him, then tipped his head, told us he'd be seeing us, and walked off and dipped down out of sight. Finch watched him the whole time.

That night, for the first time in six weeks I ate something besides canned beans and diced peaches. I never thought I'd say this, but no lie, that rabbit from Scotland was the best thing I ever ate. I skinned it and roasted it over an open fire at dusk and Finch just sat on my lap, flapping her arms and kicking her legs, watching the flames lick up and up. Gristle and fat, everything, I pulled every morsel off the bones and gave tiny pieces to Finch, too, her first meat unless you count whatever ground-up garbage was in those jars of baby food.

It was that night that I realized I was going about this all wrong, day to day, waiting for something, and what was I waiting for? A team of snipers descending on the cabin to take us, a fleet of police vehicles trundling up the dirt road. The end, that's what I'd been waiting for, but that was no way to live, and meanwhile, we were unprepared for the here and now. Our supplies were running low and we would never make it unless I started hunting. Plus I decided I needed to figure out a way to call Jake.

That night I read *The Book of North American Birds* to Finch, like I'd done each night since our arrival, and she fell asleep. By then it had gotten dark, but I was looking forward to reading the newspapers Scotland had brought. The next morning, maybe, with coffee. An action that felt almost normal. I sat at the fire and watched the silhouettes of jack pines swaying in the wind, the bats that rose and plunged, bodies flitting in the dark. I listened to Finch breathing, that fast breathing of babies that has a different sort of rhythm than adults', and for the first time since Cindy died, I felt something that was not quite peace but almost. A sense that maybe there could be something beyond the knuckle and claw of the present moment. That maybe there could be an *us* out here, Finch and me.

I told myself this could be a good thing to have someone close enough that if something ever went really wrong, I could get help, because how many dozens of things could happen out here? I could hurt myself. Finch could get hurt. Or sick. And what would I do?

What was my exit strategy? I didn't have one and now maybe I did, in Scotland.

But that night I dreamed of Cindy: a happy, sweet dream where she was holding Finch in a baby carrier, strapped to her chest, and I said, Let me take a picture. That part of the dream was a memory—it really happened, on the first warm day after Finch was born. Next, though, Cindy turned and took a few steps away but when I said, Okay, that's good, she didn't turn around, just kept walking and then there was Scotland, waiting for them, and Cindy wouldn't look at me and for some reason I couldn't move to get her and the three of them walked off and left me, only Scotland turned back and grinned and waved and his hand was covered in blood.

THREE

December 14th arrives. Finch rises early, climbing into my bed before I'm awake, so that the first thing I see when I open my eyes is her face, three inches from mine.

"Oh, good," she says, grinning. "You're awake." She presses her palms into my cheeks, scrunching my face. "Chubby cheeks. Chubby, chubby, chubby." She laughs, then rolls off the bed and begins hopping around the room like a rabbit, hands curled by her chest.

"What time is it?" I can tell by the darkness in the room that it's early. Maybe the middle of the night, even.

"Don't know. Jake's coming today. It's the fourteenth. You didn't forget, did you? Don't tell me you forgot."

"I didn't forget." I sit up slowly. "Finch, I think it might still be nighttime."

"I can't sleep. I just can't. I've been lying there awake, all night."

I know this isn't true: she was breathing heavily, deep in sleep, when I came to bed, but I don't correct her. "You know he doesn't get here till late afternoon," I say. He leaves at first light, but even with an early start, he drives all day to get here. Takes it out of him, that drive: I can tell. But he's always smiling ear to ear when he pulls in.

"You think you could go out in the main room and read for a while?" I ask Finch.

She shakes her head. "No."

It's a rare thing for Finch to say no to a book.

"All right. How about you make us some breakfast?"

"I'm not hungry," she says, "but sure." She bounces out of the room, hands still bent at her chest.

I lie in bed, listening to her. Hear her cranking the knobs on the stove, all the way left, waiting, then opening the draft and then finally adding wood from the stack in the little box. She pulls a chair from the table and climbs up to get the skillet, places it on top of the woodstove. Pours water into the kettle and sets it on to heat as well.

I doze off for a while, I realize, because all of a sudden she is back, holding a cup of coffee out for me to take. I sit up in bed, prop the pillows at my back. "Thanks, sugar. Breakfast in bed. I could get used to this."

She shrugs, hops out of the room again, and returns a minute later with a plate with an egg and an apple sliced down the middle. She climbs up beside me with her own plate, but she barely eats breakfast, saying her stomach is doing somersaults and there's no space for food. By the time we're finished, it's just getting light. She reads for a while, sets up a target with an old can and takes her slingshot out to practice, fusses over her cardinal drawing for Jake, writes him a note.

I try to keep her busy. We get three apples from the root cellar and cook them in the Dutch oven with the last of the cinnamon. We chop some firewood, take a walk south of here and try to rustle up a grouse. The hours slog past with a painful slowness, with Finch's demeanor shifting from excitement early in the day, to bursting elation, to a heartbreaking sense of disappointment. She wanders out of the yard, peering around the bend, leaning.

As dark folds in, she stands at the window, watching. "Where *is* he?" she asks, nose pressed to the glass.

Since suppertime a sense of dread has been tugging at my chest, heavy. I wipe my hands on my pant legs. Swallow, force my voice to hold strong. "Well, Finch, maybe he isn't coming this year."

"Not coming?" Finch asks. She narrows her eyes and wrinkles her nose: an almost-scowl. "Why would you say that? He would never just *not come*."

"I know, sugar. He would never leave us high and dry if he could help it. He'd never give up a chance to see you. But you've got to realize: if he couldn't come, he wouldn't have a way to tell us, would he?"

"He probably just got a late start. Or something." She leans against the window again. "He'll be here," she says, looking out into the dark, her breath fogging the pane.

I agree to let her stay up late. We sit on the couch and she reads to me while I add another square to the quilt I've been working on. All the clothes that no longer fit her have been in garbage bags up in the loft, just taking up space, and I've decided to put them to use. The blanket she uses at night was fine when she was little, but now it's a tad small. So I've been cutting squares out of her old things—onesies, shirts, dresses—and sewing them together, piece by piece. Which is taking longer than I anticipated and I sort of regret deciding to do it, but we've got the whole winter stretching ahead of us, long evenings since dark sweeps in early these months. Anyhow, there's no getting out of it now, since she's excited about having a bigger quilt. Plus she gets a kick out of looking over her old things. And, me being the sentimental fool that I am, I figure this is a good way to preserve for her a piece of her history. A way to remember those early days of our time out here.

After a while, sleep overtakes her—she has been awake for nineteen hours—and she lies on the couch, knees tucked tight to her chest, while I finish sewing.

I stack the squares and tiptoe over to the door. Slip into my jacket, pull the beanie down over my ears. I step outside into the night, frost diamonding the grass, the air cold and dry. A jet blinks red across a sky that is bright and full of stars. I shove my hands into the pockets of my jacket and lean against a porch beam.

The year before, we'd sat at the campfire, Jake and me, on a night not unlike this.

He'd poked the embers with a stick. "You know if I don't come, one of these years, it's because I can't."

I'd told him I knew.

"What I mean is that I'm not going to die of old age," he'd said, and then he'd grunted. "That's the way my neurologist put it."

"Doctors and their bedside manner."

"Well, it's sort of good to know, don't you think?"

Had he held my gaze, then? Had he stared at the fire, avoiding eye contact? Because now, a year later, I can't help but look back on that conversation and wonder if maybe Jake was trying to tell me something. Maybe he had a premonition, maybe there was something about his situation that he just couldn't bring himself to say out loud, maybe it was a cry for help, even. What was it I'd said to him when I'd helped him into the house that night? *Don't go dying on us.* Which in hindsight feels insensitive, I realize. Selfish. The thought of him alone, suffering, or worse. The one and only person in this world I could fully trust, who was there for me despite everything that had happened. After all he'd done for us. And I couldn't help him. Couldn't even be there. I kick loose a piece of gravel. Pick it up, grip it tight in my palm, cold.

I've always known this was a possibility, that at some point we'd need to fend entirely for ourselves. For years I've been trying to get more out of the garden but the truth is, the soil is bad out here, rocky and acidic, and the additional food we've been able to grow—it's still not enough. I've mapped out routes to stores, calculated the timing, fine-tuned my annual list. I've just hoped the day when I'd need to act on those plans wouldn't come.

Thing is, I did go out, early on. The first time, it was just to call Jake at the nearest gas station pay phone. We grabbed a few items inside the store since we were there. Milk, bread, a jar of peanut butter. The second trip went smoothly enough. But the third one went so poorly I can hardly bring myself to think about it. I haven't gone out since.

Finch was about twenty months old and far too squirrelly to take along. She'd recently learned to walk, and she had this thing where she would kick and bite and scream *no, no, no!* any time I tried to pick her up. I mean a full-on tantrum. Taking her to a store would almost certainly result in a scene, and I couldn't risk drawing the attention of bystanders, especially when everyone knows the first thing that comes to a person's mind when they see a man scooping up a kid who's carrying on like that. So, after weighing the risks, I decided to put her down for a nap in the playpen and then sneak out for a quick trip. She was a reliable sleeper in those days, so I knew I had a solid ninety-minute window. I was back in seventy and feeling good, but when I pulled up in the Bronco, there was Scotland on the front porch, holding Finch on his lap. She was snuggled up and sleeping.

I almost lost it, then. Really. Don't know that I've ever been so close. I had the Ruger in my pocket and I yanked it out and rushed to them and grabbed Scotland by the collar. Finch startled awake and began crying, and I scooped her out of his arms. I held her, but she immediately started pushing to be let down. I set her on the ground and stepped closer to Scotland.

"What the hell is going on here?" I leaned in close and could smell the wintergreen and woodsmoke. Crow was perched on the gutter and began to hover and caw, and Finch pointed and squealed.

"Easy, Cooper. Easy. Just lending a hand, that's all."

"Don't give me that. She was fine, she was sleeping."

He shook his head, adjusting his shirt. Then he held my eyes in that way of his. "She wasn't."

"And how would you know that?"

"I was here. On the porch."

I ran my thumb along the stock of the Ruger. Heart roaring, the edges of my vision beginning to blur.

Scotland shrugged. "I saw you leave, alone. I came down here to keep an eye on her. Thought maybe you were too proud to ask, but I figured I'd go ahead and do you a favor. And it's a good thing

I did. Because she woke up and climbed right out of that little contraption in there, quick as a whip." He folded his hands on his lap. "Cooper, you can't leave a child her age unattended. It's just not safe." His scar flickered silver in the sunlight. "Lucky I was here."

I clenched my fist, palms soaked. A result of fear but also rage. "How'd she get out here on the porch, with you?" I was afraid to know the answer. Did he have a key? Did he break in?

He grinned. "Well, I confess that was a bit difficult. It took some cajoling. But we played a game and eventually I got her to let me in."

I'll never know what really happened that day when I was out. Still burns me to think back on it because I never should've left her. Well, after that, the next time Jake came, I sent him home with a list, and that's how we've been getting our supplies ever since. I fling the rock hard, way off into the dark, wait for the sound of it hitting whatever it is it collides with. I head inside. Slide both locks, prop the shovel. I carry Finch to bed, blow out the candle, and then tumble into sleep myself.

At lunch on the fifteenth, I decide to tell Finch. I figure it's time to release her from waiting because I can tell it's driving her crazy, listening for his truck, watching for it to appear in the yard. Hoping. It's just not fair, her thinking he'll arrive any minute, and me knowing that if he didn't come on the fourteenth, he isn't coming at all.

She's at the table, finishing her meal, and I'm wandering aimlessly through the house, trying to determine how to do it. Should I sit and hold her hand? Pull her onto my lap? She isn't too old for that, not yet. I'm at a loss here, never done this before. She uses the paring knife to slice an apple, careful and precise, just like I taught her.

"Well, what is it, Cooper?" She looks at me, pushes a chunk of apple in her mouth, and chews slowly.

"What?"

"Something's got you riled up."

"How—"

"You're pacing." She presses the knife down, struggles at the red-green skin, wiggles it back and forth. "Go on, spit it out."

I'm fairly certain she's reciting that part, that I've said those exact words to her before. *Go on, spit it out.* I slide into the chair beside her and take a deep breath. "Jake isn't coming."

She holds my gaze for a moment, her wide green eyes taking this in, then her face flinches, a flicker of something. Pain, confusion. "No. He's just running behind. You've got to be patient. You're *wrong.*" She picks up the knife and cuts another slice.

"Finch, I'm not."

She shakes her head, presses the blade of the knife into the table. "How do you know? You didn't talk to him." Her mouth turns downward, a scowl.

"You're right. But we had an agreement, the two of us. An understanding. If he ever just didn't show up on the fourteenth, it's because he couldn't. That's what he said. So, something must've changed for him. Something happened where he isn't coming now." I think of the pump in his leg, the way he grimaced as he climbed onto the porch. All the years, all those antibiotics, fighting that infection. Was he lying in a hospital bed somewhere, suffering? Or had he finally succumbed?

I reach out and try to pull her onto my lap but she resists, tugs her wrist from my hand because, in that moment, I'm the one causing her pain. I'm the one to blame.

Lucky, I think to myself then, that we never went through this with Cindy. All this time, I'd been thinking it was too bad that Finch never really knew her mother, that she had no recollection of her at all, that when I showed her the picture or talked about Cindy, Finch would listen and smile politely, but there was no memory at the sight of her, no pain that would twist and burn. But now I see that if we had to lose her, we were lucky to have lost her when we did.

"You should've told me."

"I didn't know."

"Who's taking care of him? Does he have someone?" She wipes her eyes with the purple sleeve of her shirt. "We should go help."

"Aw, Finch. That's nice of you to think about. But you know we can't do that." I pat her back.

"I know we have rules. But it's Jake," she says, biting her lip. "Don't you think we could make an exception?"

"Sorry, sugar. We can't."

"But why?"

She's been pushing back, this past year. Wanting to know more about why we're here and why we can't leave. I take a deep breath, run my thumb along a crack in the table. We've been over the story, many times. Well, an abbreviated version. I look at her, waiting. "You know why."

"Because you did something you shouldn't have, once. To keep the two of us together." She pauses, raising her eyes. "And there are consequences for that. One of which is that we can't go into the world." A recitation: same words each time.

"Good girl."

She winds a strand of hair around her finger. "What you did, Coop—was it something bad?"

A thorny question. "I did what I had to do." I reach out and press my hand over hers. "He has a sister," I say, remembering: many years ago, a girl who tagged along on that fishing trip, her nose in a book. The last I heard, she was living in England.

Finch seems to take some comfort in this. Still, she picks up the rest of the apple and climbs onto my lap and cries hard, her sobs filling the cabin with a sound that lances and burns. Stomach, chest, throat. This is a new agony for me—to hear her suffer, to not be able to take it away. It's not like the cuts and bruises and bee stings of life, hurts that will throb but then fade away: the skin healing, the swelling going down.

"It's not fair," she sobs. "It's not fair at all."

I rest my chin on top of her head and hold her and tell her I know: I know it's not fair. She sits there with me, knees tucked beneath her chin, and it's a long time before she stops shaking.

FOUR

Scotland materializes in the yard. I say it that way because that's what he does each time, just shows up, appears out of nowhere, like a ghost, like fog. We never see him coming through the woods, we never hear him, and let me assure you: I keep an eye out. Never once have I seen him before he got to the yard. Never once have I heard a noise. No sticks cracking, no rustle of leaves. He's that quiet. I am fairly certain he takes some sort of sick pleasure in surprising us because each time, I know the look on my face must be one of sheer terror, and each time, he breaks into a laugh at the sight of it. He throws back his head and shows his ugly teeth and roars, his whole body shaking hard, delighted.

"Where's Jake?" His raspy voice, just *there*, all of a sudden.

I'm at the edge of the garden, cutting back the raspberry bushes, absorbed in thinking about what Finch and me are gonna do, how much time we've got. "You ever think about finding some sort of hobby, Scotland? Something besides spying on your neighbors."

Well, maybe that sounds rude. Unnecessary. But here's the thing. That first time he showed up in the yard with the flare and the rabbit—those newspapers he brought, they weren't just a random assortment. They were carefully selected. Every single one of them had an article about me. Turned out Cindy's parents had exerted their influence and gotten the word out, far and wide. Made me look like some kind of lunatic. One of them even had a big headline that said AMERICAN PRODIGAL, just like what Scotland had called me. Scotland, in that subtle and insidious way of his, was sending a message that he knew who I was, what I'd done, why Finch and me were in the woods. He wanted me to know he had me. I pictured him watching us through his spotting scope, reading the papers, curating the ones that had something about me in them, then making his delivery with the AK-47 strapped across his back. Well, I never mentioned those papers and their content to him—I refused to give him the satisfaction of knowing just how much they ruffled me—but I decided right then and there that I could never let my guard down around him. I could never trust him.

I continue cutting the bushes to the ground, piling the branches behind me. Working faster. Crow is perched on Scotland's shoulder, and when I look at him, he opens his beak and caws, mouthing off.

"No time for hobbies," Scotland says, placing a stack of newspapers on the porch. He still brings them, from time to time. Finch likes to read them, I never even look. "Besides, 'Idle hands are the devil's workshop.' That's what the Good Book says. Now, back to the matter of Jake. Tell me what's going on. It's the fifteenth. He should be here by now."

I shake my head. It's only been a few hours since I had to tell Finch. "You sure do like to keep track of things, don't you, Scotland."

"As a matter of fact, I do, Cooper. I've always kept a calendar. A journal, you might call it, though it's more just a log of what happens each day. Fastidious. 'Attentive to and concerned about detail.' That's what my daddy used to call me, and I do believe he was right."

Finch, who'd been at the back of the house paying respects to Susanna the chicken, bounds around to the front yard. "Scotland!" She runs to him, wrapping her arms around his waist. "Jake's dead," Finch says.

"Finch." I look at Scotland. "We don't know that."

"He is," Finch says. "I can feel it in my soul. He has departed this world."

Scotland shoves his hands into his pockets and turns away from us. He walks out of the little garden and heads over to one of the apple trees. "He helped plant these trees. I remember. Oh, I bet he wasn't any bigger than you, Finch."

"You knew Jake?"

He cocks his head to the side, twists his mouth. "I knew he was here, with his family."

"Did you look after them, like you do with us?" Finch asks, finding a spot on the grass and plopping down.

"You could say that."

"With your spotting scope?" She rolls a stick back and forth in her palm.

"The very same one."

A red-tailed hawk sails overhead, casting a shadow that waves across the yard. Crow flaps off to a nearby white pine.

Scotland lowers down and sits cross-legged beside Finch, his knee touching hers. "You doing all right, little bird? I know how much he meant to you."

"He was my friend," she says. She places the stick in her lap and folds her hands across her chest. "'O past! O happy life! O songs of joy! In the air, in the woods, over fields, Loved!'"

Whitman. I look at Scotland and shake my head.

"He was a good man," Scotland says. "A very good man. With a kind spirit and a heart of gold."

"And now we won't ever see him again."

Scotland reaches and holds out his hand and she takes it, her tiny hand swallowed in his fat, dirty fingers. "It's terrible to lose someone you love, terrible. Makes you hurt in ways you didn't know you could hurt."

Finch begins to tremble, and I keep pruning, a little stumped by Scotland, as usual: this unexpected wisdom. And also just a little irritated at the way he is so at ease with extending comfort, how he just knew what to say, how he offered his hand. Over the years he and Finch have grown close—unavoidable, perhaps, given our lack of social opportunities, not to mention her general propensity to get so attached to people—but still, I don't like it.

"It'll get better, Finch. Right now the sadness is all there is. Maybe it feels like there's something so heavy pulling at you that you'll sink right down into the earth and never feel light again. But you will, in time. I promise."

She wipes her eyes and then asks, her voice shaking, "How long? How long does it take?"

Scotland shakes his head. "I can't say, Finch. Wish I could. It sort of differs from person to person. But time will tell. Most likely, you'll just realize one day that you don't feel as sad as you did the day before. And the day after that, you'll be a little better, and so on. I'm guessing it'll never fully go away, but it gets better."

Finch looks at me, her green eyes wide in question, like she wants me to confirm that this is how things will happen.

I nod. "Sounds about right."

Although I'm not so sure that's how it happened for me. With Cindy, there was this initial feeling that reminded me of one of those amusement park rides, where you ride up and up and then they let you drop, all of this controlled with some grand mechanics, but still, the sensation that you are falling fast and hard and your body is dropping without your heart. That's how it was. Like I couldn't catch myself, like there was nothing to hold me up. But then things shifted and all of that feeling of being lost turned into something different, something savage and animal. Then there was only Finch and me, staying alive, and me holding on to her and taking care of her and knowing nothing could keep me from doing that.

"I have a loose tooth," Finch says, remembering, and like that, her sadness seems to dissipate, float off into sky. There is some comfort in this, I suppose—the way a child can swing right up from grief. The way there is always something else, something beyond just the sadness. She opens her mouth and tilts her head, pointing and wiggling the tooth. "See?"

Scotland obliges, leaning in and taking a look. "Won't be long," he says, throwing me a glance. "You gonna put it under your pillow so the tooth fairy can come and give you a dollar?"

Finch cocks her head to the side, narrows her eyes. "I'm eight, you know."

"No harm in pretending." He nods in my direction, winks. "For your daddy's sake."

She grins. "I'll put it under my pillow and Cooper will probably keep it, knowing him. I mean the tooth. He'll put it in the yellow Raisinets tin on the shelf, where he keeps the lock of hair from my first haircut and his dog tags from the military. Won't you, Coop?"

"Oh, I reckon so, Finch."

Scotland rises and walks to me. "What're you gonna do about supplies?"

I shake my head. "Don't know yet."

"I almost forgot," he says, sliding off his backpack and setting it on the ground. "I brought something for you, Finch."

She is whittling a piece of wood with my pocketknife, but she stops, looks up and smiles. "What is it?"

Scotland eases down beside her and slowly pulls something else from his backpack, something the size of a large human head and wrapped up like a mummy. I stop trimming.

"Careful, now. I got it all wrapped up because it's fragile." Scotland peels off the layers of fabric: a blue sweatshirt, a pink shirt, a purple scarf. Good Lord: girls' clothes. Now, why would he have those things?

Scotland unravels the scarf to reveal a skull, clean and white and completely monochromatic, the eye sockets two gaping holes, the teeth long and menacing.

Finch gasps. "What is it?"

"It's a bear skull."

"Can I hold it?"

"Sure, just be careful. Hold it by the bottom. The jaw's not attached."

Over the past year or so, Finch has developed an intense fascination with skulls and bones. Not sinister, but maybe strange. When we find them in the woods, as we sometimes do, she brings them home to add to her collection. Whenever Scotland shows up, she asks him what animal it is, and he always knows. That's a raccoon, he'll say. This one's a groundhog. You can tell by the teeth. See how they curl up like that? That means it's a rodent: its teeth never stop growing. This little guy's a porcupine. This one's a deer.

Now, she runs her fingers along the top of the bear skull, the little dip in the middle, the gaping spheres where the eyes would've been. She traces the long, white teeth. "It's so beautiful."

"Isn't it? Found him in the woods a few weeks back. Whole body, actually, though I just took the head. Sawed it off. Had to use a chain saw, the spine was so thick."

I picture it: Scotland out there with a chain saw roaring and stuttering, cutting the head off the rotting corpse of a bear, like that's a normal thing to do. I'm telling you: the man has no boundaries.

"Didn't find any wounds on him," he says, "so I'm guessing he was just old. His time had come, and he just lay down in the woods and let the scavengers have him, let the earth take him back." Scotland tilts his head to the sky. "Not a bad way to go, if you think about it. Just lie down and surrender yourself to it."

"How'd you get it so clean?"

I'd been wondering the same thing myself. The skull almost glows white, every scrap of flesh picked clean: not natural, especially if it was true what Scotland had said, that he'd found the bear dead in the woods just a couple weeks ago.

Scotland runs his finger over the dip of the bear's nostril. "Well, I got these bugs. Flesh-eating beetles. Dermestids, they're called. Useful little critters. I keep them in a big metal drum, and anytime I got a skull, I just drop it in there, and it's all done within ten days or so. They pick it completely clean, all the hair and flesh, eat every morsel till there's nothing left but bone."

"Cool." Finch turns the skull over in her hands. "Can I see them sometime?"

"No," I say, throwing Scotland a glance and then jabbing my thumb on a thorn. I decide not to ask him why, exactly, he has flesh-eating beetles in his possession.

Scotland shakes his head. "They need to stay put. Can't have flesh-eating beetles on the loose, now can we? Who knows what they might get into." He winks at Finch and grins. Folds the blanket and the clothes up carefully and slides them in his backpack.

She giggles. "I guess not. I guess that wouldn't be good." She clicks the pocketknife closed. "Are they creepy? The beetles."

"No, not really. Just doing what they need to survive, like the rest of us."

Finch has dirt smudged on the side of her mouth, and Scotland licks his thumb and reaches out and wipes it from her face.

"Listen, Finch. Old Scotland's got to get home now."

Finch stands and wraps her arms around his waist and he rests his hand on her blond hair and closes his eyes and stays there a minute. If I could see my face, I suspect I'd be scowling because I hate it, their closeness. That she trusts him. That he allows it. He squeezes her shoulder and then pulls away and wanders off into the woods, downriver, just as quietly as he came.

FIVE

Finch and me didn't always live in the woods. There was a *before* for us, a different life.

It's a long story, but here is the abbreviated version and I guess I will start with this: when I was seventeen I fell in love. Not that twinkle-eyed, see-no-wrong type of love. Sure, that was part of it, but it was bigger, what we had, me and Cindy.

I guess you could say it began on the high school track-and-field bus. That was the first time I ever talked to her. Cindy. We did track together, and that day she was late for an away meet and the only seat on the bus was next to me.

She walked up the aisle with her blue track uniform on and her yellow backpack and sat down by me and said, "Hey, you're Kenny, right?"

I didn't know she knew who I was, but I knew her because she was Cindy Loveland and everybody knew her. She was rich and beautiful, a cheerleader and a track star, too, the three-hundred-meter hurdles, and she made it look like she was just stepping right over those hurdles, like they were nothing. A lithe animal. A gazelle. And so beautiful. Which I guess I already said. What she ever saw in me, I don't know.

She nudged me because I guess too much time passed and I didn't say nothing, but I was still a little shocked she was talking to me. "Kenny, right?"

"Yeah, Kenny."

"Cindy."

"I know who you are."

I didn't know then that the reason everyone loved Cindy was because you couldn't help it. All that time I'd just watched her from a distance, the way people seemed to pull to her, the way they looked at her. And I figured it was because she was popular and her dad was the district judge and they lived in the Heights. But no. It was her kindness. Her laugh that soared up and up, head back, teeth white and not quite perfect but almost. The thing about Cindy was when you were with her, there was no one else, just you. That's how you felt, like the whole world and everyone in it just slipped out of sight.

We became friends after that time on the track bus. Just friends, technically, but deep down I was a goner. From that first day, I barely even looked at another girl. The next year, I graduated and got a job at the hardware store, stocking shelves and ringing people up, and the whole time, every day, I would think about seeing Cindy. She was a class behind me so she had another year of high school left, and sometimes, she asked me to pick her up after school and drive her home. Then eventually she graduated and geared up for college, and Aunt Lincoln told me I couldn't just sit around and wait

for Christmas break; I needed to do something. And I got to thinking, Cindy would be in college for the next four years, and I ought
to use the time to make something of myself because chances were,
she wouldn't graduate from college and be interested in a guy that
worked at the local hardware store.

Meanwhile this was in the time of the War on Terror. Troops
shuttling into Afghanistan, hunting caves and skirmishing that rug-
ged country, and soon we were in Iraq as well. There was an Army
recruiter in town and one day I walked into their little office and
signed up. They gave me a big signing bonus, and told me I was
doing the right thing, serving my country, and they said this would
give me a sense of purpose and discipline and I was nineteen and I
believed them.

Sailed right through basic training. I'm not bragging or exag-
gerating when I say that—it really wasn't hard. I was a runner, I'd
done manual labor, I could shoot, I was strong. Plus I was nineteen.
So young. Free of all the aches and betrayals that begin to catch up
with you, even a decade later. And unlike some of the people there,
I didn't have a hankering for home that pulled and distracted. The
truth is, I liked it. Back home, everyone knew me as Kenny. Kenny
the boy whose mom left him, Kenny the kid who used to trip over
his shoelaces in elementary school, Kenny the distance runner. The
Army gave me a chance to turn over a new leaf, become someone I
was not, and when I realized this, I began to thrive. I made friends.
Jake was the first, of course, and the best, but I made other ones,
too. I was good at something, and I don't know, I guess it was like
something transpired inside, like for the first time people saw me in
a different light. Which made me see myself in a different light.

It shouldn't have surprised me when my CO told me I should

consider trying out for Ranger School, but it did. Like I said, I guess I was still getting used to the notion that I was good at something. Boot camp, Airborne School: people complained about those. But then there was RIP, which at the time felt hard but later seemed like a walk in the park. Then, if you were able to hack RIP, Ranger School. And let me tell you: Ranger School is where you start to see yourself for who you really are, because they strip everything right off you. That's where being physically strong isn't enough anymore. Three phases of that—Walk, Run, Crawl—and by the end you can mountaineer, you can traverse a swamp, you can fly. What the Army calls us Rangers is "Lethal, Agile, and Flexible." And that's exactly what I was.

Anyhow. Cindy went off to her expensive college to study and join a sorority and write for the school newspaper, things she would tell me about but which I couldn't really picture. We emailed each other sometimes, and I suspect the things I told her about my life were just as hard to imagine.

By the time my first four years were up, I'd done three tours overseas and the thing about it—I hated everything I'd done but I was good at it. Shooting, hiding out, jumping out of airplanes, that feeling of soaring through the dark. Flight. All of it a type of high but then there was also all the death. They tell you, it's war; it's different. But it's not, not really. That's just what they say so you can try and live with yourself. Thing is, though: you will always know what you did and what you took and what you lost and it's your life, it's all part of you, like it or not, and you can never truly separate yourself from it. I signed up for it, I followed through. I accept responsibility. My point is just that you can never really be free from the things you've done, and that's that.

I guess I came back Stateside with a strange mix of self-confidence and anxiety. I could mostly hide the anxiety, especially when Cindy was around, but it was there, and often. The self-confidence came from a number of factors. First, I'd grown about four inches. Late bloomer. I'd put on a lot of muscle, maybe twenty pounds. I looked different and felt different and was different. Stronger. Like I could go places—grocery stores, restaurants, bars—and know my way out. See it all happen like a movie. I could trust myself. Before, I was always afraid. Nervous. Nervous about how people looked at me, nervous about what they thought. When I got back, that wasn't the case anymore and I liked that. People looked at me different, and in our little town, I was a bit of a hero. Yellow ribbons in the windows and men coming up and shaking my hand, and once, one old lady came up and held my face in her wrinkled little palm and said, "Thank you, son."

But there were other changes, too. Bad ones, and this is where the anxiety kicked in. Dreams that would swim to me and slink and lurk, and sometimes I forgot where I was and who. I called Jake, who'd gone through all of it with me, and asked him, Did he have them too? Did he duck for cover when a car backfired? Did he have nightmares? Did his heart race every time the phone rang? Did he feel sure sometimes that people around him were looking at him and judging him? He said he was having trouble but he was seeing someone, a doctor at the VA hospital, and maybe I should consider it.

Jake said his family had a cabin way off in the woods, and if I was up for it, we could meet there and just relax for a few days. A long time ago, when Jake was a kid, his father had visions of living full-time in the woods. Which meant the place was nicer than a cabin, by most people's standards. They'd planted a small orchard, some brambles along the southern side of the house: blackberries and raspberries. There was no electricity or running water, but there was a well that had water, cold and sweet. They'd done it for a while, lived out here, Jake told me, his mom and dad and him, but when his sister came along and his mother miscarried a third child, they called it quits. Jake didn't go into the details, just said that after she recovered, his mother told his father: it's the kids and me, or the cabin, and Jake's dad chose the wife and kids and left the cabin behind.

Anyhow, I told Jake sure, just pick a date, and he said how about next weekend. I packed up the Bronco and followed the directions I'd scribbled out on a piece of paper, and after about a thousand turns, I made it to the cabin. There was still some snow on the ground, I remember that. I went down to the river and caught some fish, and we cooked brook trout on a grill over the campfire. His sister tagged along. Read the whole time, mostly, though she did catch a fish. At the end of the weekend Jake handed me a key to the place and said if I ever needed to just get away for a few days, I was welcome there anytime. He and his sister were the only ones who had the keys, no need to call him if I decided to come. I told him I might take him up on that, and thanks.

It wasn't long after that me and Cindy got together. By that point I'd been in love with her for almost seven years and I finally just told her. She'd finished college and was home and meanwhile her parents were pushing her to work as a paralegal for a while and then go to law school and follow in her father's footsteps. Which she didn't want to do, or at least she wasn't sure yet. But they were pushy like that, both of them. Used to getting their way, no matter what.

Cindy's parents never liked the idea of the two of us being together. We were from different worlds, Cindy and me. The Lovelands, they had a big white house with a fountain in the front and people to do their cleaning. All their money was on account of Mrs. Loveland, who was filthy rich and always had been.

Anyhow. Cindy found out she was pregnant and I'm telling you: I'd never been happier. I guess you could say she felt torn about it, and the fact that her parents tried to convince her to put an end to it didn't make it any easier on her. But after a while I convinced her to move out to Lincoln's place with me and to keep the baby because it was ours—it was our baby and we would love it and take care of it, and we could be happy. The thing was, we really were happy for a while. The two of us and then the three of us.

But then. One night me and Cindy and Grace Elizabeth were driving home. We'd run out of diapers and we went to the Shop 'n Save to get some. With the new baby, we didn't get out much, so it was sort of our big trip of the week, something to do, a reason to leave the house. Cindy had fixed her hair and put on makeup. Anyhow, on the way home it was raining and dark and a deer ran out and I slammed on the brakes and we slid and the car rolled and rolled. Me and Grace Elizabeth were okay but not Cindy.

So then it was just me and Grace Elizabeth.

Gone, just like that. How your life can go from the three of you, so happy, to—

Well. A lot of things happened in those days after Cindy died. Things I'd rather not relive, things I'm not proud of. The long and short of it is this: we needed a place to go, the baby and me, somewhere we could be safe and together, sheltered from all of the forces that were trying to keep us apart. I thought of Jake's offer and the key he'd given me. The rutted road that was barely a road. The little cabin, so beautiful. The hundred acres of woods surrounding it and then the hundreds of thousands of acres of national forest beyond its borders. The stream where Jake and me had caught trout that glimmered and twisted in our palms. And that's where we went.

SIX

The day after I tell Finch about Jake, I'm at the woodstove, frying eggs like usual, and Finch is reading at the table, her finger tracing the fine print, her voice full of meaning. She always reads like that, with passion, just like Cindy. The eggs hiss; the woodstove crackles and hums.

Then, footsteps: someone crossing the front porch.

Heart scuttles up to my throat, stomach drops. I slide the skillet from the heat. "Root beer," I say, and Finch bolts from her chair and darts toward the root cellar, fast. Instinct. A thing we have trained for, dozens of times. She's there before I even turn around.

Rap, rap, rap.

And then a face peering in through the window. Scotland. Been a long time since he's come to the door. He presses his face against the glass and gestures to the door.

"It's all right, Finch," I say.

She's already halfway down the ladder, so she climbs back up, sees him at the window. She grins and bolts toward the door, sliding the two locks. I close the root cellar and straighten out the rug.

Over the years, we've had snoopers. A hunter who was technically on national forest land but close. He raised a hand, I waved back. That was all. But another time, we had a forest ranger who wandered onto our property. We were outside that time, and took cover in the woods. He peered in the windows, plucked some ripe blueberries. About a year later, two hikers who were lost. We hid then, too. Dashed into the root cellar so fast I forgot to lock the front door. They knocked, opened the door, called out. Then they plopped themselves right onto the front porch and ate granola, no lie. We could hear them talking. So, not that many trespassers, but enough that it has warranted our having a game plan, should someone appear unannounced.

Finch flings open the door. "Scotland!" She throws her arms around his waist and leans her head against his chest.

"Careful, little bird. Careful." He pats his chest. "Something special in here and it's fragile." He stands in the doorway.

"Might as well come in," I tell him.

He steps in, closing the door behind him and looking around. Probably casing the joint. "Here," he says to Finch, kneeling down to her height, pointing to his jacket. "Unzip me and you'll see."

Finch squeals and steps forward. Slowly, she pulls at the zipper of his coat.

"Can't you do that yourself, Scotland?" I stab the eggs with the spatula.

A nose emerges at his chest, pink and whiskered. Then eyes, ears, paws. A white kitten.

"Oh, Scotland," Finch whispers. "It's the most beautiful thing I've ever seen in my whole life. Can I hold it?"

"Of course."

Finch reaches over and pulls the rest of the kitten out of Scotland's jacket. So small it could fit in my hand, scrawny and fluffy and bright. I have to admit: it's a cute little devil.

Finch sets it on her lap and strokes its back. "Just look at it, Coop."

"Nice, sugar. Very nice."

Scotland stands up and walks over to the stove, peers into the frying pan. "Smells good."

"What's its name?" Finch asks.

"It's a he. And his name—well, that's up to you. He's yours."

Finch gasps. "Really? For real?"

Scotland looks at me. "Well, as long as your daddy says it's all right."

As far as I'm concerned, it's common courtesy to ask a parent before giving a kid a pet. But of course that's the opposite of how Scotland operates. Because now if I say no—and, given our circumstances, it wouldn't be unreasonable to do so—I'm the one who's a jerk.

Finch stands up carefully with the kitten. She carries him over, tight against her chest. "Can we, Coop? Can we keep him? Please?"

I glare at Scotland. "Let me think about it, Finch."

"But look at his face. Look at his blue eyes and long whiskers. He'll be good, I promise. Please, please, please?" The kitten crawls up her chest, perching itself on her shoulder. Delighted, Finch begins walking around the room.

I lean toward Scotland. "You should've asked."

"I figured you'd say no."

"Exactly."

"Listen, Cooper. The girl lost a friend yesterday. She's grieving. Studies show that a pet can lift one's spirits, make a person generally more at ease. Did you see Finch's eyes light up? That kitten can be her companion. Her friend, since she has none out here, aside from you and me. He'll be a comfort to her, he already is." He nods toward the couch, where Finch has the kitten nuzzled against her neck.

"Another mouth to feed, when we're already in a pinch and you know it."

Scotland shakes his head. "A feline is a competent and merciless predator, Cooper. People tend to forget that. They feed their cats, let them lie around the house all day and play with fluffy little toys. It's a disgrace, really. To the cats and to us humans. Sure, give the cat scraps here and there to keep him around. Let him know he's wanted. But don't feed him. Trust me, I've got a whole gang of cats in my barn, and I don't feed them a thing. They're robust and efficient, just as God intended them to be."

"If he's trouble, I'm getting rid of him."

Scotland frowns. "I don't like the way you say that, Cooper, with a sinister tone. And just so you're aware, felines are sensitive creatures. He will sense your distrust, your malice, and he won't like it. The two of you won't be friends." He leans against the cracked edge of the counter. "But fine, if he's trouble, I'll take him back. How's that sound?"

Finch looks at me from the couch. "I'll take care of him myself. You won't even know he's here. He'll be no trouble at all. I promise." The kitten licks her chin. "Please, Coop?"

I scrape the eggs onto two plates. "Guess I don't have much choice in the matter."

Finch carries the kitten over to the table and sits down. "Thanks for my kitten," Finch says, leaning against Scotland. "It's the best thing anyone ever gave me."

He rests his hand on her shoulder, runs his finger over the kitten's snout. "Glad you like him, little bird. I knew you would." He turns to me. "Listen," he says. "You gonna try a supply run?"

I set my plate of eggs on the table, the steam pouring off. I pick up the saltshaker, pat it on my palm. It's empty, I know, but there's something about the gesture of it, the habit. "I don't see a way around it."

"You can't go anywhere in town," Scotland says. "Not with a big order like you're planning. You know that. People will notice. They'll talk. There's a Walmart about fifty miles south, down in Somersville. Right off 93. Can't miss it."

I've already accounted for this and mapped a route to Somersville, but I nod.

"You want me to come down and look after Finch?"

My mind gutters back to the last time Finch was here alone, when I came home to an unlocked door and her sitting on the porch with Scotland. But also to the more recent discovery of footprints by our hunting blind. The idea of someone in our woods, close. "She'll ride along."

"Risky, the two of you out together."

"We'll be all right."

"Well," he says, moving toward the door, "I'll keep an eye out."

"I'm sure you will."

SEVEN

I've never minded it before, the onset of winter, because Finch and me make the most of it, the cold nights and short days. We play long rounds of Rummikub and checkers, we read and memorize poems and cook our more elaborate meals. There's a part of me that sort of enjoys it, a slower time of year after we've spent the rest of it toiling hard. I like the safety of it, too: knowing that for the majority of time, the forest roads are closed and we don't need to worry about trespassers.

But of course this year is different. After breakfast I open the cupboards and take everything out. Chicken noodle soup, baked beans. A very small amount of sugar, maybe a quarter cup. I lift the door to the root cellar and climb down the steps, the wood creaking beneath my feet. There, I count up what's left of our fall crops. Apples. Three butternut squash, fourteen carrots, seven potatoes. After eight years, I've learned to do a good job of rationing our supplies so that we're just running short in November. It takes some planning, and we have to be careful, but we eat well, Finch and me, balanced, wholesome meals. As I divvy up the remaining food into portions, it becomes clear: we will be out of food by Christmas.

Me, I can make do. I'm a grown man and if I don't eat great for a few months, no big deal, I'll survive. But Finch. All this time I've taken care of her, made sure she had protein and grains and vegetables and even fruit. I've given her the best life I could, and I've been able to justify keeping us both out here, because she has never been in need or want. She's always had clothes that fit and a warm place to sleep. She has never gone hungry, not once, thanks to Jake. But yesterday, I caught her stuffing an apple in her pocket, stealthy-like, and trying to slip out the door before I could see. I didn't say anything about it. I couldn't. The thought of her feeling like she had to steal and sneak.

I will not let her starve.

One trip. There's the Walmart Scotland referred to, fifty miles away, and a gas station about twelve miles out the road, and I'll go to Walmart and then stop and get fuel on the way home. A simple excursion, the kind most people do every day of their lives, groceries and gas, only I will be buying everything in bulk.

The list.

Produce: oranges, lemons, bananas.

Dried items: Prunes, raisins, cherries, apricots. Various types of beans. Oatmeal, rice. Nuts.

Canned goods: peas, mushrooms, corn, green beans, peaches, pears, soups.

Candles. We are down to the last one, the wax nearly gone. Matches. Batteries.

Flour, salt, baking soda, vinegar, sugar, coffee, powdered milk, cooking oil.

Toothbrushes, toothpaste, fluoride rinse, toilet paper.

New pants, shirts, socks, and underwear for Finch. A winter jacket, snow pants, gloves, boots. She has outgrown these things and I won't have her hunt and help outside without proper attire.

Luxury items. Paper and pens. Hot chocolate mix. Milk, butter, and five big slabs of sharp cheese. Now that winter's here, we can keep things cold in the icebox out back.

Birdseed. Cat food, litter.

I organize it into categories, based on how I remember things being set up in the store, and I figure with time for travel, plus my shopping, plus the stop at the gas station, if everything goes perfect, we can be back in four hours. Two hundred forty minutes of risk for a whole year of security and sustenance, and I figure it's worth it.

Well, not like we have a choice.

Here are the risks, and there are so many that I hate to even think of them, but if there's one thing the military taught me it's that a person must be prepared for what he might encounter.

First, traffic or any other unforeseen holdup along the route. Second, nosy or suspicious people at the store. Little old ladies who have nothing better to do than poke around in someone's business and ask questions. *What are you gearing up for, the apocalypse? Going somewhere? Why so much stuff?*

Third, the truck breaks down and we have to ask for help. Fourth, we're in an accident. Fifth, on the way home the gas spills all over the supplies, leaks down into the wrong place and we blow ourselves up.

Well.

I suppose all of this sounds ridiculous. Paranoid. Which of course I am, I admit that: paranoid through and through. Deep down I know that the only real risk is the sixth one, which is that someone will catch my eye, see something familiar about me. Someone with an uncanny ability to recognize a person. That someone makes a phone call, the police show up, I get arrested, and the last time Finch sees me is with handcuffs, getting hauled off, and I never get a chance to tell her what really happened, the truth about us.

I'll wear a baseball cap. Plus I have a beard now, and it has come in long and thick, and though there is a hand mirror in this house, I've hardly seen myself over the past eight years. Still, I suspect I look different. Age and stress: they have taken their toll. But clearly, this is the greatest risk of all, being recognized. It's no easy thing to disappear, and we've done it. I'm putting all of that at risk now, I realize that. But we are almost out of food and once the snow comes, we could be stuck at the cabin for weeks and there is no other way.

Early the next morning, Finch is buzzing with excitement, all riled up, and who can blame her, this being the first time she's left the woods since she was an infant. I tell her to fill the canteens and get her pillow. I pull the blankets from both of our beds and carry them to the truck.

"Bundle up, sugar. Don't want you to get cold."

She grabs her jacket, hat, and gloves, and bunny-hops around the room. Then she stoops to pick up the kitten and tucks him under her arm. "Come on. Let's go."

"Walt Whitman's staying here," I say, shaking my head. That's what Finch decided to name him.

"But he'll be lonely. Scared. He might get into something."

I shrug. "Then leave him outside."

"He's too little. These woods are crawling with predators, you know that. He could get killed." She narrows her eyes and looks at me sternly. "Think about what happened to Susanna, Cooper."

"Well then, leave him here and tell him to stay out of trouble."

She mopes about this, dragging her feet across the floor, moaning. At last she settles the kitten into an old sweatshirt, tucked in a wooden crate from the root cellar. She leaves a small dish of water beside his bed.

Finally, I tell her we need to go. "You can sit up for the first part of the drive, but when I say so, you've got to duck down on the floor of the back seat and cover up." She's small enough that she can slide down between the front and back seats and tuck under a little nest of blankets and pillows.

Her face falls. "You mean I can't go into the store?"

As hard as it is for me to deny her this, I know it's for the best. No getting around it—she'll slow me down. So many things to see and touch and ask about. It will nearly double our time. Plus who knows what she might ask or say, and someone standing close by might overhear. "Sorry, sugar."

"But I thought we were both going. Together."

"No."

"I thought maybe since Jake didn't come, it changed things. Like maybe we were operating under different rules now."

"Well, we are, sort of. But not in the sense that you can come with me. I wish things were different, Finch."

"Me, too."

"But they're not."

"Okay." Disappointment lingers on her face.

I promise myself to grab something special for her at the store, try to make up for this. "So can I trust you to follow directions?"

"I'll follow directions. I want to go." She starts bunny-hopping again.

"You'll need to be real still in there. Someone walks by, we can't have them see you squirming around. It'd be suspicious." She's still hopping. "Finch, are you listening?"

"I'll be the stillest girl you've ever seen. I'll be so still you'll think I'm dead."

"Finch."

"Okay, I'll be so still you'll think I'm a statue."

"Good. That sounds perfect."

I fire up the engine and we drive out the long dirt road, stopping at the gate. I climb out, unlock it, pass through, stop again, and lock it. There's nothing more inviting to snoopers than a gate that's usually locked standing wide open. People see that, and they consider it an invitation to mosey right on in, regardless of any NO TRESPASSING signs. Once the gate is locked, we drive out the rest of the dirt road. White pines tower overhead, tall and thick. After a while we pass the gas station where we'll stop later. There's a green Ford Ranger outside, as well as two pickups and a silver sedan. We pass a little collection of houses, a village, I guess you'd call it, one with a big trampoline that must've been flipped on its side in a recent windstorm. "Look at that," Finch whispers, her forehead pressed to the glass.

We veer onto the highway and drive, the miles soaring past. When I see the sign for Somersville, I tell Finch it's time for her to duck down into her hiding spot, which she does. We pull into the parking lot of Walmart, and I peer over into the back seat, checking to make sure she's fully covered and inconspicuous. Tug at a corner where her shoe is sticking out.

"I'll be as quick as I can," I tell her. "Stay right there and try not to move too much, all right? I won't be long."

"Okay," she whispers, and the covers move a little.

I open the door and climb out.

"Finch?"

"Yeah?"

"I love you."

"I know. Love you, too."

EIGHT

For a person who, for the better part of a decade, has not stepped foot inside any building other than a small cabin tucked in a hundred thousand acres of woods, Walmart is a startling and bewildering place. The lights, endless ranks of fluorescents, shine with devastating brightness. The rows and rows of gigantic televisions all blast the same scenes, in varying degrees of clarity, and with the slightest amount of difference in timing, so that if you stop and stare, one screen is maybe a millisecond behind the one next to it. Dizzying, baffling. Blue and yellow signs hang everywhere: LOW PRICES! HUGE SAVINGS ON ELECTRONICS! It doesn't help that the holidays are right around the corner, so they've got Christmas trees and ornaments and plastic reindeer and a giant blow-up Santa Claus that bobbles back and forth. The sheer abundance of it all: so much, so much of everything. There is nothing muted about it, nothing held back.

The moment I step into the store, I feel a swell of panic coming, grasping at me like a drowning swimmer with a rescuer within reach. Which, you know what happens. The person pulls you under. Down, down, down. I blink, focus. No. Not today. Today there is a mission, a job that must be done, and at the heart of that job is Finch. Finch, who is waiting, tucked in a heap of blankets on the floor of the back seat. Finch, who is counting on me. I glance at my watch: a little past seven. I planned the trip so I'd be here early in the morning, before it gets busy, but not so early that they have a nighttime security guard on duty, wandering the store, hopped up on caffeine and bleary-eyed and bored.

I pull a cart from the rows at the front of the store, tug the list from my shirt pocket, and start walking toward a big blue sign that says PRODUCE. I gather my items from this section quickly, and I'm making good time and feeling better. But then things go south a bit.

How had I forgotten that the simple act of buying oatmeal is not so simple at all? There are whole grain oats, quick oats, steel cut oats, multigrain oats, and then there are multiple brands. Which one? And are they really different, or is this some scheme from the big companies to get people to buy more oatmeal? I try to picture the container, the tall cylinders that Jake always brought, try to recall the words on the side, but with six different options—six!—I can't remember.

"Don't usually do the grocery shopping, do you?"

I'm squatting, leaning over and squinting at the labels on the oatmeal, which happens to be on the bottom shelf of an aisle laden with maybe eight thousand boxes of cereal. I turn around, and towering above me is a middle-aged woman with a paunch and a blue cart crammed full of groceries. I look around, like maybe she is talking to someone else, or she's on her phone or something.

She points to the oatmeal. "I saw you reading all the labels. My husband's the same way. I ask him to pick up some yogurt, and without fail, he'll call me and ask me which brand, which flavor." She shakes her head. "We only ever buy the one kind. Dannon Light and Fit, vanilla. The same brand, the same flavor, every single time. It's the only kind we ever have in the house. You'd think, after all these years, he'd at least recognize the container. Wouldn't you?"

I can't quite put a finger on whether I'm supposed to answer, but she stands there looking at me, like she's waiting on a response. "I guess so, ma'am." I turn back to the oatmeal, pick up one of the containers and act like I'm absorbed by the nutrition facts, hoping maybe she'll take a hint.

No such luck.

"Yeah, that's why I do the shopping. Me, I can sweep through here in thirty minutes, load up the cart with groceries for the whole week. Plus everything else. Toiletries, paper towels, napkins—I call those sundries."

This is not the first time in my life such a thing has happened: a stranger, someone lonely hankering for a conversation, a whole world full of people that could fill such a need and who do they find? Me. I don't know how or why, me being a "poor conversationalist"—at least that's what the guidance counselor told me in the eleventh grade when I had the required appointment to figure out what my plans were after graduating. I had none, and told him that right off, and then when I didn't have anything else to say, that's when he said it. Cindy gave different words to it, and hers were nicer: "You're a good listener" was how she put it.

Anyhow. This little draw of mine, people I have no desire to speak to pulling right up to me, I call it a curse, because that's what it is. True story: once, I was having coffee, minding my own business, as usual, and a woman came up, sat down across from me, and told me she was having an affair, thinking about leaving her husband, except there were kids involved, and I'm not lying—that woman asked me what I thought she should do. A total stranger, telling me her whole life story and then asking for advice. Another time, this was in the eighth grade, and I was stuck after school for detention, the only person that day. The teacher in there, Mr. Marks, he plopped down in the seat next to mine and started telling me about his troubles with his girlfriend. I was a smart aleck back then, let me tell you, and I wanted so bad to say to him, *What do I look like, a priest?* But I just listened and watched the clock tick away the sixty minutes of detention.

"Old-fashioned," the woman says.

"What?"

"The oats. Get the old-fashioned ones." Finally taking the hint that I'm not interested in a conversation, she pushes her cart away, the wheels rumbling down the laminate floor.

I grab eight canisters of oatmeal and stack them in the cart and move on.

There is something about Walmart that makes you realize all that you've been missing out on in life. I remember this, about halfway through the trip. Yogurt, for instance. Ice cream and the little cardboard-wafer cones on which it sits. M&Ms, pretzels, lotion, colored pencils. Thinking of Finch and the look on her face when I told her she couldn't come in, I grab all of them. None of those items are on the list.

Halfway through, I'm out of room in the cart. I check out, take the supplies to the Bronco, whisper to Finch to sit tight: I'll be done soon.

Back inside Walmart, I pick a pair of snow pants for Finch, a coat with a removable liner that I hope might get her through the spring and summer rain and the cool but not cold days of next fall. Both items from the boys' department because they have to be camo. I grab her a set of camo gloves but also a pink pair, with sparkles. Before I left the cabin, I traced her foot on the back of the list, and I go to the shoe section, hold up the outline to various sets of winter boots, then pick one that seems appropriately larger than her foot.

I walk past the electronics, screens blaring and offensive, ten million pixels of color and light. The small section of books. I think of Finch, the allure of a brand-new book calling like a siren from rocks, but I glance at my watch and keep moving because she's waiting in the truck, tucked beneath her blanket. Hopefully. The cart is packed precariously high.

I throw a box of battery-powered Christmas lights onto my heap of purchases, take one last look at the list to make sure I haven't forgotten anything, then begin pushing the wobbly and overburdened cart toward the front of the store. The cashier, a woman with two chins and fat elbows like clubs, has no desire for small talk, doesn't even look at me, and for this I am grateful. She works through the items, scanning quickly, adding them to a fancy platform with multiple bags that she rotates once each one is full. When I hand her six one-hundred-dollar bills, she heaves in disgust. Annoyance about the lack of a credit card, I assume. She holds each one up to the light, checking for the watermark, and then punches numbers into her register. She hands me my change and I mutter thank you, and she flips off her illuminated sign and waddles away from her post.

Outside, free from the loathsome abundance of Walmart, I find that the day has warmed, and as I push the cart, now overflowing with gray plastic bags, rumbling through the parking lot to the truck, I admit: there's a little hop to my step. A happy and victorious sense of having accomplished something worthwhile, of having overcome a fear that nearly took me under. Or maybe it's just the fresh air and the sense of freedom I feel in having gathered the supplies that will carry us through the year. There's a richness in that feeling, knowing Finch will be warm and cared for and even enjoy some luxuries.

The parking lot has filled up a bit since we arrived, and when the Bronco comes into view, I see a man standing beside it, peering inside. I push the cart faster, half running, trying to maintain my cool.

"Can I help you with something?" I say. There's an edge to my voice but at least I don't tell him to get away from the truck, which is what first came to mind.

He's old. Wrinkled and feeble and wearing a newspaper-boy hat and a plaid scarf and gray coat.

"What you got in there?" he asks, pointing. "It's moving."

"A puppy," I lie. "For my daughter. Just picked him up. Threw some covers over the top so he didn't get cold."

He leans in closer to the truck, looking. A roar blooms in my ears: if Finch hears my voice right at the door, she might emerge.

"I knew it," the man says. "I knew it was a puppy." He adjusts his glasses. "For Christmas?"

"That's right."

"What kind?"

"Oh, he's a Lab," I say, glancing at the heap of blankets. Finch's blond hair is poking out from beneath a corner of the blanket. "A yellow Lab."

The old man is eyeing up my cart of supplies. "I had one when I was a boy. He was yellow, and we called him Patton, like the general." He shifts his weight. "I don't mean to overstep, but would you mind if I had a look?"

I attempt to clear the lump in my throat. "Well, to be honest with you, sir, he was awful upset about leaving his mama this morning, and I don't want to rile him up more, getting him out here in the parking lot. It'd probably be best if we just head on home, no offense."

He nods. "Of course. Poor thing just needs to get to your place and settle in."

"Exactly."

"Well," he says, "you enjoy yourselves. You and your daughter. Merry Christmas."

"Same to you."

He hobbles away, shuffling across the pavement.

Close. Far too close. Just when it seemed like we were in the clear. I'd thought this was the safest plan, Finch hiding in the vehicle, safer than her coming with me into the store, safer than leaving her home, but this little incident is reminding me that we're never safe. Not really.

Once the old man is fifty yards off, I open the truck door.

"Finch, stay down," I say softly. "Just a few more minutes. I still have to unload the cart. You all right?"

"I'm cold. I have a cramp in my calf. It could be a deadly blood clot."

"Sorry, sugar. Almost done."

Once everything is packed, I take the cart back. I hold tight to the handle, prop one foot on the bottom, and with the other foot, give myself a good push. Sail, glide, the skinny wheels howling over the pockmarked pavement, the cool air on my cheeks.

I trot back to the truck, climb in, crank the heat, and drive toward home. Once we're out of town, I tell Finch she can sit up. I turn on the radio and find a station that plays country music, which is strange to hear, guitars and drums and the banjo, I think, and a woman's voice that is sweet and sad and twangy, like you always think of with country-music singers. I don't know any of the words to these songs, all new, I suppose, but for the first time in years, I think about how I used to drive around and play the radio, and I knew the songs, not just the words, but I could anticipate the rises and drops and the way the music would turn. As I head out of Somersville toward the cabin, toward the gas station where we will make our final stop, the music on the old radio buzzing in and out, the winter sun casting a golden haze on everything, the sparse trees and the brown fields, I'm feeling triumphant—no, more than that. Jubilant. Giddy, even.

"One more stop, Finch. One more stop and then we're home."

"Can I go in with you this time?"

I debate this. The gas station is a rinky-dink place, a small square building, painted mint green and in the middle of nowhere. Plus, given what just happened at Walmart, taking Finch in doesn't feel so unreasonable.

"I've never been in a store, Cooper. And it's freezing in the truck."

We'll only be in there for a minute or two, and more than likely,

there will be no surveillance cameras. It would mean the world
to her.

"Please, Coop? Please?"

"If there's no other cars in the parking lot, you can go in."

"Yes!" She flutters her legs.

"And no talking, no matter what. Someone talks to you, just
smile and look away. You got that?"

She presses her lips tight. Nods, eyes wide.

NINE

The only car at the gas station is the old green Ford Ranger that was there three hours earlier: the cashier, I assume. I pull up to the pump, tell Finch to climb out, and the two of us head in to prepay. Finch grips my hand, her palm sweaty with excitement.

Inside, the cashier has a name tag that says SHEILA, and even though it's only midmorning, she is drinking a Mountain Dew and twirling a skein of licorice around her middle finger. Sheila is watching television on a tiny screen, *The Price Is Right*, and I can't help but notice: where the heck is Bob Barker? Finch stands at the counter, staring. A lady with white hair is spinning some giant rotating thing, and the new host is grinning. Finch has never seen a television before.

Sheila peers over the counter and eyes up Finch. "You like *The Price Is Right?*" she asks.

Finch glances at her, then at me, then back at the screen.

"She's shy," I tell Sheila. I point to the four red containers next to the truck. "Ten gallons of kerosene, ten of gas, plus let's put fifteen gallons in the Bronco."

"I was shy when I was your age, too," Sheila says. "Wouldn't talk to anyone. My mother went to her first parent-teacher conference and the teacher told her I hadn't said a word the whole school year. That was in November. Quiet, all those weeks."

I force a smile, place a stack of twenty-dollar bills on the counter.

"You been in here before," Sheila says, looking at Finch and then me. Doesn't even acknowledge the cash.

"Naw." My pulse begins to roar. "You must be mixing us up with someone else."

She squints, tying the licorice in a knot. "No, it's been a while. Five, six years. Maybe more. But I remember."

This is where we came to call Jake, all those years ago. We used the pay phone out front but also came in to grab a few supplies. "I have one of those faces," I say.

She clucks and grins, big and lopsided. "That's the thing. I don't remember your face. What I remember is that Bronco." She points out the window. "Nineteen ninety-four, right? Used to have one myself. Same color, same year. Except yours had that Army sticker."

My stomach flicks and my heart pounds and I nearly choke and I wonder—can Sheila see it, that flare of panic? I want to drop my stuff, forget the fuel, hightail it home because the two of us are at a gas station and there are people everywhere and what was I thinking, bringing Finch out into the world—

I take a deep breath, hold the air in, exhale. *Stay calm, Cooper. Breathe.* "Best vehicle I ever owned," I say. I pick up a candy bar, not sure why, and put it on the counter. My hand is shaking, and I shove it into my pocket.

Sheila nods. "I totaled mine. Slid into a ditch, last New Year's Eve. Now I got the Ranger." She has not yet touched her register—apparently she'd rather chat—but I push the money closer.

And then a jangle at the door, a flicker of light. Never even heard the vehicle pull up outside, with Sheila yakking and *The Price Is Right* blaring from the television.

A man walks in. Tall and lean and wearing cowboy boots and a tan and brown uniform. Badge pinned to his chest pocket. He is maybe my age, hair buzzed short, good looking, a military stiffness to him.

"Morning, Sheriff," Sheila says.

Of all the luck. The room begins to burn white, the objects take on a glow.

After everything you've overcome, you can't just let your own mind get the better of you in a little gas station on the fringe of wilderness. You are almost home, Cooper. You're nearly there. You've got a whole year's worth of food in the truck. And think of Finch. She's counting on you. You cannot let her down. Not here. Not now.

Finch turns and stares, jaw open. A woman on *The Price Is Right* begins to bounce up and down, clapping her hands.

"Sheila." The man tucks his hat under his arm and pulls a Styrofoam cup from the stack. Opens a packet of sugar, dumps it in.

"Miss," I say, and try to force a smile. This is something I remember Jake telling me: always default to 'miss' rather than 'ma'am.' Makes women feel old when you call them ma'am, he told me. "I don't mean to be rude, but I need to get on home."

"Of course." She punches in the numbers, slides the bills into the register. She hands me my change.

"Appreciate it." I nudge Finch to move, and she shuffles out in front of me, head down.

"Get in the truck, sugar."

She climbs into the back seat. I fill the Bronco first, then I grab the fuel containers. My hands are shaking as I pump the gas and kerosene. The pumps are old, nothing digital, no buttons. Which also means they're slow. Finch watches out the window as the numbers on the pump roll past. At last, all four containers are full. I slide them onto the floor of the passenger side and get into the truck.

The officer is standing outside the store, looking at us. He raises his arm, pointer finger up, signaling us to wait.

I debate this. I could pull out of the station, act like I didn't see him.

He's walking toward us.

"Cooper," Finch whispers.

He taps on the passenger window.

I push the button and open it.

"That your daughter?" he asks, leaning closer.

I nod.

"How old is she?"

My heart races. There's no way he has pieced everything together after one minute of observation in the store. Impossible, impossible. I consider lying, just in case.

"I'm eight," Finch says from the back seat.

He takes a sip from his Styrofoam cup, winces at the coffee's heat. "Girl her size ought to be in a booster seat, you know."

"Yes, sir. I took it out last week and forgot to put it back in."

"Well, don't forget next time. It's for her own safety," he says. "Not to mention it's the law."

"Yes, sir. Will do. Thank you."

He steps back from the truck. "All right. You folks get on home."

As I turn on the ignition, my head is pounding and I can feel the panic swelling at me hard, a choking sensation that tightens and tightens.

Breathe.

I remove the lid from the canteen and take a swig.

"What's a booster seat?" Finch asks, as we pull out of the gas station.

"You shouldn't have talked to that police officer," I tell her. "I told you don't talk to anyone, no matter what."

"Do you think Walt Whitman's okay?"

Sometimes she does that, ignores what I say, changes the subject. "Finch."

"Well, he asked a question, and you didn't answer. He was just standing there."

"I'm serious, Finch. I need to know that when I tell you something, I can trust you to listen."

"All right," she mutters. On the fogged-up window, she draws a heart and writes her name.

I make a left and then a right and then keep on driving fast, six miles of road that coils and rolls, the dust kicking up high behind me. When I come to the gate I climb out, unlock it, pass through, lock it. We pull into the yard and I turn off the engine and rest my head against the wheel.

"You all right, Cooper?"

I nod and climb out of the truck, and a sense of relief and

exhaustion hit me hard. "We made it," I tell her as she hops down from the back seat, and she puts her hands on her hips and grins. I walk to her side of the vehicle and wipe her name off the window.

She bolts to the back of the Bronco and surveys the heap of gray plastic bags. "Just look at all the stuff."

It takes hours to unload all the supplies. First we carry everything to the cabin. Once everything's in, I move the Bronco, parking it behind the woodshed so it's hidden. Just in case. Then we have to sort the items. Walt Whitman gets underfoot the whole time, lacing between our feet, his little tail high in the air. Finch unpacks the bags, examining the contents, reading the labels.

"Ritz crackers," she says, holding the red and blue box in her hands. "These look good."

"They are. They're sort of buttery and crumbly."

"Cheerios," she reads. "Look at the little bee. I'm keeping the box once we're done with these. I could cut out the bee and attach fishing line." She waves the box around. "Hang it from one of the beams in the loft. It'll look just like a bee, flying around."

"You can pick one thing to try now," I call to her, hauling a load to the root cellar. "We can't open everything at once, or stuff will get stale. So, look things over and pick one."

At last, she lines up her top five choices on the table: Ritz crackers, honey buns, pretzel rods, peach cups, Lay's potato chips. She eventually decides on the honey buns.

Finch tries on all her clothes—a lengthy endeavor. First, we haul everything back to the bedroom, then she tries on each item and parades out to the main room, where I'm fixing a late lunch. Everything fits, thankfully. She's particularly tickled with the pink gloves and wears them the rest of the day.

As we organize all the stuff and set everything in its right spot, such a sense of satisfaction comes over me that I start to whistle, and then Finch joins in, too. There's a lightness to our work because despite the hiccups along the way—the chatty lady at Walmart, the snooping old man at the truck, Sheila and the sheriff at the gas station—we made it. We're safe.

TEN

"Tell me about my mother," Finch says, settling into bed, pulling the covers to her chin. On occasion she asks, and because I don't have the heart to refuse her, I force myself to think of her. Cindy.

I never asked Lincoln for this, for stories, but there were nights when I could feel my own mother's absence, the longing for her cold and palpable, and I wanted to think of her, imagine her there with me in my small bedroom with its *Star Wars* poster and crate of Matchbox cars. I wanted a story. I would've asked Lincoln for one, a memory—I remember thinking of it, but I knew that she was mad at my mother, maybe even more than I was. She'd been clear about that from the start.

"If your mother had died," she said to me once, shortly after Mom took off, "we would mourn her. But she did something much worse than that, Kenny. Something a mother should never do, and so instead, we'll pretend she never existed."

Let me tell you: this was a troublesome and confusing task for a kid. How could I pretend my mother never existed when the only thing I ever thought about was her? I learned, though, that Lincoln's reasoning held some weight. Over time, I didn't think about my mother as much. Slowly, slowly, she began to dissipate from my mind, like a fog lifting and burning from sight, so that by high school, I barely thought of her at all.

"Which story, Finch?" I ask, squeezing in beside her on her little bed, my back propped against the wall.

"The one where she rescued the squirrels."

"You sure?" I readjust, the round logs of the bedframe uncomfortable against my spine.

"Yes, come on with it." She giggles and squirms.

"Your mother had a soft spot for animals. I've told you that before. Always wanting to rescue something, always in tune with the critters, and they were drawn to her. By that I mean, they would look at her different, the way sometimes the birds here will look at you."

"'I knew a woman, lovely in her bones, When small birds sighed, she would sigh back at them.' Do you remember that one, Coop? Theodore Roethke. American poet, 1908 to 1963."

Finch and her regurgitations of knowledge. "I remember."

"It always reminded me of her. Well, it reminded me of how you say she was."

Something pangs in my chest. "You want me to tell the story, or what?"

She nods.

"All right, where was I? Your mother. We had a cat at the farm, my aunt's old pet, and she was a mean and feisty little thing. Hissed at you if you got too close, showed her teeth. Didn't help that she was large, maybe fifteen pounds, which is big for a cat, and all black, which made her look even meaner, somehow. Her eyes sort of glowed more, you might say. Your mother loved animals, with the exception of that cat. Now, I will say, in your mother's defense, she tried to make nice with Kitty, at first. Bought some cans of food, made her a little bed out of an old cardboard box, put some rags in it so it was soft. Well, Kitty would have none of it. She seemed to resent your mom even more for trying to befriend her. That's just the kind of cat Kitty was. Cantankerous."

Finch giggles, bites the sheet. Walt Whitman purrs on her lap.

"I asked your mother, you want me to get rid of that cat? She told me of course not. Like I said, she had a soft spot for animals, even mean ones."

Finch interrupts. "She wouldn't have approved of what you did with Susanna. My mother."

"No, I reckon not. Anyhow. One day Kitty dragged a dead squirrel, well, half-dead, up onto the porch where your mother was sitting with a glass of lemonade and a book. She was pregnant with you at the time. The squirrel was writhing and twitching, and Kitty was batting at it, playing. Which that's what cats do, that's how they're wired: they toy with something before they finish it off. Your mother shooed her off the porch, and Kitty hissed, ears back, eyes aglow, but then took off. There she went, right to the big oak tree in the front yard, clawing her way up the bark. Your mother was ab-sorbed in her book—she was like you, reading all the time, and get-ting so wrapped up in the story that sometimes it was like the world around her disappeared. Next thing she knew, Kitty was dragging a baby squirrel out of the tree, thing was in her jaws, and she brought it right up onto the porch and put it beside the mother squirrel, who for the record was not yet dead."

"What did my mother do?"

"Well, she hopped up then, picked up the broom and swiped that cat off the porch before old Kitty knew what hit her."

Finch bursts into laughter here, squealing, kicking beneath the sheets.

"Kitty was fine—we saw her later that day, and trust me, she was just as surly as ever, and none the worse for the wear—but at this point, your mother came to get me. I was in the barn, clearing out junk. Made me climb up in that tree and gather the rest of the squirrels. Which, just to be clear, if it weren't for her being pregnant, she would've climbed up there herself. She was wiry and strong, like you. Very fit, as I've told you before. Not one to ask for help unless she really needed it. So, up I went. Tucked those baby squirrels into my shirt like a marsupial and then shimmied back down, real careful. There were three of them. We put them in the box your mother had made up for Kitty, and moved them into the house where she couldn't get them. Your mother made me go to the store and buy some eyedroppers and whole milk, and we fed them, multiple times a day. Nursed them right back to health."

"And then what?"

"Well, after a while we didn't need to feed them from the droppers. We gave them other food. Birdseed."

"They love birdseed!"

Here, squirrels are always climbing up and stealing seed from the bird feeder, which is attached to a post right outside the cabin. We chase them off, holler out the door, stomp on the porch. Like everything else, the birdseed is limited, and a squirrel can put a hurting on it. We can't run out of food for the birds in the thick of winter when they're counting on it.

"Exactly. And sometimes your mother would spread peanut butter on crackers. Boy, they loved that, let me tell you."

"What about Kitty?"

"Well, once we adopted the squirrels, I knew Kitty would be a problem. So I took her down the road and dropped her off at a neighbor's farm. I suspect she did just fine. She knew how to fend for herself. She might still be around, scaring nice people and robbing squirrel nests. I wouldn't be surprised at all if that were the case." I tousle Finch's hair.

"The squirrels, were they cute?"

"Oh yes, cute indeed. Especially if you're keen on little critters."

"And my mother fed each one with the dropper?"

"Yes, ma'am. She had a mother's touch, even before she was a mother."

"I wish I could've known her."

A twinge of sadness flickers upward, catching in my throat. "I know." I lean in and kiss Finch on the forehead. "Time for bed now, sugar. Good night."

"Night, Cooper."

I head out to the kitchen and lean against the counter and look out, the clouds simmering across the sky. That story about the squirrels, it happened, but I change the ending. What really happened was we rescued the squirrels, and we nursed them with the little droppers for two days but then, one by one, they faded, not lifting their heads, refusing to drink, and by the third day all three of them were dead in the little cardboard box. Cindy was heartbroken. She cried and cried, and I think maybe everything felt a little worse on account of her being pregnant but I'm not sure. Whereas I blamed the cat, the course of nature, she blamed herself.

Truth is, I like the version I made up. Cindy and me and three pet squirrels, scuttling around the house, a happy sort of mayhem. Finch likes it, too, and even though it's not fully true, parts of it are, the important parts, the ones that help her understand the type of person Cindy was. That's what really matters. Besides, nobody needs another sad story, least of all me.

I step outside, listen. Such stillness here this time of year, with the peepers and crickets of summer quiet now. Tonight, clouds hide the skinny moon, so the yard is dark and shapeless. I slide into my boots and walk off the porch. Check the chicken coop for any sign of disturbance, shine the headlamp slowly from left to right, looking over the yard. Nothing. I head back inside, slide the locks on the door, and prop the shovel against the handle.

If there's a time of day that's hard, it's the evenings. Not sure why, but maybe it's this idea that after Finch is asleep and I'm alone, my mind pulls toward Cindy. Maybe when all the chores are done and there's some downtime, I'm more aware of her absence. More aware that I'm alone. During the short window of happiness in my life, when Cindy was pregnant and the two of us lived at Aunt Lincoln's farm, we'd sit together after supper and talk. Sometimes on the front porch, sometimes at the river, sometimes up by the pond. Didn't matter where: that was our thing, talking in the evenings. What we'd done at work, who we'd seen. That was all good and well, but there was more. We'd talk about what we wanted out of life. We'd talk about the future. Updates we might make to the farm. Places we wanted to take our children. How we wanted to be.

Well. None of those things can happen now, of course, which can get depressing if I let myself think about it too hard. In the past, I've let myself do it, talk to her. Spin into regretting and wishing and remembering, and it's a vortex, that type of thinking. It'll suck you right down and you have to kick and claw your way back. Better to stay in the present. I turn down the kerosene lamp, watch the light fade to blue.

"You would've liked it here," I whisper, and that is all I will say to her tonight.

ELEVEN

After breakfast the next morning, Finch gets back to work on her cross for the grave of Susanna the chicken. She finds two pieces of white pine and cuts them to size with her hatchet. I start splitting firewood, axe up high, down hard. I'll feel it this evening in my right shoulder, a tightness, a soreness, an injury from my second tour where part of a building collapsed and a beam fell and knocked loose a chunk of bone, which the doctor said was probably best left untouched. It mostly doesn't bother me—well, maybe I've just gotten used to it, a dull ache that never goes away—but certain activities aggravate it. Splitting wood. Drawing the bow.

Finch carefully opens the pocketknife and uses it to skin pieces of bark from the twigs, her hands steady and sure. She gets the twine I laid on the porch and begins wrapping it round and round in an X to tie the two pieces of wood together. I pick up an armload of wood and carry it to the porch. Since the woodstove is not only our source of heat but also our means of preparing food, we use it every day. Which means we go through a lot of wood.

Finch finishes the cross and takes it out back to where we buried Susanna. I hear her pounding it into the ground and sneak a look around the corner to see her kneeling and using a rock. Walt Whitman brushes against her back, wandering back and forth. The cross leans and she adjusts and pounds some more. I could offer to help her, but I've always been of the mind that my daughter should grow up to be independent and resourceful, because you never know what life might decide to throw at you. Finch is both. Besides, she would resent my offering, anyway, and she wouldn't like it if I were spying on her, either.

At last she is satisfied. I duck behind the corner and get back to splitting wood and Finch soon comes around the front. She marches into the house, and comes out with her journal, a gift from Jake, a space where she draws and takes note of all her findings in the woods. There's a pocket in the back where she keeps things. Pressed flowers, uncommon feathers. Her slingshot is tucked under her arm.

"Walt and me are gonna scout a little," she says.

I nod. "Where you headed?"

She points to her left. "East."

About a year ago I began letting her roam a bit. I still get a little nervous when she does, but she was getting antsy, pent up here all the time, watching and helping, and I felt guilty for limiting her so much. I figure a little bit of freedom—I can give that to her. She scouts the ground, looking for tracks; tucks herself down and sits real still until the critters come in. And they do. Her preternatural ability to be quiet, hide. Not sure I could find her myself if she ever decided to put me to the test. She knows the tracks of every animal that comes through here. Knows their trails, which way they move, where they bed. Knows the calls of the birds. She knows the woods just as well as I do, and she never goes far. I've made sure she understands: she cannot wander off.

I split the wood into quarters and leave them in a heap for Finch to cut into smaller pieces for kindling, which work well to get the fire hot quick on cold mornings. Then I move on to the bigger stuff. Overnighters, I call them: thick slabs of hardwood that I bank the fire with at bedtime.

After a while, I hear the call of a whip-poor-will: a means of communicating in the woods without hollering. I look for Finch, echo the sound. She glides into the yard with her journal in one hand and her slingshot in the other, and I take a good look at her, gangly and tall, all arms and legs. Her pants, which she has worn since last year, fall inches above her ankles.

"Well?"

"Three gray squirrels. A tufted titmouse and a pileated woodpecker."

"Worthwhile trip, then."

"The woodpecker's working on a red oak, about a hundred yards up the hill." She points. "The tree's dead. We could use it for firewood."

"Good find," I tell her.

She fiddles with her pencil. "That was something, wasn't it, Cooper? Driving on that big road to Walmart. Trucking along, the trees and cars racing past. It was like flying."

I murmur an agreement.

"The gas station, all those houses, the things in people's yards." She climbs on top of a log, rocking back and forth, balancing.

"And there's more, I'm sure of it. There's a whole world out there, Cooper."

Dollhouses. Libraries. School lunches on those melamine trays. Funnel cakes and Ferris wheels. Swimming pools: the smell of chlorine in your hair, those white chairs that hue with mildew. Saturday-morning cartoons. Riding a school bus. Telephones: the comfort of hearing someone's voice who is far away. Airplanes, the miracle of flight. The ocean. Crushes. Sleepovers with friends. Back-to-school shopping. Playing dress-up. Getting a driver's license. Bowling alleys. Ice cream, hand-dipped. Sharing secrets with a best friend. Proms. Field trips. Movie theaters. Walmart.

I know the list. The many things Finch is missing out on, based on my decision to bring us here. I'm well aware that there are things that she will simply not have, some of which are rather significant. And sure, there are times when I question whether it's fair to raise a child without certain facets of life that people consider to be central to an American childhood. Whether my own troubles have been forced upon her, whether, one day, she'll resent that. What I rest on, though, what keeps me from getting too tangled up in feeling bad about it, is that this life I am giving her—it's not conventional, but at its core, it's a good life. Wholesome. In terms of basic necessities, she lacks nothing. She's cared for. Loved.

I swing the axe high and pull it down hard, palm sliding up the handle. The oak splits and falls into two halves. I bend and pick them up and pitch them to my new pile. "We got everything we need right here, Finch. Food, clothes, warmth, peace. Each other." Even as I say it, a part of me twinges. It's good, for now. Good enough, anyhow. But, much as I hate to admit it, I understand: one day—and that day will be here before I know it—this place will be too small for her.

She holds Walt Whitman to her nose. "It's just sometimes I wonder what it'd be like. To be out there. All the people. And think about the castles, villages, cities, buildings. Horses! What would it be like to ride a horse? Trains, airplanes. I mean, can you imagine flying?"

"That's the nice thing about books. You can experience all different people and all sorts of places through them. All in the safety and comfort of your own home."

The wind picks up and tosses leaves that tumble and spin across the yard. I set another round log upright and swing the axe. Finch will leave, eventually. I know that. I understand that this world we've built—hunting, fishing, reading the same books over and over—it cannot last forever. That's what makes it more precious to me, knowing it's a temporary state. Well, everything is temporary. This place and this chapter: I cling to it, I admit that. But I do have an endgame. The plan being that when Finch turns eighteen, I'll put her in touch with her grandparents. Give her their name and number, their address. Tell her a little bit about them. I'll encourage her to go to them. One thing I'm sure of is this: one look at Finch, and Judge and Mrs. Judge will know exactly who she is, her being the spitting image of Cindy when she was young. I'll send the photo of Cindy along, too, in case they need more evidence. But they won't.

Now, to be clear—I hate the idea of this. Thinking of Finch leaving, stepping out into the world without me: it makes me sick. She has a life to live, though, and I want her to have it. In due time, she will.

"I think I'll fry up potatoes for supper," I say. "If it's not too windy, we'll make a campfire outside. I got something new at Walmart. Something you need to know about. Hot dogs."

One day she'll need more, I understand that. She'll not only want to know about the world; she'll want to see it. Taste it, feel it. Experience it herself. I can't blame her. And she will have it, just not yet. For now, I haven't told her the long and dreadful story of why we're really here, the details of what I had to do to get her back. No need for her to know, at least not yet. She's eight and she thinks of me as good, and I let her think it, and is there anything wrong with that—me wanting her to see me in a certain light? No. That's of the utmost importance to me, my daughter's respect, and I don't mind admitting it. The way she looks at me. The way I provide stability in the world, footing. I'll tell her someday. All of it. What the world beyond these hundred acres has done to us. What it would do to us still.

TWELVE

After Cindy died, I knew right away her parents would be a problem. Which they were. But not in the way I would've pictured. First, Mrs. Judge brought over a meat pie. Milk, eggs, bread. I met her at the door and accepted the pie and a paper bag of groceries. I didn't invite her into the house. She didn't ask. The next time, she brought lasagna, and two days later, formula and diapers. The third time, I let her in.

"I could take her for a few hours," she said, holding the baby. "I know you're tired, Kenny. Who wouldn't be? You could get some rest." It was true: I was tired. On the rare chance that Grace Elizabeth actually slept for a spell through the night, I couldn't sleep on account of the anxiety. The accident on repeat anytime I closed my eyes. Cindy's face. "We're her grandparents, Kenny," said Mrs. Judge. "Let us help. It's what Cindy would want. You know that."

So I agreed. Two days later, Mrs. Judge came to the house. I had a diaper bag ready but she said she'd already gathered some supplies at her place. She had a car seat, too, apparently. "I'll bring her back this evening," she said, and before I could even kiss Grace Elizabeth goodbye, Mrs. Judge bundled her up and waltzed out the door. A few hours later, Mrs. Judge brought the baby back, dressed in a different outfit and wearing a headband.

The next morning, two vehicles pulled into the driveway: a blue sedan and a patrol car. Nobody got out of the patrol car, but two people climbed out of the sedan, a man and a woman. Just came to the door and knocked. They were with Child Protective Services, they said.

This was eleven days after we buried Cindy, and it should not come as a surprise to anyone that things were not going well. For starters, Cindy had nursed. Grace Elizabeth had never taken a bottle, and she wasn't too keen about me shoving the plastic nipple in her mouth. Nor did I know what I was doing in regards to holding her at the right angle and making sure she was burped. But after ten or twelve tries, she took the formula milk, drank it right up; she must've been so hungry she got over the desire to fight. And I got better at giving it to her. The sleeping, as I mentioned, remained an issue. She was up most nights and slept on and off through the day, and when she was awake, she wanted to be held. So I hardly got anything done.

All of this is to say that when CPS got there, things didn't look too good. Dirty dishes everywhere: countertops, table, couch. I hadn't cleaned the bathroom since Cindy passed, nor had I taken out the trash. People had brought casseroles and stuff, and a few of them were in the fridge, plus on the counter sat a chicken carcass that I intended to pitch but hadn't gotten around to. It just so happened that at the moment they knocked on the door, Grace Elizabeth was in the middle of a diaper change, which I always did on the floor. I stood up to open the door, and when I turned back, there was the baby with her dirty diaper over her face, must've pulled it up right when I went to get the door.

"Mr. Morrison," said the man, after snooping around for a bit, "Child Protective Services has determined that it is in the best interest of the child to remove her from this home."

"Remove?"

"Yes. That means we'll take her into our custody."

"The hell you will." I scooped Grace Elizabeth off the floor and held her close. I could barely believe my ears.

The woman slipped out the door and waved to the squad car from the front porch.

"Mr. Morrison, this doesn't need to get ugly."

"You come in here, find some dirty dishes and some trash that needs to go out, and you determine that I'm unfit and think you can just haul off with my child. Well, I got news for you. You can't just take her."

"Actually, Kenny, they can." A new voice, at the door. Don Williams, a buddy of mine. He'd run track with both Cindy and me in high school. He was a deputy now.

"Donny—"

"Listen, Kenny. They have a court order for removal."

"A court order?" I shifted Grace Elizabeth in my arms. "And they brought you along, for backup." I was piecing things together. "Which means this isn't about the dishes and the trash. This has been in the works for a while, this—plan. To take my child away. To 'remove' her." I replayed the previous days. Mrs. Judge bringing groceries to the house, offering to take the baby so I could rest. I glared at Donny, pointed a shaking finger. "You could've had the decency to warn me, Don." But I knew how he was, ethical and very serious about his work, and he never would've bent a rule, not even for an old friend.

He tucked his hands into the pockets of his brown trousers. "This is a setback, Kenny. That's all. It's not the end. You have rights."

"You're damn right I do. I'm her father. If you think I'm gonna let you walk out of here without a fight—"

"I know you've had your share of hardships. First Lincoln, then Cindy. Not to mention the—" He fumbled for words. "—the challenges you've encountered, adjusting to life back Stateside."

I knew what he was referencing, one incident from shortly after I got home, and it stung. I stole a glance at the CPS worker, who was sliding her feet back, inching away from me, in movements so slight they were barely noticeable.

"It's a shame, the whole thing," Don said. "But listen. The courts, they want families to be together. You get yourself a lawyer, they'll get this thing sorted out."

"And who will preside over that? Let me guess. The honorable Judge Loveland." I shook my head. "You and I both know how that'll go."

"Kenny, he won't preside." Don gestured for me to follow him into the kitchen. "I'm saying this as your friend. Don't lose your cool here." He leaned in close. "You can't afford to make a scene right now. Not with your—history. It'll all go on record. Make things much worse for you." He swallowed. "Especially with me here. God knows I'd never want to testify against you, Kenny, especially on the matter of you and your baby girl, but I would, if I had to, and you know it."

"She came to the house. Cindy's mother. I let her in. Let her take the baby for the afternoon. I trusted her."

"I'm sorry." He shook his head. "It's not right." He reached out and adjusted the salt and pepper shakers on the counter. Finally, he turned to me. "Here," he said, holding out his hands for the baby. I knew he had two kids of his own, a boy and girl.

I held Grace Elizabeth close. The CPS workers stood in the corner, watching, the woman looking nervous. I kissed the baby on the forehead, breathed in her hair. I handed her over to Don, and he carried her out to the sedan, strapped her into a car seat in the back seat. I stood on the porch, watching, my heart pounding: a battle raging inside of me. Wanting to run and take her back but also trying to heed Don's warning about everything going on record.

"Caseworker will be by later this afternoon," the woman called over her shoulder.

And then they all climbed into their cars and drove off. Don rolled down his window and raised two fingers as he turned out the driveway. Tires crunching the gravel, then silence.

As soon as they were out of sight, I realized I'd made a terrible mistake.

Unfit. That's what they would call me. And Grace Elizabeth would be gone, too, just like that. Just like Cindy.

No.

With Cindy, it was so quick, there was no way to fight it off. Cindy seeing the deer and grabbing my arm and gasping, *Kenny*, and then the deer leaping into the passenger-side window from the bank, its hooves against the glass, and me slamming on the brakes and the rain, the car sliding on the asphalt and the back end going up on the berm and then over and over.

This time, it didn't have to be like that. I could fight for Grace Elizabeth and I would. And not in some court.

You will see that in all of the animal kingdom, creatures protect their young in the most senseless ways. They will throw themselves in harm's way. They will fight, wing and claw and tooth. The stegodyphus spider, for example. When her young are old enough, she rolls over and lets the babies climb on her and eat her. What I mean to say here is that it isn't unnatural for a person to do everything in his power to protect his young. It isn't wrong.

The caseworker showed up a few hours later, just like they said she would. By that point I'd already formulated a plan and made substantial progress on it, but I was careful not to let on. I had the Bronco loaded with everything I could think of, starting with weapons and ammunition. Three shotguns: 16-gauge, 20-gauge, and the sawed-off Lincoln kept next to her bed her whole life. Four rifles: a .22, a thirty-aught-six, a .308, my .243. Then there was the smokestick that she sometimes took out in late season. And of course I had the Ruger.

Grace Elizabeth's clothes and diapers and three pictures, one of just Cindy and one of Cindy and me and one of the three of us. Blankets and matches and towels and soap. Formula, canned goods. All of my cash, which was quite substantial because I'd never spent my signing bonus with the military, or much of the other money I'd made when I was overseas. I'd come home and cashed it all and locked it in Lincoln's safe because if there was one thing I was sure of in those days, it was that you couldn't trust the banks.

Two books, I grabbed at the last minute and put them under the passenger seat. *The Holy Bible* and Lincoln's well-worn favorite, *The Book of North American Birds.*

I'd done all of this by the time the caseworker pulled up. I was almost ready, but like I said, I played it cool.

Linda was her name, and she was nice enough. It was likely I could get Finch back, she said, provided that I could clean the place up and, more importantly, demonstrate that I was stable and reliable.

"In the vast majority of cases," she explained, "the state likes to see parents and children together." She paused, tracing the hem of her jacket sleeve. "Your case is somewhat tricky because you and the mother weren't married. You must understand: that makes things a little more difficult in terms of legal matters. Not impossible, mind you. It's just that it adds a layer of complication."

"What do you mean, a layer of complication?"

"I mean that we need to determine paternity. The gist of it, unfortunately, translates to more time."

"How much time?" I hadn't slept and I was seething by then, angry not only at Judge and Mrs. Judge and CPS, but also myself. For letting Finch go.

"Well, it depends, of course. Typically, reunification takes between six and eighteen months."

"Eighteen months!" Grace Elizabeth would be walking, talking, feeding herself. I'd miss all of it.

"Mr. Morrison, please. Try to understand. These things take time. Meanwhile, you might use this opportunity to gesture toward improving your situation. You might seek therapy, for instance. That would show that you're wanting to be healthy. And Mr. Morrison, don't take this the wrong way, but you might also work to tidy up a bit. We offer a class on that . . ."

By that point I wasn't listening, not really. Six months, eighteen months: I wasn't about to wait around for some court to determine whether I was good enough to be my own kid's dad. No, sir. Meeting with that caseworker confirmed it. I knew what needed to be done.

Late that night, I went to the Judges' house and got Grace Elizabeth. Let's leave it at this: I did what I had to do, and I got her.

THIRTEEN

Now that we've stocked up on supplies from Walmart, the second arm of our new survival plan involves expanding our hunting territory. We'll head down to the river, a place we call the valley. With a water source, it's our best chance of seeing some game, and we need meat. Usually Finch is excited about these expeditions, especially since we're heading into less familiar ground. But this afternoon, she's off. She harasses the cat. She stands close, fidgets, head hung low. I set my bow against the door and rest my hand on her shoulder. "You all right?"

She reluctantly pulls something from her back pocket and holds out her hand. "I found this," she mutters, staring at the floor. "Last night when I was scouting."

I take it, flip it over in my palm. A round, plastic disk. A lens cap, I think. Black with silver lettering: NIKON.

I think of Scotland, the spotting scope. "Where?"

"East."

"How far?"

She twists her new boots back and forth. "By Old Mister." Her name for a massive, gnarly white oak about a quarter mile away, between the cabin and the valley.

I wrap my fingers tight around the lens cap, try to hold in my frustration. At her, for wandering, but also at him. "What were you doing all the way out there alone? You know the rules."

"I was trailing a squirrel. I lost track."

"Why didn't you show me yesterday?"

She shrugs. "I knew you'd be mad I'd gone too far."

An unsettling realization: that Finch could keep something from me. Withhold information. That she could have secrets of her own. "Listen," I say, kneeling next to her. "I don't want to take it from you, the freedom to roam. But if you can't be trusted, I will. You understand?"

She nods.

I set the lens cap on the shelf above the woodstove. Her discovery confirms a suspicion I've had, which is that Scotland has been in our woods. Not just on his way to visit the cabin, but other times, too. The footprints at our hunting blind, now this, even closer. Closer to us, farther from his place. And I don't like it one bit.

Maybe this seems like a small transgression—trespassing—but with Scotland, it's more than that. Because, of course, he could've just asked, if what he wanted was to hunt. Not like I'm in a position to tell him no, him having me pinned down the way he does, knowing who we are and why we're here. He could've said, Cooper, I'll be hunting in your valley. But that's not his way. He wouldn't ask because it's not in his nature to ask. He'd rather sneak. Heck, for all

I know, he's been using our woods the whole time we've been out here, maybe even before, and he's just now made a mistake, leaving the lens cap.

Plus now he's got me wondering if maybe all along he hasn't only been keeping tabs on us here at the cabin. Maybe he tracks everything we do in the valley, too. Hunt, fish. Tap maples. Maybe he's always done that, watched us, nestled himself in that blind and I just never noticed, it being on the far end of the valley, where if he had his spotting scope, he could be tucked down in there and see us, but we wouldn't know to look for him. If that's how it's been, he could be watching us leave the cabin, then scuttling down there quick and hiding until we arrive.

But if the lens cap was at Old Mister, he's infringing beyond where I thought.

Well, frankly, I've had enough. Sure, I could just say, Hey, we found something that belongs to you. Saw you've been using the hunting blind, too. Let him know we know. But when I think back to the way he brought that stack of newspapers with all the articles about me, I decide there's a more fitting way to communicate our discovery. Besides, the thing is, I don't want him just to *know*. The man needs to learn a lesson about minding his own business. About boundaries.

So, for once, I'll be a step ahead of him.

Scotland knows we need a deer, and he'll be watching; I can count on that. I head back to the bedroom and pull the .243 from the gun rack.

On the porch, I sling the rifle over my shoulder and tuck a bullet in my pocket.

"You're taking your rifle?" Finch asks.

The plan is I'll hunt with the bow, but if Scotland happens to be in that little blind of ours, I'll be able to see him through the scope. And if he's there, I'm gonna fire off a round. Just one, not *at* him, but off to his left and into the bank. That ought to send a message. The message being: I know you're there. Quit it.

"Won't use it unless I have to," I say.

We set off.

Finch is quiet and savvy in the woods, feet soft, lips pressed, and by that I mean she has a certain look where her lips are pulled taut and she is trying to keep the words from coming out. But also the way she moves, almost animal-like, and the way she is watching everything and listening and feeling it all. It's in her blood, something inherent and primordial, instinctual, whereas I had to learn all of that. How to be quiet, how to move undetected, how to watch and see it all and also to wait. I remember Lincoln taking me out hunting for turkeys when I was a kid, the woods dark and still, and you had to be so quiet if you wanted to stand a chance, but I just couldn't. Couldn't be still or quiet. Too much to see and smell and take in, and I would pitch and shift, roll my ankles, anything to move. Not so with Finch.

Maybe it's because she has been in the woods her whole life. In the beginning, I took a sheet and made a sort of sling to carry her around because there was work to do—food to get, wood to cut— and she had to be with me. Hunting, fishing, scouting, hoeing the garden, planting. She was there for all of it, strapped to my front at first, then to my back. When we were hunting I'd get a piece of birch, cut the bark off with my pocketknife, give it to her to chew on. That would keep her quiet, and it was probably healthier than those plastic things you see kids chewing on. Pacifiers. Cruel practice, if you ask me, shoving something into a kid's mouth like that, just to keep them quiet.

Finch leads. It's a bit of a haul to the valley, but knowing her, she could probably find her way in the dark, if she had to. We wind our way through a copse of jack pines, tall and spindly. A wind rushes through: an ocean sound. The trees lean, one creaks. There are no deciduous trees here, no leaves on the forest floor, an easy place to walk without noise. I nock my arrow, just in case we sneak up on something. A deer bedded down, a flock of turkeys, drumming into the air.

We step out of the pines and pause at Old Mister, Finch running her hand along the bark. I circle the tree, looking for any additional sign. Nothing. We head to a hollow, sparse and steep and punctuated by tall outcroppings of sandstone towering along the top of the ridge, gray and covered in lichen. Finch veers off course and scrambles up on one of the rocks before we descend. She spreads her arms wide and tilts her head, sun on her face. She does this every time, just looks, takes in the view. I wait, scanning the rocks for movement. There are dens all along the rocks, some small, some big. No doubt in my mind this place is full of critters, once the snow starts.

Finch slithers down off the rock, taking up the lead again. We descend, sliding a bit: it's steep and in this part of the woods the ground is thick with leaves. At the bottom of the ravine, a stream, a trickle year-round because there's a spring, higher up. Near there, a swath of walnuts. No other trees because they leach their toxins into the soil. Finch leaps across the stream and I follow her up the other side of the ravine toward the next hollow over. The valley. We slide along the top of the ridge before heading back down again. The river runs through this part of the property, so it draws in the animals and provides good hunting. Farther upriver are the maples, so in the spring, we're there tapping the trees.

We have a treestand in a sycamore with wide and ambling limbs, a perfect and magnificent tree that Finch has christened the King of Trees. Which is a fitting name. It's close to six feet in diameter, with a fat, round trunk that opens its long branches, broad and white and luminous on this December day. You can hear the river, deep and slow. You can see the bend where it hugs the wall of rock, carved over so many years of the water running its course. Come spring, the wetland will bloat, and the river will gush, a treacherous torrent with all the snowmelt. This time of year, though, it's a soothing sound, hushed and peaceful. The sun will inch its way across the sky, throwing light over the valley, casting shadows, and we will sit with our backs against the King of Trees.

We push our way through the cattails with their tufts and the arching alder, our feet sinking into the mud, and at last we arrive at the King of Trees. Three years back, I built the stand: a ladder with a platform at the top and a big notch so that it sort of hugs the tree. I put it together back at the cabin and then dragged it down here. Trust me, this was no easy task, but worth it, since I'd been hunting on the ground with Finch for five years, which with a bow is almost impossible.

I tie my bow to the rope that hangs from the tree. Finch climbs up first, and I follow close behind, so that just in case she were to lose her footing, I could catch her. Then, once we're both in the stand, I slowly pull up the bow. We tuck down against the tree, settle in, pull the large camouflage blanket over our bodies, tuck it in at our sides. The bow's ready, the arrow's nocked.

I could almost lean into it, the peace of this place—the world quiet except for the whisper of slow-moving water, the breeze and the trees tossing the very last of their leaves, the thrushes darting through the purple-red stalks of alder, and Finch taking it all in, tucked in next to me—except we're not just hunting, today. I'm waiting for him.

The first thing I do is use the scope on the .243 to pan the whole valley, looking for Scotland. I stop and take a good long look at our blind, and it's clear: he's not in there. At least not yet.

Finch kicks her small legs, knees bending, feet twitching and rubbing along the plywood.

"What is it, Finch?" I whisper, close to her ear. "No deer's gonna come anywhere near us if you don't sit still."

Her legs quit moving and she turns to look at me, eyes wide, wrinkling her nose, showing her baby teeth, the one loose and hanging on by a thread. This is a new look for her. Her bear face, she calls it. I think she imagines it's scary but Finch is eight and beautiful, and even her ugliest face isn't scary. I'm not just saying this because she's my daughter, though I suspect all parents see their children through a certain lens that makes them more attractive than they truly are. Finch, though—she really is an exquisite little creature, with her blond hair and her eyes like water, clear and changing, somehow green and gray and blue all at once and sometimes more one than the other. A spitting image of Cindy when she was a kid.

She plucks a leaf from a branch, leans back against the King of Trees, and begins tracing its veins with her pointer finger. I reach out and squeeze her hand and lean back next to her, and I think, no matter who you are in this world, you'd be hard-pressed to experience a moment better than this. The December sun warm and still high in the sky but dropping, flinging light through the saplings.

The breeze. The air heavy with pine and dirt and whitetail, too: the promise in that smell, the hope of something to come. All of us hoping. I close my eyes and listen—

Leaves. Step step step. Finch, hearing it too now, presses her fingers into my palm. Step step. Whatever it is, it's close, but behind us, the King of Trees is blocking it from view. Stomp. Hoof pounding the ground. This is a deer, sensing something isn't right. But step step step step, and in a moment, they walk into our line of view, their bodies tight and alert. Two of them, doe and fawn, their coats in the midst of turning from that amber color of summertime to the darker gray-brown of winter.

I've always hated it when this happens. Mother and young. You take the mother, the fawn is left to fend for itself. You take the fawn, you're killing a baby in front of its mother. And I know animals are animals and maybe they don't feel love, but still. It's an ugly situation either way, and I wish it could be avoided but it can't. Well. We need to eat and my rule has always been to take the mother, more meat. Slowly, I move my hand to the bow.

The deer step from the woods into open ground, the mother looking around, assessing everything, cautious. I still need to draw back the arrow, which means they need to get farther out ahead where they're not right next to us. A delicate matter, hunting with a bow. The deer has to be far enough away that I can pull back without her seeing me, but she can't be too far away, or she's out of range. The doe raises her head and sniffs the air, then seems to relax a little, snout to ground, grabbing grass. They are so close but we're downwind so they must not smell us. Step. Beautiful, delicate creatures. So close I can see the silhouette of the doe's thick lashes. Her watchful brown eyes. They inch forward, and by now my heart is pounding, waiting for the moment because when it comes, I'll need to be fast.

Step step. Yes. Now stand. Draw back, aim, breathe.

But no. Something on the other side of the valley. A noise.

The deer take off, mother first, fawn right at her heels, leaping high over the alder and small dogwood, darting back in the direction they came, their fluffy white tails disappearing and reappearing as they bound out of range.

More noise, then. A ways off, still, but loud. Rustling and thrashing. Scotland. I hand the bow to Finch, lean down slowly and grab the .243. I press my pointer finger to my lips and signal to Finch to keep quiet. It's thick on the far end of the valley, and though we can't see what's coming, we can see the tall tops of the alder and dogwood shifting, their silhouettes bending and shaking. I could fire into the air, which would send a message.

But then a voice, singing. Not Scotland's. No— It dawns on me: he would never be so loud.

Coming closer and closer and suddenly, she's there. Emerges from the thicket. A young woman. A girl. Hard to say, exactly—not sure I'm a good judge of age and I guess maybe she's somewhere in between. Thin and pretty and wearing a large blue backpack. Tripod tucked beneath her right arm. Big, fancy camera slung from her neck. The wind picks up and the girl's hair blows across her face. Long and red and lustrous as it catches the sun. She comes closer, still singing, but then she stops, leans over, takes off the backpack. Slides it off her shoulders and rifles around in there and then sets it up against the base of a maple.

She is too close. Much too close. A hundred yards away, maybe less.

I press my hand against Finch's chest to hold her still, and I feel her heart thumping against my palm. I glance at her face. Not afraid. No, enthralled. Rapturous. For a minute the girl just stands there: listening, looking. Waiting. My mind starts bounding ahead because Finch and me, we cannot be seen. Cannot.

The girl sets up the tripod, presses its legs into the ground. She screws in the camera, spinning it round but looking up and around as she does. Next, she leans down, peers through the viewfinder. Pans left, right, snapping photographs. How long is she there, adjusting the lens, looking, taking everything in? Seems like hours, Finch and me frozen there in the tree, hearts racing. The girl stands up from behind the camera, looks in our direction, raises her hand to her brow. She tilts her head.

Dear God—is she looking at us?

FOURTEEN

At last she turns and packs up her gear. Straps the tripod to her backpack, slides the camera over her neck, and heads off west of us, crossing onto national forest land, disappearing into the pines.

I drop my hand from Finch's chest. Right away, a loud and unnatural sound starts thundering through my head: like standing right next to a train but worse.

"Coop, you all right?"

I grab Finch's hand and hold it. Throat tight, no words, just noise and the sun that is starting to sink, so unbearably bright and everything—trees, cliff, cattails—spinning and blurred.

"Did she see us? Cooper, are you okay?"

I shake my head, hold up one finger. I realize I better get out of that tree, so I turn and start climbing down, quick.

Breathe.

At last my feet touch the ground, and I let the rest of myself drop. Finch is there, too, must've scrambled down right after me.

"Cooper, it's happening." Finch leans down, her face close to mine. "Can you hear me? Your face is white and you're sweating." She looks around, fishes out a canteen. She twists the cap off and holds it to my lips, but I can't drink.

Fear, pungent and metallic in my mouth, sour and burning. My heart is roaring now, pumping so hard my chest feels like it's in a vise. Everything is hot hot hot; everything is too close. Tree, sky, air, all of it pressing down. I stand and tear off my jacket and stumble, foot catching on a root and then I'm facedown, on the ground, the grass in my teeth, and I'm shaking and so afraid.

"Panic attack," Dr. Shingler said, years ago, when I sat at one of my appointments at the VA hospital and told her how sometimes an overwhelming sense of fear would take hold of me, make the world spin hot and vicious, like some kind of brush fire licked by wind and bursting into something bigger. I resented that term, "panic attack," because it sounded like a name some hoity-toity person in a white jacket had made up. But the truth is, it did ring true. It felt like I was under attack, like the world was caving in on me, like I was trapped. Plus, if there is one thing I have learned in this life of mine, it's that the mind is the cruelest of all weapons. Battles, skirmishes, they did their mean work and then they were over, but the wounds on the mind remained: scabs, welts, pockmarks. They never really went away. They could come back, strike again.

"You witnessed a lot of trauma over there," Dr. Shingler told me. "You lost friends. You experienced terrible things. At the time, you probably didn't have the opportunity to process all of that. You had to survive."

I hadn't even told her about the worst of it: the thing I did that sealed the deal for my ugly heart and guaranteed me a spot in the hottest corner of hell. The thing that would swim back to me in the darkest of dreams. The thing I never told a single soul about. Not Jake, not Cindy, no one.

"You've got to ride them out," Dr. Shingler said. "They feel terrifying, but you need to tell yourself that there's nothing physically threatening. By that I mean that you're not in cardiac arrest or anything, though it may feel that way. Has it happened at work?"

"Once." I'd gone to the bathroom and locked the door until it passed and then told my supervisor that I must've eaten something bad for lunch.

"Well, if it happens again, try to keep working, if you can." She took off her glasses. "I'll teach you a breathing exercise. It might help."

I sat and just looked at her, and she must've sensed that I was skeptical.

"Come on, Kenny. Let's give this a try. Take a deep breath in through your nose," she said. "Then breathe out through your nose. Slowly, gently. Think only about the breathing, nothing else. The breathing is all there is."

I breathed in, I breathed out. Let me tell you, I felt a little stupid sitting there practicing how to breathe with Dr. Shingler. But it did work, and when my medication ran out, six months into our time in the woods, I remembered that day in her office. The big window, the little electric fountain in the corner that hummed and bubbled, the sound of it supposed to help patients relax, and Dr. Shingler with her blue eyes, telling me to think only of breathing.

Deep breath in, deep breath out.

Finally, what I smell is earth. Rich, sweet dirt. Grass bent and poking at the side of my mouth. At first I'm not sure where I am. But then the river murmurs close by, and I remember: Finch and me, hunting. The doe and fawn, the girl. I push myself up to sit and look around, but it's almost dark, the woods a wreckage of shapes and shadows. Everything spins.

My lips are parched and stiff, but I attempt a *whip-poor-will*. "Finch?"

"Here." Her voice floats out of the darkness and I see the silhouette of her, huddled close by, tucked next to the King of Trees, the camouflage blanket wrapped tight around her body.

"You all right, sugar?"

She nods, and even in the dark I can tell she's been crying.

"I'm sorry. How long was it this time?"

"A long time. I'm cold."

I stand up, legs weak, and then take a few steps to her. I kneel down and pull her small head against my chest. "I'm sorry, Finch." I apologize, always, because I know it's hard on her to have to witness it, to have to wait it out. I tousle her hair. "Come on. Let's get you home. We'll make some hot chocolate."

She nods, and we stand and start making our way back to the cabin, stumbling on tufts of cat grass, our pants getting hung up in the brambles. The fact that my feet are numb from cold doesn't make the trek any easier. I keep the headlamp in the backpack, and we use it to guide our path, but tonight the clouds are thick and the night is unforgivingly dark. Finch holds tight to my hand.

Her jacket gets snagged in a thorn, and we stop. "I get scared when it happens," she whispers.

"I know. I do, too." What's the point in trying to hide it or come up with some line about how there's nothing to be scared of? Finch always knows the truth, anyway.

"Do you think it'll happen to me someday?"

I stop then, squat next to her and pull her against me, her long hair cold against my cheek. Terrifying, the thought that I could pass any of it on. That Finch could suffer from these very same things, and it would be entirely my fault. Genetics, proximity, influence. "Tough to say, Finch, but I don't think so. I didn't always have them. Not until— Well, I never had them until I was a soldier, in a place far away. There were things that happened over there that were hard for me, hard for all of us, and sometimes when you come off a thing like that, your mind and body have a hard time readjusting. Anyhow, that's how it all started. And since you probably won't ever be a soldier, I'd say you'll likely be fine."

She nods, her face still pressed to mine. I squeeze her hand twice, and we keep on walking.

"How come you never told me?"

"Told you what?"

"That you fought somewhere far away."

"Aw, I don't know, Finch. Never came up, I guess."

"Where were you? Where did you fight?"

"Mostly a place called Afghanistan."

"What was it like?"

"Brown. Lots of different shades of brown. Light brown, dark brown, green brown, tan. Yellow brown. Dusty brown."

She giggles. "Cooper."

When we get home, I light the kerosene lamp in the kitchen and the candle on the trunk. Finch heads straight to the bedroom and gets her notebook and colored pencils. She pulls the chair from the table and starts sketching. Walt Whitman leaps onto her lap and settles in, purring.

I step outside. Pump some water from the well, splash my face, hoping to wash off the fatigue. A screech owl hollers nearby, fluttering in the dark. Other than that, silence, darkness, cold. Inside, I stir the stew on the stove, scraping the sides of the pan. I grab two bowls and ladle us our food, giving Finch a little extra.

"Dinner, sugar." I set the bowls on the table and nudge the cat. "Off you go, Walt."

Finch slides her notebook to the side. She has already rendered an image from the woods: the King of Trees, the river, a girl with a blue backpack and long red hair.

FIFTEEN

We eat our stew in the almost-darkness, the light of a candle throwing shadows across the walls, the woodstove purring. My body aches from the panic attack, burdened by a heaviness, and my vision is still blurred a little, slow to return. A headache flares behind my eye sockets, pushing at the temples.

"What do you think she was doing?" Finch asks.

I rise from the table, put the kettle on the stove. "I don't know, sugar."

"I mean, why was she there?" She pokes at her stew. "In our woods."

I shake my head. "I don't know, Finch. I've got no idea why she was there."

"That thing she had, the black thing she was looking through—that was a camera, wasn't it?"

"Yes." The kettle begins to hum.

"I wish I had one." She takes a bite of stew. "Think of the pictures I could take. How close I can get to animals. She was so pretty, wasn't she?"

I pluck a mug from the cabinet and don't answer her.

"Her hair, the way the wind blew it." She winds her hair around her pointer finger. "Do you think I'll be like that, someday? I mean that pretty."

I scoop half the suggested amount of powder in the mug and pour the hot water over it. "You're the prettiest girl I ever knew, Finch. I'm not just saying that." I set the mug in front of her and squeeze her shoulder. "Even prettier than your mother, if you want to know the truth."

She grins and leans forward, blowing on her hot chocolate.

I walk the bowls to the counter and submerge them in the washbasin. Look out the window, scan the yard. My mind is twisting and weaving through all the things to consider about our run-in with that girl, but I don't want to think about them until Finch is tucked in for the night.

Once I finish my two squares of the quilt for the evening, we head to the bowl in the kitchen and brush our teeth.

"Open," I tell her, and she obeys, mouth stretched wide. I brush each quadrant, counting to myself. No dentist out here, so I make sure I take good care of Finch's teeth.

"Okay, spit," I tell her, and she leans over the stainless-steel bowl and splatters it with foamy toothpaste. I take the towel from the kitchen and wipe the sides of her mouth.

"Don't brush so hard, Coop. You know I have a loose tooth."

"Sorry, I forgot."

She opens her mouth and points to one of the top center teeth, wiggling it back and forth. "See?"

Once Finch is tucked in, I go back to the main room and pull the lens cap from the shelf, because as my head is clearing from the panic attack a troubling thought has come to me. I walk the cap over to the candle. Lean in close, have a good look at it. Maybe it wasn't from Scotland's spotting scope, after all. Maybe those weren't his footprints in our hunting blind. Which means that girl could've been around for who knows how long, snooping, and what if she knows about the treestand, the cabin, the chickens, *us*?

I pull a long tube from the coffee-table trunk and take out the big rolled-up piece of paper inside, a hand-drawn sketch of the property that Jake's father made at some point. It details everything, not just the cabin and the small clearing where it sits, but other things as well. It's only because of this map that I know that there used to be two sweet cherry trees in the yard next to the apples. I'm assuming they didn't last long, because they weren't here when we arrived, not even a trace of them. But the map shows the wild raspberries and blackberries at the yard's perimeter, the outhouse, the pump for the well, a compost pile out back, close to where we buried Susanna. All of this is in great detail, and from what I can tell, to scale.

But the map shows the rest of the property, too. The steep hollow we cross. The swath of sugar maples we tap for syrup. The river that coils through the valley, the swamp that is only a swamp certain times of year, but which, in a tiny patch in the southwest corner, has quicksand, and that, too, is noted, in small print. The patch of huge, lichen-covered rocks, where there is a cave that I eventually searched for and found, and also a stretch of rock on the ground that's so flat it feels like a road but it's not. Even the square of huckleberries that flushes red with fall is noted. You see, this was drawn by a man who loved his land, who wanted to know it the way a good father wants to know his child. In the dim light of the kerosene lamp, I lean in close and study the sketches and notes.

There is a thing I've always been good at, one of the few worthwhile abilities I never had to work for: a preternatural sense of direction. As a kid I used to wander the state forest behind Aunt Lincoln's land, hours sometimes, just walking and tracking and following sign. Footprints, scat, the pressed grass of animal beds. I was a boy without commitments or rules, mostly, so on days when Lincoln was working long hours, or wherever it was she would disappear to, I went to the woods.

Never once did I get lost. Never once did the possibility cross my mind. I don't know how else to put this, but I just always knew where I was, and I always knew how to get back, even if it involved going a way I'd never gone before. And because this wasn't something I'd learned to do or learned to fear, I never gave it any thought.

Then one day Lincoln took me hunting. We trekked way up into state land, and Lincoln shot a deer. It was wounded bad but didn't fall. Deer, sometimes they can take such a hit, and bleed and bleed and you wonder how on earth they can still be alive, but they are. They keep on moving, resilient creatures, with an irrepressible drive to live. Well, dark folded in quick and Lincoln slumped down against a tree and said, "Heck, Kenny. Did you bring yourself a snack? I think we might be lost."

I was eleven then, and hungry all the time, but more often than not, there wasn't much to scrounge from Lincoln's cabinets, so I told her no, I didn't have a snack. But the good news was, we weren't lost. I knew exactly where we were, and in thirty minutes we were home, back at Lincoln's kitchen table, eating Chef Boyardee from the can.

Lincoln sat across from me and shook her head. "How'd you do that, Kenny? How'd you get us home?" Her face was red, the way it would always get when she'd been outside for long, and her eyes were moist. The one always teared up and spilled over when it was cold.

I shrugged.

"You been out there before, to that spot where we were?"

"Nope." I shoved a ravioli in my mouth.

"Never?"

"Never."

She pointed her fork at me. "That's from your mother."

I stared at her. Lincoln never spoke about her—my mother, her sister.

"She could know how to get somewhere, even when she'd never been there before. We were in a city once, somewhere neither one of us had been. I'm telling you, I was all turned around, felt like I was spinning. But she knew her way around, like she lived there. Crazy thing, that a person could know a place they've never been."

In the military, I learned, and so did my superiors, that my ability to know my way around unfamiliar territory was a useful skill indeed. And let me tell you: they did not let that skill go to waste. "What street was that where you saw the woman with the radio, Private?" I didn't know the name—couldn't say it—but I'd point on a map. "Can you get us to the spot where you and Williams found that cache of weapons? In the dark?" And I could get them there. A roundabout way, a different way than I'd gone before. I could find it. I always did.

Anyhow. I guess when I take out the map to double-check, I'm not really double-checking. I know where the property line is that separates this land from the national forest. I know that, sitting against the King of Trees, we were a quarter mile from that line because I paced it off, a long time ago. I know that girl headed back through the national forest by walking an old logging trail that winds a mile and a quarter through a swath of towering white pines and all the way back to a small parking lot. In fact, come to think of it, I believe it's called Old Logging Trail: a flat, comfortable walk that, on some pamphlet, experts have designated as "easy." I know, too, that she would've passed the NO TRESPASSING signs I posted years ago and that she must've paid them no mind.

What I don't know is whether she's been here before. Whether maybe she's to blame for those footprints we found at the King of Trees. The blind, too. How close she has come to the cabin, whether she'll be back. And, most troubling of all, whether she saw us. Whether she took our picture. Because if she has been snooping around and it's a habit of hers, if she's out there roaming around with a camera, of all things, it changes everything for me and Finch. Everything. Our whole world now in a more tenuous state than it already was.

And the question is, what am I gonna do about it.

Because somehow I can't shake the feeling that us crossing paths with that girl—it's trouble.

SIXTEEN

The day after Finch and me see the girl in the woods, we make another attempt at a deer and head out in the opposite direction of the valley, west. The snow will be coming soon, and I want meat hanging before it does. We're lucky, that morning: the two of us creeping up over a ridge, coming upon a six-point bedded down in some broom sedge. Almost didn't see him but then the white of his antlers jumped out to me, forty yards ahead. Easy shot.

We sit down, our backs against a thick black oak. Give the buck time to run and wear himself out and die.

Finch pulls an apple from my backpack. "Can I track him myself?" she asks.

"You can try."

She smiles, sinks her teeth into the apple, winces. "My tooth."

I lean close and take a look: the baby tooth, twisted to the side and hanging. "Want me to give it a yank?"

She makes her bear face. "No."

After twenty minutes, we stand and head to the spot where the buck had been lying, the grass matted down. A smattering of blood.

"Here," Finch says, pointing to a patch of blood smeared on some cheatgrass. She steps forward, her eyes searching the forest floor. "And here." More blood, drops on a lichen-covered rock. Such focus. She bends, squinting. Circles back. Sometimes the blood trail stops. She stands up straight, looks around, momentarily stumped. "I don't need your help," she says, waving me off.

I linger behind.

She catches sight of something and dashes forward ten yards. "Found it." A large swipe of blood on some grass. Tuft of brown hair. She reaches out, presses her finger to the blood. Looks some more.

"There!" Triumphant, she points: twenty yards ahead, the deer. She darts off.

"Don't get too close." It could still be alive, and if so, frantic. Any creature on its deathbed will fight for those final moments. I've learned that the hard way.

"It's dead," Finch says. "I see its tongue hanging out."

I nudge it gently with my boot, just to be sure.

Finch and me gut the deer in the woods. She kneels down, leans in. "Can I do it?"

I hand her the knife, point. "Slide along here. Good."

"How old do you think she was?"

"What? Who?"

She stops cutting, looks at me and rolls her eyes. "The girl we saw yesterday. Who else?"

"Oh." Of course she would obsess over this. First time we ever run into someone in the woods and it's a girl. A young woman.

Whatever she is. "Sugar, I really don't know. I can't say I got a good look at her, to tell you the truth." I point to the bladder. "Careful here. Go along this way. You don't want to cut this. You'll have a real mess on your hands."

"Do you think she's a nature photographer? Or an artist?"

"Hard to tell." I reach out and guide her hand as she cuts.

"I know, but we can guess. Or imagine." She stops working and looks at me. "We can make something up. I like thinking about her."

Whether to allow this, whether to engage or shut it down altogether. "All right, fine."

She turns the knife and hands it to me. "I'll go first. I think she is a princess who has run away. She has always wanted to explore the land beyond the kingdom gates, and finally, at the annual winter festival, she sees her chance to steal away, and she does."

Should I be reading into this? A girl who wants to explore beyond her kingdom. I look at Finch. She grins and the wind tugs hair from behind her ear and blows it across her face.

"I think she was probably out in the woods taking pictures and accidentally wandered off national forest land and ended up in the valley." This is what I hope. But, given our recent findings in the woods, I'm not convinced it's true.

She sighs. "I sure would like to see her again."

I give her a look, but she's staring into the treetops, squinting at a bird.

"She was lost but found her way and she won't be back," I add. (If we're imagining, why not fulfill the fantasy?)

"I hope you're wrong about that, Cooper. I really do."

Once we've finished field-dressing the deer, I sling the backpack over my shoulder and grab the buck by one antler. Drag him back toward the cabin, over the long stretch of lichen-covered rock; up the hill and through the pines. Taxing work, and I'm sweating hard by the time we're home. In the yard I take a swig of water and catch my breath, then get to work on hoisting him up in the shed while Finch works the hand pump and rinses the blood from her hands. She bends down, dries them in the grass, disappears in the cabin.

When she returns, she's got her slingshot and notebook. I've got the deer hanging upside down, and I'm using my pocketknife to remove the skin. Walt Whitman is sliding between my feet, licking drops of blood, his white face and whiskers stained.

"Tenderloin for supper, Finch. Your favorite."

She nods. "I'm going to set some traps."

I slide the knife along the rib cage. Ponder this. The girl, the camera. But also the fact that scouting and wandering—they are small freedoms and joys I can give Finch. And once the snow hits, she'll be even more limited. "I don't want you near the valley. Don't forget."

"I'll head north, behind the house. I saw lots of sign back there. I'll set some deadfalls."

Deadfalls. She notches branches, creates a figure-four. She props up a heavy rock and places some bait on the ground. Never once has she caught a thing, but she gets a kick out of it. I hold out my hand. "Here, take my watch. Come back in twenty minutes, okay?"

She unfastens it from my bloody wrist and slides it in her pocket.

"And take this darn cat along, would you?"

She grins and shakes her head. "He'll slow me down," she says, and with that, darts off, waddling just a little in her thick camouflage pants and jacket.

"He's slowing *me* down," I mutter, nudging Walt Whitman with my boot. He looks up and meows and then begins attempting to climb my leg.

I watch her go. She jogs along, the wide legs of her camo pants swishing. At the edge of the woods, she turns and raises a hand. I wave back. And then she is gone, slipping into the thickness of the pines.

"You two were out late last night." Scotland: his raspy voice, there in the yard, just a few feet away.

Finch is back by this point, shooting rocks at a target with her slingshot. She's getting good at it, better than me. I'm digging carrots, a pathetic crop of short, gnarly stumps, and I throw one into the basket and stand up to look him in the eye. Heart in my throat from him just showing up like that and he can see it, the panic.

Laughter. Mirth. He's roiling with it. "The look on your face." He wipes his eyes with his sleeve.

"You're a son of a bitch, you know that, Scotland?"

"Language, Cooper. Language," he says, turning serious and glancing meaningfully at Finch. "There's a song children sing in Sunday school." He clears his throat and then starts singing. "'Oh, be careful, little ears, what you hear. Oh, be careful, little ears, what you hear.'"

This life and its contradictions. The sun overhead, warm and bright against the still December sky. The black-capped chickadees quivering at the bird feeder. But then Scotland there in the yard, singing church songs, eyes locked on Finch.

He keeps going. "'Oh, be careful, little tongue, what you say. Oh, be careful, little tongue, what you say. For the Father up above is looking down in love. Oh, be careful, little tongue, what you say.'"

"Give it a rest, Scotland."

"I like it," Finch says. "You have a nice voice."

I have to agree: it's sort of startling, how good he can sing. Rich and smooth. Like he can transform it entirely from his speaking voice. Like he has had some training.

"Thank you, Finch," he says. "It's a good song. A good message." He leans in close to me. "You need to watch the way you speak. Your foul language. I mean that. She's listening. Learning. Finch is a beautiful girl. She'll grow up to be a lovely young woman. Before you know it, too. Just look at her, halfway there already." He shakes his head. "Nothing worse than a pretty lady with a dirty mouth."

Jake raised this issue with me a few years back when Finch cursed when she tripped in the yard: the fact that she was learning every word and action and mannerism from me and I better do my best to model good behavior. Which, coming from Jake, he said it in his usual gracious way, and I took it to heart. Since then, I've tried to clean up the way I talk, in part out of respect for Jake and in part because I could see his point.

But Scotland—he has a way of bringing out the worst in me, and besides that, I have no interest in child-rearing advice from the likes of him. "What do you know about raising kids anyway," I mutter, turning my back to him.

Scotland kneels down beside me so that our faces are so close I can smell him: dirt, animal, woodsmoke, wintergreen. He looks past me, to the woods. "Oh, neighbor. You don't know the first thing about me, and I'd be obliged if you'd bear that in mind. Also"—and he looks at me, here, holds my eyes, his pupils small in the bright light, his gray eyes gleaming— "'Judge not, and ye shall not be judged.' Luke 6:37."

Not much I can say to that, so I just turn away from him and start pulling carrots again.

Scotland peers into the basket of carrot stumps. He shoves a hand into the dirt, holds a handful, squeezes it, lets it drop. "You need to sift this dirt, too many rocks. And with all these pine trees around, I'm guessing it's far too acidic."

"We've been composting. It's getting better."

Scotland grunts and gestures toward the basket. "Looks like it."

I dig and pull up a good carrot—three inches in length, our best one. "See?"

"You should haul up some dirt from the river's edge. That rich, good stuff from the floodplain. Full of nutrients. That'll get things going. Put your ashes in, too. Now that Jake's no longer coming, you've got to do better with this garden." He hops up, curls his feet under him and stands quickly, and for the hundredth time I wonder how old he is and how he can possibly get around the way he does. My own knees and back and shoulder are always nagging at me about my age.

He saunters over to the porch, leans in, and looks up. Then he grabs one of the chairs and drags it to the edge of the porch. Climbs onto it, reaches high, grips the edge, and shimmies up, onto the roof, lickety-split, like a kid on a jungle gym, body contorted and bent at impossible angles. Such agility. I admit it, I'm impressed. Jealous, even.

"Gutter's broke," he calls down. "Better get that fixed. Don't want to be up here on this metal roof, once the snow hits. You got a hammer and some nails? I can do it now if you want."

I stand there and debate this. Think about whether I want to owe him a favor.

Finch pokes her elbow into my side. "What size nails?"

He holds out his finger and thumb, demonstrating a length.

She bounds into the house, grabs the nails and hammer from the drawer in the kitchen, and reappears. I reach up and hand them to him.

"Hey," I say, trying to sound casual. "Your spotting scope. What brand is it?"

"Why?"

"Just wondering."

"It's a Vortex." Up on the roof, he starts hammering.

I kick at a clump of dirt in the yard. It belonged to her, then. The lens cap. Which means she'd been on our land before. But how many times? And will she be back? I swear under my breath.

Scotland pauses, holding the hammer midstrike. "What's that?"

"Nothing."

"You been down to the river lately?" he asks.

I can't help but wonder what all he knows about our trek down there last night. Whether he was close, whether he was watching. Whether he saw her, too. Whether he has known about her all along and was just waiting for us to encounter her ourselves. "No."

"Yes," Finch says, giving me a look. "We saw a girl yesterday. That's why we were so late getting back. Cooper had a panic attack. Sometimes he has those, on account of him being a soldier."

Scotland tucks a nail between his lips and looks at me, then scans the woods. "A girl, huh?" He is a good pretender, I know. A master at holding tight to information and then releasing it when he sees fit.

"A girl or a woman," Finch continues. "I'm not sure. How do you tell the difference, anyhow? Well, either way, she's very pretty."

She runs her hand down her braid. "With long, red hair. Today I determined that she's a wood nymph. We were down by our hunting spot. There's a big sycamore, and it's beautiful and majestic. We call it the King of Trees." She gestures, holding her arms wide. "Do you know where that is?"

"I don't get down there much," he says. He shimmies down from the roof and hands Finch the hammer. "That ought to do it, neighbor."

I press my thumb and forefinger into Finch's shoulder and she wrinkles her nose and bares her teeth. "What?" she hisses.

I've explained to her before that she doesn't need to go sharing every detail of our life with him. That she can have a filter. What I haven't told her is that he knows about the thing I did to keep us together, that he knows we're hiding, that he's had us in a vise all these years and there's nothing I can do about it but be civil enough toward him and hope he doesn't decide to make a phone call and end everything for us. He's a neighbor, not a friend—there's a difference. But of course I haven't laid this out for her. She adores Scotland, trusts him. Which is precisely what makes me so uncomfortable. Precisely what makes him so dangerous.

SEVENTEEN

The next evening, as dusk folds in on the cabin, I slip into my coat and pull on my hat and boots, then step outside. The sky is low and light gray and ominous, like it's holding snow and waiting, which is all right because we're ready, the cabin is stocked with supplies, and besides that, a good snow would keep that girl from coming back, coming closer. I tilt my head to the sky as if to say, Go on, then. Let her rip.

Finch shuffles out, grinning, decked in her new camouflage gear. She points to the back of the house. "I need to check my traps."

"It'll be dark in a few minutes."

"You know I have to check them. What if there's an animal, suffering? That's the first rule of trapping. Always check your traps. That's what you taught me."

"Take them down," I tell her, nodding, and she scuttles off. "And hurry," I call after her.

I pry the lid off the bucket of chicken feed, which makes the girls get extra wound up and pushy, wanting it. I toss three handfuls into the fenced-in area. At the well pump I fill a bucket for them and then dump it into their pan.

"The way I see it, as soon as the snow comes, we're in the clear for a while," I tell the chickens as they peck at the ground. "Me and Finch and Walt Whitman, we'll hunker down here and just wait it out." After they've had their fill, I get my stick and use it to encourage them up the ramp and into their coop. "Go on in now, ladies."

I head up to the porch and decide to sit down for a few minutes, take a breather. Slide the Ruger out of my pocket and set it beside me. Sit with my back to the post and stretch out my legs. A junco darts into the feeder, then another. The woods are still and gray, no wind at all, and the birds are plain and lovely and reliably indifferent.

This place—it has made me whole. Well, as whole as I will ever be, after what I saw.

After what I did.

We were on our third tour when things really went south. Everything wrong from the start, beginning with trouble on the flight to Germany: something bad with the plane. We had to deplane and then we sat around for eleven hours. Waiting, playing solitaire, fielding questions. Some people playing games on their phones, anything to pass the time. There was something about that, thinking you're leaving, and then not going, that was hard. You would get yourself into a certain mindset, shift gears, so to speak, and then you had to change back. Plus everyone knows that it's right after leave that people get killed. You come home, you let your guard down, you die. Well, after sitting in the airport, we finally got rerouted and sent through Morocco of all places, then Anders got some kind of horrendous stomach bug that spread to the rest of us, so by the time we actually hit the ground in Kabul, we were dehydrated and jet-lagged and worn out. Four continents in three days and nobody had slept hardly at all, other than Jake, who could sleep anywhere, any time of day, God love him.

Anyhow. It would've been good for us to take a day or two to rest up, get a handle on ourselves, but no time for that. Five hours after we got there, they sent us out. We were reliable, we'd all been there before, they were counting on us, they needed us. That's what we were told. So we juiced up on energy drinks and coffee and packed up our gear. By midnight we were heading west in a Humvee on a search-and-rescue. Two of our guys had lost contact the day before and we were supposed to find them.

Well. Find them, we did, but they were dead, strung up in the street and a sorry sight, an image that I will never shake off. We radioed it in. But meanwhile it was like the bodies were bait for us, like the insurgents had known we'd come for them. We were tucked in along a building and we needed to cross a wide street to get back to the Humvee, which was about a mile out. I said I'd go first and that's when Jake stepped on the IED and then they knew where we were and everyone started shooting and the two of us got separated from the rest of our team.

I slung Jake over my shoulder and we ran for cover, hunkered down in a dark building. I set him on a table and took a look at him, and it was worse than I'd thought: he was in poor shape and bleeding bad. I dug in my pack, poured coagulate on the wounds, pulled out a shard of wood that was stuck in his armpit. Part of his face was gone, too. That was the hardest part, seeing his eye and part of his cheek ripped right off. I gave him some water and then held his hand and sat next to him.

After a while the skirmish died down and people were back on the streets, resuming their lives because that's how it went. When things got heated, civilians would scoot off the streets, and real quick, it would be clear and quiet except for those of us who were fighting. But once things settled down, people were back out again, resuming their everyday business, which always struck me as strange, how they could live like that, though I guess they had no choice.

No one knew we'd gotten pinned down there, with nowhere to go and the radios lost in the blast. Before long, we ran out of water, and Jake's face and leg were looking bad, his whole left side a bloody, charred mess, and the flies were seething now, too many for me to keep away from him. That bothered me, the way they just descended upon him, like he was already dead, and I couldn't keep them back. How long, I remember wondering, how long until he'd die on that table on that unknown street in an unknown town.

It was December 14th and things were looking bleak. Jake started reciting Psalm 23, which if you don't know it, is a death song, in my opinion. *Yea, though I walk through the valley of the shadow of death.* I told him to quit it. Bent down and got right in his face with blood and sand and muscle and bone and looked through all of it and said, "Don't you dare."

He changed his tune.

"'Not, I'll not, carrion comfort, Despair, not feast on thee.' Is that better?" he asked, looking at me. His face monstrous. The left eyeball a space of dried black blood but the right one, the same:

kind and knowing. And yet he was smiling, I could tell. He'd been a handsome devil, before.

I squeezed his hand. "Sure, brother."

"That's Gerard Manley Hopkins."

"Tell me about him." I said this to get him out of the mode where he was brewing an infection and knew it and therefore gearing up to let go. I needed him to shift into English-teacher mode. I needed him to stay alive.

My tactic worked. He started talking about Hopkins and the Victorians and sonnets, none of which meant anything to me, but with him distracted I could scout the building a bit and not worry about him dying on me.

And so it was that Jake was talking poetry when I crept up and up, four flights of stairs to peer out a window. I had a pretty good sense of where we were but I knew I could confirm it from a higher vantage point. Once I got a look at things, I knew I could navigate our way back to base. Anyhow, like I said, people were back on the street. The bazaar was open, three kids were kicking a ball. From up there, I saw two figures closing in on the building, and they were headed right toward the entrance close to Jake. Jake lying on a slab on the brink of death and both of them sneaking, heads tucked, shoulders down.

Quick quick I darted back down the stairway, skipping steps, all those flights, and into the room and all I had was my AK, which would've alerted everyone that we were still there. And I couldn't have that happen, not with Jake incapacitated and hours to go until nightfall. I remember running my hand along the wall in the stairwell, the steps that turned and turned. The rough feel of the stucco on my fingertips, the sound of my boots echoing down and down.

By the time I reached Jake they were both there in the room, standing over him and I thought he was dead already, that they'd finished what little was left of him, and a sudden fury swept over me, a thing so forceful I lost sense of everything I knew and was and all that was left was that room: my friend on the table, two people there to cause him harm, the flies that hummed and feasted, the heat.

I killed both of them. A man and a woman. Quick, but still.

The thing the woman had been carrying—it was a cake. Later, I fed it to Jake, crumb by crumb, because he wasn't dead. They hadn't touched him. Looking back, I've tried to convince myself that maybe they really would've hurt Jake, after all. Maybe both of us. Maybe I could've told them to get lost and they would've walked out of there and then told someone, and Jake and me would've gotten strung up in the streets. Regardless of what would've happened, though, whether they were there by accident or there to harm us, the fact is, I killed them, and I have to live with it.

Well. Bad things happen to people during war, even good people, as it did with Jake. It is no respecter of persons, war. Even if it doesn't damage your body, it damages your soul. As it did with me. And now I've slipped into reliving that dreadful day yet again. Can't ever seem to get away from it, can't ever be free.

"Finch?" I rise from the porch, tuck the Ruger in my pocket, and head toward the backyard. It's almost dark, and she should be back. I round the corner of the house. Pause. A sound. A motor? Not far and we never, ever hear a motor here, except when Jake comes, the main road being too far for sound to carry. The noise growing louder. Someone coming. For a second I allow myself to think it: Jake? No. "Finch!"

Tires on gravel. I scan the woods, looking for Finch, any sign of
her. Nothing. My mind racing and toiling: Scotland, the girl we saw.
I tuck behind the back side of the house. Headlights flicker through
the almost-dark. The vehicle rounds the bend and comes into sight.
A blue car, not sure the make, and inexplicably quiet. I turn around
and search the woods again. No Finch and the sun is slipping behind
the hill, throwing off a magnificent array of winter colors: yellow,
salmon, red, pink. Within minutes, it'll be completely dark, and now
someone is here. Where is she?

The car pulls into the little flat spot in front of the cabin. Still,
I have no plan except the Ruger in my pocket, but I wait and hope
that something comes to me.

EIGHTEEN

The driver's-side door opens and a woman steps out. I squint, fairly certain that nobody else is with her. She reaches high, stretching, then leans back into the car and pulls out a coat. She wears a long gray skirt and a baggy white sweater. Curly brown hair, short. No, pulled back and tied in a bun at the nape of her neck. She closes the car door and walks toward the house.

"Hello?" she calls, climbing the porch steps.

The door is unlocked, of course. She knocks, takes a few steps, I'm presuming to peer in the window, but I can't see her. "Hello?" she calls again.

What to do. Behind me, rustling. I turn and see a small figure, skirting the edge of the woods. Finch. I *whip-poor-will*. She stops in her tracks, startled. In the dark, she can't see me. I make the noise again, and this time she places me and stumbles toward me. I pull

her close, press my chin to her head. Despite the cold, she's sticky
with sweat.

"You all right? Why are you out of breath?"

"I saw the car coming," she whispers. "The headlights. I tried
to hurry."

"Is someone there?" The woman on the front porch peers
around the side of the house, her voice coming closer. "Bloody hell,"
she mutters into the dark. "Bloody hell!" She steps off the porch
and I can barely discern her outline in the dark. "Now what?" the
woman says, looking at the sky. Followed by more muttering that I
can't quite hear.

Finch turns to look at me. I can feel her head moving against
me, her heart beating against my palm. I press my finger gently over
her mouth.

The woman shoves her hands in her pockets and begins pacing
back and forth between the blueberry bushes and the cabin. Spins
on the ball of her foot and we can hear her skirt swishing. With what
appears to be a sudden sense of purpose, she marches to the car.

Leaving, thank God.

No— She leans in, rustles around in there, and fishes out a
headlamp, strapping it to her head, the light flickering through the
trees. She tramps over to the outhouse and disappears inside. Almost
like she knew right where to go.

"Who is she?" Finch whispers. "Why is she here?"

"I don't know."

"I'm cold."

I unzip my coat, slide out of it, and wrap it around her shoulders. Walt Whitman prances up and glides against my knees.

Around us, the dark thickens. Finch shivers. "We can't stay out here all night, you know," she says. "We'll get hypothermia. We'll die. I can hardly feel my toes. If they fall off, I won't be able to walk. You need your toes to walk."

"Stay put," I tell her, then I stand up, knees and back stiff from squatting. She's right: we can't just hide behind the cabin all night. I walk around to the front of the house just as the woman is exiting the outhouse.

She starts when she sees me, gasps, steps back, nearly falls: she's surprised and clumsy and she shines the headlamp right in my face.

I shield my eyes. "Can I help you?" I say. I'd planned on opening with "This is private property," but up close I can see how scrawny she is, how pathetic and scared.

She looks at the Ruger. "I'm." Her voice shakes; the headlamp shudders as she adjusts its angle. "I'm looking for a family. A man and a little girl." She looks toward the car, sizing up the distance.

I take a step closer, and fear flickers across her face, her features accentuated and strange with the angle of the headlamp. "Who are you?" I hiss. The possibility that Judge and Mrs. Judge have found us and coordinated some sort of plan to take me down flickers through my mind. Because if they were gonna do it, they would do it with stealth and flare, same way they did before. Get my guard down, then make their move.

"I'm very sorry to have disturbed you," the woman says in her shaky voice. She has the slightest hint of an accent. "It's clear I've come to the wrong place. I must've gotten turned around on the back roads. It was getting dark. I apologize." She steps sideways toward her car. "I'll be on my way now."

"Not before you tell me who you are, you won't."

She swallows hard. I see the movement of her throat, gray in the shadow of her jaw. "I'm just making a delivery, that's all. My family owns a cabin out here, and supposedly my brother's friend is staying in it for a while. He gave me a list and asked me to bring supplies. That's all I know. I'm late, but again, I'm just making a delivery. Please—"

I'm still suspicious. Which, if you knew Judge and Mrs. Judge, you'd understand. "How late?"

Her brow furrows, the headlamp flickering its light. "A week. I was supposed to come on the fourteenth. But I had to work and then my car was in the shop and I couldn't."

"You got the list?"

She nods, begins searching her pockets. "Here," she says finally, handing me a piece of paper. "I have food in my car. Food and batteries, all sorts of stuff. Everything on the list, actually. You can have all of it if that's what you're after. Take it, please. I just need to be on my way." She takes another step toward the car.

I hold the note in the light of her headlamp: it's my handwriting. Things begin to make sense.

It has been ten years since we saw each other. "Marie?" Jake's baby sister.

She tilts her head. "Do we know each other?"

"We met once, years ago. You and Jake met me here."

"Kenny?" She squints, studying my face. "I didn't recognize you."

Strange, hearing that name, after all these years. "Yes."

She seems unsure.

"I go by Cooper now," I add.

"Oh." She frowns. "Jake didn't tell me."

"Is he all right? Jake."

She shakes her head, the light of the headlamp flickering in the dark. Her face falls, and that look—I know it, all too well.

Jake's dead.

"Six weeks ago." She wipes her jacket sleeve across her eyes.

I turn away because I want to let it all spill—sadness, anger, loss—but I know I can't. Not here, not now. Not with Marie and a car full of supplies and Finch hiding behind the house and dark pressing in and a thousand things to figure out. Jake, my only friend. Jake, who kept us alive all these years. I'd known, I guess, based on our agreement, and then him not showing. Well, I'd known something had happened. Something was wrong. But still. Suspecting something is different from having someone tell you for sure that it's true. Now the news pushes down on me, a heavy, dragging thing that pulls and yanks. My knees threaten to give so I let them. I lean against the hood of the car.

Marie clears her throat. "I'm sorry to be the one to tell you. And please understand: I don't mean to be insensitive, but I should get the car unloaded and be on my way."

"No, you can't do that, just turn around and drive home. How many hours you been on the road to get here?"

"Nine."

I shake my head, my senses blurry but returning. "Naw, Jake wouldn't have that. It's not safe. You need to rest up a bit. We've got supper on inside." I slide the gun into my back pocket. "Sorry about the gun. Sorry for scaring you. It's just—nobody ever comes. I didn't know who you were. Have to be careful out here."

"Yes," she says, looking at me. "One does have to be careful."

Well, I guess I can see how that might've sounded a little off to her. Me with the gun, me towering over her and scaring her as she exited the outhouse. Meanwhile it's fully dark now and here she is, out in the woods with a complete stranger. She wrings her skirt. She walks to the car, opens the trunk, grabs a reusable blue bag packed with groceries, and heads up the hill to the cabin.

Finch darts out from behind the cabin, her cat a flash of white, bouncing in her arms.

"My daughter," I say, grabbing two grocery bags. "Finch. This is Jake's sister, sugar. Marie."

She extends her hand to Finch, who stares at it, then holds her cat up for Marie to look at.

"This is Walt Whitman."

"A fine name for a fine cat. May I take a closer look inside?"

"Sure." Finch leaps onto the porch and opens the door. "This is our cabin," she says, and the truth is, I cringe a little when she says that, because it's not our cabin. Not really. It's ours but not ours, and Marie's presence makes me aware of that, in a way that Jake's never did: how the ground on which we've built this life is borrowed.

Inside, Marie and me fumble around the small kitchen, bumping elbows and grazing hips, and finally I just tell her maybe it'd be best to let me put everything away since I know where things go. I try to say it nicely. She's just brought us supplies, after all. Finch offers her a tour of the place, and Marie trails behind, Walt Whitman cradled across her chest. The various skulls, some of which she has found herself and some of which are from Scotland, all piled in a wooden crate in the corner. On the windowsills, shards of mussel shells from the river, the black insides of which glimmer in the sun. Also fossils. An old metal spoon she found once, in the middle of the woods. Pressed inside the pages of books we rarely read, red and yellow leaves from the fall. Queen Anne's lace from summer, violets from spring. Dried lavender tied together with twine, hanging from the ceiling.

Finch begins a barrage of questions. Where do you live? (Jake's house, for now, in Michigan.) What does the house look like? (Tan brick with a front porch.) Do you have a job? (Librarian.) What's your favorite food? (Chocolate.) Do you have children? (No.) Do you own a bicycle? (Yes, a red one.) What's your favorite book? (Too many to list.) Do you have friends? (A few.)

"I have a new friend," Finch says, reaching out and rubbing Walt Whitman behind the ears. "She has long red hair and lives in our woods."

"Supper," I say, giving Finch a look. I ladle the stew into bowls and set them on the table.

"Have you ever been to a store, Marie?" Finch asks, pulling out her chair.

"Of course. Many times." Marie frowns and glances in my direction. "Have you?"

"Once, I think. I was a baby, so I don't remember."

"Finch," I say, seeing that Marie is about to ask another question, "let's take a break on the interview and eat."

Finch makes her bear face and slides into her seat.

"I remember these bowls," Marie says, running her finger along the rim of hers.

"Did you live here with Jake?" Finch asks.

"When I was little, yes. I don't remember much, honestly. But I do remember the bowls for some reason. Smells wonderful," Marie says, taking a deep breath of the steam. "I'm famished."

Finch stares at Marie. "You look like Jake," she says.

"You think so?"

"Only prettier."

Marie clears her throat, takes a drink. "Well, I have nicer hair, at least." She fluffs her curls and laughs, her brown eyes bright and brimming. Jake was balding, even when I first met him, and he was the type of guy who just kept it shaved, once it started.

Finch giggles. "You *definitely* have nicer hair." She stirs her stew. "Did he say anything about us before he died? Did he give you a message for me?"

Marie looks at me and swallows, then looks back at Finch. "As a matter of fact, he did. He told me there was one thing he needed me to do for him: to bring supplies to his very dear friends. He also said that there was a lovely young lady to whom I should send his warm regards. He always wanted children, and he thought of you as a daughter. I'm sure of that."

"I loved him."

Marie reaches out and covers Finch's hand with her own. "We all did."

Walt Whitman pokes his little white face up between my thighs and I shoo him away.

"Cooper and Finch, if it's not too much of an inconvenience, I'll stay the night because, well, to tell you the truth, I'm not sure I could find my way out of here in the dark. I'm also well aware that there are no hotels close by. First thing tomorrow, I'll be on my way. Does that seem like a suitable arrangement to you?"

"You can stay forever if you want," Finch says.

"I can sleep on the couch if you'd like the bed," I offer.

"The couch is fine," Marie says. She twists a strand of hair around her finger. "I'll be good there. And more than likely, I'll be gone by the time the two of you are up. Stew's delicious, by the way."

NINETEEN

After dinner, upon Finch's insistence, Marie reads a page of *The Book of North American Birds,* and I wash the dishes and listen.

"'Eastern Phoebe. Hailed by many as a harbinger of spring, the eastern phoebe migrates early. It's characterized by its buoyant fluttering flight with shallow wingbeats.'" She's a good reader, Marie, with a smooth, lulling voice. Which I guess shouldn't surprise me, her being a librarian and the daughter of a literature professor. Still, with the woodstove pushing heat and the strain of the day and my hands in the hot, soapy water, there's something in me that wants to go lie on the couch, just listening until I fall asleep.

Finch takes a good while to settle down, all wound up because of our guest and the day's excitement, but at last, she curls up in her bed and sleep overtakes her.

Marie heats some water in the kettle and asks if I'd like some tea. I say sure because why not. The new candle on the counter flickers and flares, a small glow in the dark room.

"I forgot how beautiful it is here. How peaceful." She leans against the counter and peers out the window. "Look, full moon."

I move to stand beside her, and high in the sky the moon hangs round and white, pockmarked, stricken with gray. The ground glistens with a dusting of snow. Still a few weeks until the bigger storms usually come, but not entirely out of the realm of possibility that one could push through. "You ought to plan on an early start, just in case this snow amounts to something."

Our arms touch and it's nothing, arms touching, but it has been eight years since I've touched a woman and there's something in that small contact, the converging of skin, the feel of another person, that nicks at a thing deep inside of me, that wounds and burns. And also thrills. Yes, I admit it. I'm a man, after all, with urges and needs: can't be helped. I pull away and turn and move the kettle from the stove before it begins to sing. "How long has it been since you were here?"

"Oh, years. I haven't been here since that time I tagged along with you and Jake. So, I don't know. How long ago was that? A decade?"

I nod. I can't help but think: Consider how much has happened. How a life can veer and stretch and retract and shatter. How it feels in this moment, as though things could crumble yet again with just the slightest alteration. Tenuous, this life. Nothing sure at all.

"My dad's dream of living off the land," Marie says. "This place. His father passed away and he built it with every cent of his inheritance. To my mother's great disappointment, I should add. I was five when she finally said she'd had enough, so I don't

remember much. Bits and pieces. Picking raspberries, digging potatoes. Jake was older so he remembered a lot more." She turns
from the window.

I hand her two mugs from the cabinet. "Tell me about Jake. If
you can."

She pulls a fancy metal tin from her supplies and opens it. "It
was bad at the end. He was so small and weak. I doubt you would've
recognized him." She places a tea bag in one mug and pours the steam-
ing water over it. "Funny thing. When he asked me to come here, he
was so heavily dosed on morphine, he was in and out of conscious-
ness, and I honestly wasn't sure if you were real, or a figment of his
imagination." She catches my eye, smiles a little. "I came anyway,
obviously. Found the list—it was right where he'd said it would be—
and went shopping. I questioned myself the entire time, wondering,
doubting. I guess when I pulled up here, I really wasn't sure what
I'd find." She tugs at the string on the tea bag and dunks it up and
down, then pulls it out, places it in the second mug, and adds the
water. "He came often?"

"Once a year."

She hands me the mug and our knuckles graze and it's there
again, the shiver and sting at her touch. I realize right there in the
moonlit kitchen that I have been lonely and that although I've been
telling myself all these years that any primordial sense of desire
died in me with Cindy, that was a lie. A thing I've believed, from
the marrow out, so deeply that I didn't know it was false. Foolish,
though, the thought that the very pull and push of nature could die
with a person, that it could only be about love.

Marie takes a sip of her tea. "Jake said you lost someone very
dear to you. That you were staying here until you got your footing."

So that's what he told her. Just like Jake to figure out a way to explain our circumstances without lying.

"That's right," I say. "Awful generous of him to take us in the way he did."

"How long have you been here?"

"A while." Best to avoid specifics.

"And do you envision yourself staying?" She traces the handle of her mug. "I mean long-term."

"Jake said—he told me we could stay as long as we needed to."

"I see."

The situation dawns on me: We're not living in Jake's cabin, anymore. We're living in *her* cabin. Which means. "You were thinking of selling the place, weren't you?"

"I considered it. Before. Like I said, I wasn't sure what I'd find, coming here. But, you're using it. Living here." She runs her fingers through her hair. "Obviously, that changes things."

"We can pay rent. I have money."

"Please forget I mentioned it. I'm not thinking clearly. It's been a long day." She leans forward, elbows on her knees. "It's been a long year, really."

I nod, take my first sip of tea. This is a concern, of course, and one I hadn't thought of. The possibility that our home could be sold right out from under us. But my mind goes to Jake. I think of his drawn-out decline: the years of suffering, the way his body had taken the initial hit with such mettle. How he'd fought and recovered but not really, how for so many years he was slowly wearing and withering, his own body deserting him, cell by cell. I wonder if maybe holding Cindy in the two minutes between when the car stopped rolling and she died, maybe that was the better way to go. Finch wailing in the back seat but Cindy quiet and breathing but barely, and bleeding bad on the inside. In the newspaper they would write that she died upon impact, but I know the truth: she was alive for two minutes. She blinked and blinked. She squeezed my hand.

Of all the nightmares and memories that surface and blend and cycle through my mind, of all the terrible things I've seen and done, that one is the worst. I run my finger around the rim of the mug and take a sip of the hot tea, shake it off, that image. Cindy at the end.

"He was all I had left," Marie says. "My parents are gone. Thomas."

I look at her, small boned and plain and somehow also pretty, in an old-fashioned, innocent way. "Thomas?"

Her voice quavers. "My husband. Ex. He had an affair and I told him it was over." She turns and rifles through the bag where she got the tea bags and pulls out a box. "Want some? Dark chocolate with caramel and sea salt. The best."

"How long ago?"

She uses her fingernail and struggles to break the seal on the box. "What?"

"Your husband."

"Oh. Not long. Seven months." She hands me the box. "Can you help with this?"

I pull the pocketknife from my jeans, flip it open, and slide it along the edge of the box. "Heck of a year," I say, handing it back.

"It wasn't the first time. So yes, a bad year, but really, it's been bad for years. I should've ended it a long time ago, but I didn't. I just kept hoping maybe he would change. Maybe I would somehow be enough for him."

Here we go again: people spilling their secrets to me. My Confessional Curse. "Naw, don't say that. It has nothing to do with you," I tell her. "Men like that, it's just how they are. Nothing you could've done to change that." I don't know where that comes from, advice. Words to soothe. All these years, all the times this has happened— the woman at the café, Mr. Marks in eighth-grade detention—never once have I offered any solace. Never once have I uttered a single word of response.

She plucks a chocolate and offers me the box. "Usually I slice each one thinly and eat a little sliver at a time. You savor each piece. It melts in your mouth."

I hand her the pocketknife.

"Finch is a wonderful girl."

"She is."

"Her mother?"

"Car accident. Finch was a baby so she remembers nothing."

"Were you married?"

One of my biggest regrets in life, not marrying Cindy. I'd bought the ring right after we'd discovered she was pregnant. It was a nice ring, too. I'd proposed down at the river where she'd first kissed me. But she'd wanted to wait on the wedding. Didn't want it to be a shotgun type of thing, didn't want to be pregnant in her wedding dress, didn't want her parents to think that the only reason we were getting married was because there was a baby on the way. I understood all of that but I also thought maybe things would be a little easier, a little better, if we were married. I'd insisted and then one day we got into a big fight over it and I figured, who gets into a fight over when to get married? Cindy pregnant and crying and telling me I just didn't understand and why couldn't I just trust her. I'd pulled her into my arms then. The fullness of her, everything about her bigger and puffier with the pregnancy, not just belly but arms, legs, ankles, face. *We'll do it when you're ready*, I told her. *Just say the word. You know I've loved you since that day on the bus.* It was something I would say to her sometimes, and she would tilt her head and smile, only that time, she just buried her face in my neck and cried.

"Engaged," I tell Marie. "But not married."

Marie hands me a sliver of chocolate. "Well, you've done a good job with her on your own. Finch. She's sweet and imaginative and bright."

I slide the chocolate into my mouth and for some reason think of communion, the wafer melting on the tongue, the burn of the wine. I took it, once. "Thank you. She takes after her mother."

"Where does she go to school?"

School. Of course Finch would love school, her mind and its sponging up of any type of information, her voracious appetite for words and books. Sometimes I imagine taking her to a library, not even a big and famous one, just someplace small would be enough. The look on her face, her green eyes wide with wonder, mouth open. The joy of it for both of us. Sometimes I picture her coming home from school, leaping off the bottom step of a school bus and then bouncing home to tell me all about what she learned that day. Nothing special, just regular things that kids and parents experience. But these things will never happen for the two of us. For her, yes. When she's older and I have to let her go. I know this and always have, but Marie asking about it sparks a crushing sadness in me. "She's homeschooled," I say.

"Oh. What a shame. I mean, for her to have to miss out."

All of a sudden I can't wait for Marie to be gone. The moonlight spills in through the window and illuminates the mug she's holding, yellow, a small chip missing from the rim. It has been too much. The girl in the woods, the car driving up the gravel road, the news of Jake's death. The fact that Marie owns the cabin and could, if she wanted to, sell it out from under us. But it's not just all of that. It's that Finch is already falling head over heels for her, attaching like a limpet. Marie reading, Finch nestled up against her, the warm soapy water and the tea and the chocolates—it's too painful, it's too much, these glimpses of a life we will never have, when all this time, I'd convinced myself that what we had was enough. I finish my tea and place the mug on the counter. "Well, I'm gonna turn in," I say.

Marie looks at her watch. "It's eight thirty."

"Been a long day. You sure you're all right here on the couch?"

"I'll be fine. Do you think it'd be all right if I use my headlamp and read for a bit? Will that keep you up?"

I tell her it won't bother me. "Thanks for the tea and chocolate, Marie."

"Good night, Cooper."

In the morning we'll make breakfast. I'll fry eggs and help Marie load her car. Finch and me will watch her go, watch her negotiate the ruts and rocks on the dirt road. Finch will say that she loves Marie, that she wishes she could stay, and I'll rest my hand on her shoulder and lie and say, Me too. She'll be sullen for a few hours, shoulders sagging, maybe even some tears over Marie's departure, as there always were when Jake had to leave. We'll split some firewood, maybe see if we can bag a turkey or a grouse. Maybe I'll ask Marie if she can leave the chocolates, and Finch and me can have them later in the evening, with the door of the woodstove open so we can hear the fire hiss and crack, a special treat and a tribute to Marie.

We'll read *The Book of North American Birds*. By evening, Marie will be back home in Michigan, and Finch and me will be okay. Still the girl in the woods, and still the ongoing issue of Scotland, but at least the added complications of Marie and her quiet little car and the reminder of all that we are missing out on will be long gone.

TWENTY

But no. By first light the trees are draped in snow, the weight of it bowing the pines, the branches bent at strange angles so that the woods, familiar to me in their shape, have transformed into something different. Everything white and new, and still the snow is coming fast and hard, a hypnotizing blur. I watch from the bedroom window, and the first thing that comes to mind is Finch and her sled. Finch and her new camouflage snow clothes from Walmart. It's barely light, the sky that unholy gray when there is snow, and she is still asleep on her little bed, tangled in the sheets and heavy blanket, but she'll wake soon, almost the same exact time each morning. Finch and me gliding down the bank to the west of the cabin, first making tracks for the sled, then slogging back up the hill, then going, over and over, until we're tired and hot in our winter jackets. Once we're really tuckered out, we'll come in for hot chocolate. I won't even skimp on the amount of mix I put in.

And then, as my senses return, I remember: in the main room of the cabin, Marie. Took me a long time to fall asleep but then I slept so hard I forgot all about her. Marie with her reusable grocery bags packed with teas and chocolates. I stand and press my head to the thin glass and feel the cold against my forehead.

I pull on my jeans and flannel and then sneak across the room, the floorboards moaning and cracking in the cold. Time to get the fire going and gather the eggs and see about breakfast. Maybe it'll warm up by midday, melt the snow. Maybe she can still go.

Once I open the door, I'm hit—"hit" is the word—by the scent of bacon. How had I not smelled it from the bedroom? In the main room, Marie is at the woodstove, which is hot and purring nicely already, the small fan, powered by heat, on top spinning fast and pushing warmth around the room. She's wearing an old red apron from the bottom cupboard, and she's leaning over with a spatula in her hand, inspecting something in the cast-iron skillet.

She turns to me and smiles. "Coffee?"

What is it about the sight of her in the kitchen that makes my heart simultaneously quiver and sink?

"Here," she says, filling a mug from a fancy glass pitcher with a black lid.

I take the mug because frankly, I'm still a little flabbergasted by the humming stove and bacon and a woman in the house making me food. I take a sip. Over the years I've grown accustomed to the instant coffee that Jake brings in an enormous plastic container from some bulk food store. It's fine; it does the trick of getting me going in the morning, and Finch likes it too, on a special occasion, with some sugar and powdered milk. But this. I close my eyes because this is rich and smooth and delicious. "What is this?"

"Let me guess. Jake had you drinking the instant stuff."

I nod.

"We disagreed regarding whether or not that garbage could be considered coffee." She tucks her curls behind her ear and smiles: bright, perfect teeth. And there is something about her when she smiles, the way her brown eyes tilt downward, that radiates warmth. The way Jake did. I realize right then that I haven't washed my face or brushed my teeth. *When was the last time you took a look at yourself, Cooper?* There is a small mirror, eight by ten with a wooden frame and small tiles pressed into it, that I found in the top drawer of the dresser, but I never take it out. I mean, it's been years.

She points to the snow. "Do you think I can get out?"

"In that little contraption of yours?"

She folds her arms. "It's a Prius. It gets forty-eight miles per gallon."

"Not in the snow it doesn't. In the snow it stays right where it's parked." I grin despite myself. "I'll take a gander, but I'd say it's unlikely you're going anywhere today."

"So I might be here for another day?"

"Or more. Unfortunately."

"Thanks for that." She wrinkles her nose. "Very hospitable of you."

"I didn't mean it like that. I just meant you probably have things to do. Commitments. And now you're stuck here."

"Sure you did. It has absolutely nothing to do with your wanting me out of your hair." Her eyes glisten when she says it, mouth curving into a smile.

She is too pretty.

"My high school guidance counselor said I was a poor conversationalist."

"Well, the thing is, we both want for me to be on my way, but it seems that Nature had other plans today, so I say we just accept that and make the most of it." She raises her coffee mug. "A snow day."

"All right." Inside, I'm recognizing that it's unlikely to be a snow *day;* it'll be several days. For a moment I wonder how long it would take me to shovel two tire-width paths to the gate. But even at the gate, there'd be miles to go until she'd come to a road that was plowed.

"And your guidance counselor shouldn't have said that." She cracks an egg on the rim of a big Pyrex measuring cup and whisks it. "Even if it's true."

"Is someone gonna miss you?" The thought drifting in. Marie not showing up for a lunch date with a friend, Marie not attending work. Neighbors, noting a lack of activity in the house. Someone who might call, someone who might track her down. "I mean, will someone be worried?" I don't add—and come looking for you, or worse, call the police and have them come looking for you.

She wipes her hands on her apron and stares out the window. "Nobody will be looking for me. Not for a while, anyway. I'm a school librarian, and the district is on winter break. And. The divorce, Jake. I just moved back to the States last summer, when things got bad for him. I haven't had time." She fumbles for the words. "I don't have any friends. Yet."

"Well, that's something you and I have in common, then."

She smiles a little and turns back to the woodstove.

"I'm making pancakes with blueberries. Five bucks a quart this time of year but Jake made me promise to add a few surprises to the list." She looks away, but not before I catch a flicker of sadness cross her face. "The coffee, the chocolates. These blueberries. The bacon. I forgot the syrup."

"We have syrup."

"Well. Then I guess we're set, after all. Want to try the bacon?" She gestures toward a plate, where slices, crisp and brown and drenched in grease, lie in neat rows.

I'm at a loss. Here in the kitchen that isn't really mine but that has effectively been mine for eight years. The place where I know every corner, every spice, every chip in every plate. Never once has there been someone else at the stove, least of all a woman. Jake with his messed-up face and infected leg, he would try to cook sometimes, but I could tell it hurt to stand and lean. Not to mention he'd just spent all those hours driving, which also took a toll. *Just sit*, I would tell him. *You brought the food, you done your part. Now sit.* And he would, right on the stool in the corner.

The truth is I can't stop watching her, and I feel a tiny bit ashamed to admit that because I always thought I was more progressive when it came to such things. That is, I didn't think I was that kind of man, drawn to the sight of a woman in the kitchen. Cindy, she was a full-blown hazard in the kitchen. Her parents had a chef, so before we got together, she'd hardly set foot in one. She couldn't even cook mac and cheese from a box without burning it, and I was okay with it because that was my thing, cooking, something I brought to the table that she couldn't, and she loved it about me, and I loved that she loved it.

Marie flips a pancake.

"Did you sleep all right?"

"Sure, once I rearranged the pillows so my head wasn't below my feet." She grins. "I slept well. Great, actually. It's so quiet. I've been living at Jake's since—since I left England. And there's always noise. The garbage truck on Wednesday, recycling on Thursday. Street cleaner on Mondays. So today I just woke up when I woke up."

Walt Whitman wraps himself around my leg, purring. I turn to the window. Outside, the snow continues to fall, thick and blinding. I finish the coffee and grab my jacket and hat, hung on the posts behind the door.

"There's nothing quite like it: waking up to all that white." Marie walks to the window in the kitchen and stands on her tiptoes. "There was a hill at the college where my father taught. We lived a few blocks away, and Jake and I would walk there in all our snow gear, two waddling ducks, our sleds in tow. We'd just go and go."

I slide into my boots. "Did you close the gate when you came through last night?"

She pours batter into the skillet. "I didn't. Is that a problem?" She says it nonchalantly, like it's not even a question.

"As a matter of fact, it is."

The way I say it has an edge. She looks up, frowns. "Sorry."

"We always keep it locked. An open gate invites people. Sends the message someone's here and it's fine to come on in."

"Do you have trouble with trespassers out here?"

"No, but like I said, we keep it locked, always."

Marie bites her lip. "I didn't know."

It's a source of stress, knowing that gate's open. Cars won't get through in this snow, or trucks. But snowmobiles. Unlikely they'd be out this far but you never know. And now I need to keep an eye out.

I open the door and step out onto the porch, protected by the roof and mostly clear of snow, although some has blown in, and the edges are white with fine dust. So quiet there, so intensely white and pure. Cold, too. The whole world swathed and bright.

Torn, that's how I feel. Pulled in too many directions. Irritated about the gate being open, frustrated by the snow and yet somehow also grateful for it. Lulled by the warmth of the stove, the bacon, the coffee, the intimacy of Marie's confessions. That she's even here: another adult, a beautiful woman. All of it. Can't afford to get caught up in that, let my guard down.

I step off the porch, the snow halfway up my boots. I take the shovel and clear a small path to the chicken coop, just wide enough for one person to cross because it's heavy, all the snow, and we only have the one shovel, a square-shaped garden tool. It does the job but it's not ideal. I should've picked up a decent snow shovel at Walmart.

"One problem solved," I tell the chickens, who are huddled in the coop and not pleased about how snow flutters in when I open the door. I mean the girl with the camera. She won't be back out here in this snow, all those national-forest roads closed, at least for a while. "But another one gained," I say, peering into the coop. One of the hens eyes me cantankerously and refuses to move. "Marie. What are we gonna do about her?" I push at the hen with the back of my gloved hand and she clucks and then leaps to the side. "Got a woman in the house with me and one day in, I start thinking things. What? Yeah, so maybe I was. Maybe I did steal a look when she leaned over to pour the coffee. I didn't look long, anyhow, so don't go making me out to be some kind of pervert."

I brush the pine bedding back from the ledge of the coop, tidying the chickens' mess. "And yes, she's attractive, okay. I find her attractive. I did, years ago, when we first met. And I still do. There, I said it." One hen seems to change her mind and comes back toward me, beak out, intending to peck. "Easy," I tell her and swat her softly on the head. "You're lucky I need you, or you'd end up like Susanna." The hens stand in a row at the back of the coop, watching me as I tuck their eggs into the deep pocket of my coat. "Sorry," I say. "That was uncalled for. What happened with her was about putting her out of her misery. You understand that, don't you, ladies?" I close the door and latch it and shimmy back through my skinny path to the porch.

You're talking to chickens, Cooper. You're confessing. You're apologizing to them. Critters with brains the size of a pea. You're losing your mind.

I stomp off the snow, turn to look once again at the woods. Even though I'm close, the birds are fluttering toward the feeder, pulled there by hunger, by the situation of snow. Two, maybe three years back, Jake brought the feeder, and after much debate—not right off the porch (bird seed all over the place), not on the clothesline (bird crap all over the clothes)—we dug a hole with the post-hole digger and sunk a straight and skinned piece of locust and installed the feeder just outside the window so that Finch and me could watch the birds when we ate our meals. Scotland had come shortly thereafter and taken the opportunity to point out that Finch's childhood would be lacking if I didn't see to getting her a pet crow. Which she has been harping about every spring since: finding a baby crow to nurture and tame.

Now, juncos, plain and gray, tremble in from the woods, gathering at the base of the feeder, but the snow is deep there. I grab the shovel from the porch and walk toward them and they scatter. I clear a spot so that when the seed spills, they can get it from the ground.

I step back and lean on the shovel and wait and see if they'll come back with me that close, and they do. Beautiful, fragile little things, quivering. I look up and see Marie at the window, Finch tucked in against her, and Marie's arm across Finch's middle. It's a happy sight, the two of them watching in wonder and smiling, and I smile back, but inside I'm seeing that in spite of everything I can give Finch out here—and it's a good life, and the best I can do—there is also something missing. A woman to love and soothe and guide her. A mother.

TWENTY-ONE

There was an incident, before. Before the cabin, before the car accident and CPS, before Finch. Six weeks after I got back from Kabul. Aunt Lincoln had died while I was overseas, so I was unable to fly home and attend the funeral, but I know she wasn't the type to hold such a thing against a person. Anyhow, she'd left me the place, so I was living out there on the farm but not farming it. I'd gotten a job at the lumberyard. Nothing fancy, just unloading wood and keeping inventory and sometimes sweeping sawdust. It was hard work and I liked it: the strain on the body, the counting and tallying in my little chart with a clipboard. After everything I'd lived through over the past four years, there was something reassuring about the simplicity of it, wood and numbers, that was all.

I was at the diner in town, eating a Reuben sandwich with french fries and pickles and a Coke. It was 2007 and I was sort of a hero in my little corner of the universe. They were good people in that town, Vietnam veterans scattered among them, people who'd learned their lesson from that conflict and who realized it was okay to feel mad or confused about the war, but it wasn't us soldiers who made the decisions about who to fight, and where. They hung yellow ribbons in their windows, plastered stickers on their bumpers. When I came home, they threw a big parade to welcome me. Sometimes people gave me free stuff, and at the bar they would always tell me my drink was on the house.

I'd only been home six weeks, and the truth is, sometimes I would have nightmares. Horrid, visceral dreams that were almost memories but not quite. I'd wake up screaming, sweating, twisted up bad in the sheets. I guess this happened most nights, and I didn't really like going to bed because when I did, I knew where I'd end up: back there. Those hot and spinning days. The stink of death that hung heavy in the air. Jake's leg rotting and the two of us pinned down with nowhere to go. What I did to get us out of there.

But the dreams didn't bother anyone but me. Aunt Lincoln's house was way out of town, and nobody would hear. I figured it would end, the visions that haunted my nights. I figured probably all of us had them in some form. I just needed time. I didn't tell anyone, not even Cindy. The two of us weren't a couple yet, not officially, but we'd been spending a lot of time together.

At the diner, I was talking to Kelly Ramsey about her chickens, which one of them laid olive-green eggs, she said. Kelly was a waitress there, and we'd gone to school together, only now she had two kids already, both boys, and we talked, most days. Kelly Ramsey was talking about those green eggs—"same size as any other egg, only green, olive green."

And then a jangle at the door, the little Christmas bells that hung from the handle hitting the glass. When I turned there was a certain slant of light. Two guys walked in, and they were armed, they were there to kill all of us. They were there, crossing the threshold, and I had seen them before, and they intended harm. One of them had a gun and the other was hiding something behind his back. The look on their faces. Meanwhile, men women children there in the diner, almost every booth full of people eating their lunch, all of them talking and laughing and having a grand old time. Only nobody seemed concerned about it, so it was just me, trying to figure a way to stop them.

"You got an egg carton at home? Bring it with you next time, and I'll get you some." Kelly going on about those green eggs.

In a high chair close by, a baby squealed and flapped her arms. Jim and Jada Miller's youngest. Phil Williams raised his arm to get Kelly's attention and said, "Kelly, can I get some ketchup when you have a chance?"

The men were spreading apart, one on each side of the room. Sneaky, those two, because although there was malevolence in their eyes, they moved in a way that was nonchalant, in a way that nobody took note of them at all.

I had my Ruger on me. I had a license to carry a concealed weapon, everything legal, and I wasn't about to let this go down without a fight, all those innocent people having lunch, and two armed psychos about to let loose. So I slipped it from my pocket, the gun, and fast. "Everybody down!"

Then. So much screaming and moving, the whole room flooding with noise and turmoil. A shipwreck, a kingdom falling. The mosque collapsing on Doyle and Turnbull. Phillips bleeding out on my fatigues. Blood blood blood. Everything reeling and white and where was I and where were the two men with their guns?

The baby in the high chair crying now. Phil Williams and his wife tucked beneath their booth, hunched low, heads down, and also crying.

How long did I stand there with the gun? Minutes? Seconds? The room a vault of whispers and cries.

"Kenny." A voice, somewhere in the room, far away, like it was coming from a long tunnel, but quiet and calm and familiar.

Another voice. "Don't, Kelly. Think of your kids."

Where were the two men? Where had they gone?

"Kenny! Kenny, it's all right. Put the gun down, Kenny."

An unnatural quiet in the room.

"The men. There were two of them." Something hammering loud and roaring, like a jet taking off. My own heart, I realized. I put the Ruger in my pocket and walked out of there, out onto Main Street, the day sunny but cool. May. The wind picked up and tossed crabapple blossoms that floated down onto my shoulders.

Judge came to see me later that day. After I walked out of the diner, I guess someone called the police and also him and this is what they must've arranged: a visit from the judge. I would rather have the police, to tell you the truth, but what I got was him. I heard the engine and watched from behind a curtain in the living room. Rolled up in his Lexus, stood outside the car for a moment, eyeing up the house, doing what he did best, I suspect: judging. Aunt Lincoln had not been the most fastidious when it came to upkeep, so there were tires and scraps of metal and a huge heap of five-gallon buckets that she used for growing fat, juicy tomatoes, all of this littering the yard.

There was a mattress on the front porch, and an old green couch that was perfectly comfortable but an eyesore all the same, plus the steps were starting to rot. Though I'm sure Judge couldn't see it, I'd already put quite a dent in the mess, hauling four loads of junk to the transfer station, cleaning up the place. I'd taken a chest freezer from out back, three gas grills, nine filing cabinets. Plus I'd been burning all the papers Lincoln had held on to. Insurance policies from 1989, catalogues, receipts, magazines.

The thing is, me and Judge had never gotten along, and here's why. He always saw things in black-and-white, which is maybe what judges are supposed to do. Me, I saw things how they really are: not black-and-white but a hundred shades in between.

I walked outside and stood on the porch. Didn't want him in the house, which, frankly, was worse than the yard, Lincoln being a bit of a hoarder. But like I said, I was working on it, honest to God. "Judge."

"Kenny."

"What can I do for you?"

Judge stood there in the afternoon sun in his black suit and shiny shoes that probably cost more than two weeks' worth of groceries for regular people. He was wearing sunglasses and he tipped his head down just a little to show me his gray eyes. "Well, Kenny. I suspect you know why I'm here."

"Someone pressing charges?"

Judge shook his head and used his toe to nudge at a witch ball that had rolled off its stand and lay beside the walkway. "No, nobody's pressing charges, at least not yet. Good people in this town, Kenny. You can be grateful for that. They see you as a hero. At least they did, before yesterday. But."

He paused there, and I thought, *I bet this was something they taught you in law school:* to pause at the right time. To make people wait so that what you said next had more heft to it.

"You pulled a gun at a diner, Kenny. On a Saturday. There were children, old folks, babies. People are scared, and they should be. They're worried about what might happen next time."

"It won't happen again."

"You can't be sure of that, son. You know that as much as I do."

It made me mad, him calling me "son," like we were friends, like he cared, because he didn't. The midday sun beat down hard, and I sort of liked the idea of him standing there roasting in his black suit. I was hot in my old T-shirt and shorts and no shoes, so I was sure he was uncomfortable. But I'd grown used to the heat, the way it could take it out of you—that's one good thing that had happened over there—so I just stood there and didn't say anything, thinking about how hot he probably was.

Judge pulled a fancy handkerchief from inside his coat and blotted his forehead. "People are saying maybe it'd be good for you to take some time away," he said. "Talk to someone. Professionals."

"People?"

"Like I said, Kenny, folks are willing to forgive you for what happened, but they want to know it won't happen again. That you're getting help."

"You mean like at a hospital. For crazy people."

"There's a VA hospital up in Bridgeport. I've already made a call, and I can take you there myself. You pack up a little bag, we can go right now."

And Judge could take credit for solving everything, for helping the poor wounded warrior. He'd tell everyone how he came out to the house and talked me into going, talked me off the ledge. How brave, people would say. Oh Judge, you could've been killed, who knows what might've happened. Judge, who didn't know the first thing about war or what it took from you, because he was well connected and had dodged the draft for Vietnam. While Lincoln's husband, Uncle Bill, was squatting in a ditch, earning his own nightmares about burning villages and little children with skin on fire, Judge was sitting in a college library somewhere, learning about the Constitution. No, sir. Judge wasn't taking me anywhere.

I shook my head. "Don't think so, Judge."

He took off his sunglasses and wiped his brow with the sleeve of his black suit. Judge with his changeable gray eyes that could go from sad and sympathetic to mean and disapproving in a matter of seconds. Right now the eyes were kind, but that was probably fake. Something else he'd picked up in law school, probably, an ability to change his face like that. "This is a mistake, son. And what I worry is that someone's gonna get hurt."

A breeze picked up and the wind chimes on the porch began to clang and sing, two different sets, one made of colorful glass and the other made of tubes of bamboo, two different tunes, dissonant. I was done talking to Judge, but I didn't mind letting him stand there in the heat, so I pretended maybe I was thinking it over. I rubbed my thumb along a piece of paint that was peeling up from the railing. And finally, after he'd taken his jacket off and loosened his tie, I shook my head. "Can't do it."

"Well, I'm sorry it has to come to this, Kenny, but you need help and you're refusing to get it. Like your aunt in that way, I suppose. Apple don't fall far."

I hated him for saying that about Lincoln, who'd been dead six months.

"I came here as a concerned citizen. As an ally. But since you won't have any of that, now I'll speak to you as the father of a young woman who is on the path to being happy and successful. Let me be clear on this: I don't want you anywhere near Cynthia. You were never good enough for her. She knows that. You know it, too. Everyone does. And now not only are you not good enough, but you're also dangerous. And everyone knows that, too, so don't expect any sympathy from all the people in town who used to see you as a hero."

Remember what I said about Judge being able to change all of a sudden, shift into something utterly different, like a chameleon? Well. That's what had happened. An ugly miracle, right there in the sun and heat. Kind and concerned Judge was gone, and now the real Judge was here, cold and vicious.

Something mean and dark began to weave inside me. I felt the sweat begin to spill down my face, felt my fists clench. "She's an adult," I told him. "She can make her own decisions." I said it strong, like I was spitting at him, like he hadn't gotten under my skin, but inside, I was feeling the stab of his cruel words, the truth of them. Cindy was too good for me, and everybody knew it, especially me.

Judge stepped closer, skipped all three steps and was up on the porch right next to me, so close I could smell the lunch on his breath. Pickles. Now, mind you: I'm a hair over six foot, but Judge, he was taller, and he positioned himself so that I could sense the height he had on me, so he was looking down on me. "You come anywhere near her. You so much as look at her. I will ruin your pathetic little life. We clear on that?"

I held his eyes but didn't answer him. I could sweep the legs from beneath him and take him to the ground before he even blinked. The truth is, I hated him and always had and who did Judge think he was, telling me I was worthless and pathetic? After everything I'd been through. All those years away, I'd been dreaming of Cindy, hoping for something more between us, and the possibility of it— well, it had kept me alive. And aside from all of that, what Judge didn't know was that my pathetic life, it was already ruined.

I turned away from Judge. Left him standing on the porch with his nice black suit. Unharmed, by the way. I'm fairly sure he hollered something after me about not walking away from him, but I went into the house and let the screen door slam shut. I think he knew better than to follow me. Through the screens I could hear the wind chimes jangling their songs. After a while Judge turned and walked away. He kicked the witch ball hard before he got in his Lexus and drove off, shattered it all over the yard. Now a thousand pieces of iridescent glass in the yard to clean up as well, but when I peered out the window, it looked like a pool of water there, shimmering in the sun, shiny and beautiful and bright.

I never could bring myself to go back to the diner, and I missed the Reuben sandwiches and french fries and pickles. Kelly, too, her chatter about the chickens and kids and her husband's motorcycle. There was something comfortable and reassuring about all of it. I kept on working at the lumberyard, kept whittling away at the junk out at Lincoln's. The hard labor, the pull and strain but also the chance to see that I was actually accomplishing something—that was good for me. Lincoln's place was still a wreck but I was making progress, and I had a good vision for how nice it could be, once everything was cleaned up and repaired. The land was beautiful: a small valley cleared of trees, the creek that cut right through the middle of it. Truth is, even then, even before Cindy was pregnant, I was picturing a life out there, with her.

I didn't have another episode like that, where I was seeing people who weren't really there. Which trust me: that was a relief. But still. You can see why, when Child Protective Services showed up after Cindy passed, when my friend Don leaned in and advised me to let Finch go without a fuss, you can see how after what unfolded at the diner—me wielding a weapon and everyone ducking under tables and screaming—you can see how Finch and me had to come out here. You can see we had no choice.

TWENTY-TWO

Marie brought boots and a coat, but no snow pants, so I tell her she can use mine. She puts up a fuss about that, saying she doesn't need them, she'll be fine, but I point to the thermometer on the porch and tell her it's nineteen degrees outside, and she gives in. Waddles out from the bedroom in the insulated camouflage pants that are six inches too long and also too big at the waist and falling down. She holds them up with one hand, the extra fabric balled in her fist.

"These aren't going to work," she says with a shrug.

Finch giggles, slipping into her snow boots. "You look like a cowboy, the way you're walking."

"Hang on," I tell Marie. I grab my belt from the drawer in the bedroom and bring it out. Kneel down, my face level with her waist. She holds her parka up and I loop it through the belt holes for her, elbows grazing her rear. When I reach around the back, my face presses to her abdomen. I cinch the belt and stand up. "See? They're perfect."

She looks away.

"I thought maybe we could go down to the valley," Finch says, tugging her hat over her ears. "See if the river's freezing up."

Marie smiles. "Sounds fun."

"No need to trek all the way over there," I say. "I can guarantee you it's not frozen yet."

Finch holds my gaze. "But maybe there would be something else to see. Something interesting or unusual."

I glare at her. "Not today. Too much snow."

"It's light, though. The snow. We could get there."

"Marie doesn't want to go trekking all the way over there," I say.

"Don't cancel your plans on my account," Marie pipes in.

Finch grins. "See?"

"I said no."

She kicks the leg of the table, sloshing the last of my coffee. Marie's eyes grow wide. "I need to," Finch snaps. "I need to go there today."

"Excuse us for a minute," I tell Marie. I motion for Finch to follow me to the bedroom, and she follows, moping, walking slowly. "Is this about that girl?" I whisper, closing the door. "Because if it is, I can assure you: she's long gone."

She folds her arms across her chest. "You don't know that."

"Of course I do." We saw her leave. Two days later, a foot of snow.

"But it wouldn't hurt to go back down there. Just to be sure."

"The only thing I need to be sure of is that you're going to let this thing go."

"But—"

"Drop it," I hiss. "Don't bring it up again. You hear me?"

She makes her bear face then bursts out of the room, stomping past Marie and right out the front door.

Marie looks at me. "Everything all right?"

I shrug. "You know how it is. Kids."

She steps toward the door, tucking her gloves into her jacket. "I'm heading out."

"I'm right behind you."

I get dressed. Long johns and jeans and thick wool socks that are thinning in the heels. Jacket, hat, scarf, gloves. For the second time this morning, I step onto the porch, the snow still falling but lighter now, the flakes sailing down, slow and gentle. Footprints everywhere, my own, covered in a layer of snow already, and also two sets of smaller ones, but no sight of Finch and Marie. I follow the prints around the side of the house. Nothing. Look to the woods. Swing back to the front of the house. Heart beating fast now.

"Finch?"

Smack. Something hard hits me square in the face. Knocks me back a step. Cold cold cold, and I nearly lose my balance.

"Gotcha!"

Laughter that flits up and up.

I wipe my face with the sleeve of my jacket. A snowball. Marie shuffles closer, wading through the snow in my pants. "That's for copping a feel," she says, looking up at me.

"I didn't—"

"Close enough," she says, pointing at me with her gloved finger. She signals to Finch. "Fire away!"

From the ditch at the edge of the yard, Finch pops up and

launches another snowball that hits me in the chest. Marie plucks a snowball from her pocket and hits me again in the head. She runs toward Finch and ducks into the ditch.

"Two against one. No fair!" I squat and ball some snow and hurl it at Finch. Miss, which gets her laughing. Make another one, fling it at Marie, hit her on the head, the ball crumbling down over her beanie.

On and on the morning goes, the hours flitting past. Snowballs and snow angels and sledding up and down the little dip just beyond the yard: a short run, nothing too thrilling but fun all the same, especially since it's Finch's first time on a sled, ever. We take turns, the three of us, sometimes doubling up, sometimes headfirst. We build a ramp for one of the runs. Heap the snow up and pack it down so that the sled lifts off and then slams down hard and sometimes, whoever is riding topples over. I haven't laughed so much in years.

The whole morning, I don't think of Cindy at all, not once. I keep an eye on the woods—instinct—but I don't worry. I don't fret about Scotland, either, although when Finch and Marie go in for lunch, I wonder if he is watching with his spotting scope and so I turn in the direction where he says he lives, take off my glove, and flip him the bird, just in case.

So of course he shows up, later that afternoon, when I'm shoveling a path to the outhouse again. Slogs right into the yard on a pair of snowshoes that look like they're about a hundred years old, only this time in the snow's silence I heard the *swish swish* of him coming through the snow. Saw him from way off, first time ever he didn't catch me off guard and send my heart shooting into my throat.

"You have a guest," he says, gesturing toward Marie's car.

"Jake's sister, Marie."

"You holding her captive?" He laughs, his voice filling the deep silence of the woods.

"The snow."

He spits to the side. "I saw the car coming down the road last night. I was fixing to head down here, but then I determined you could handle it. Told myself if you needed my help, you have the flare."

I shovel the spot where Scotland spit, the tobacco a brown spot in the snow. "That's right. If I ever need you, I have the flare." I'm hoping he'll take a hint: quit showing up here and meddling in our business. Quit watching us. Given how the past eight years have gone, I doubt he gets the message.

He pulls a chunk of ice from the roof of the outhouse. "I saw the two of you unloading her vehicle and figured it must be someone Jake sent. With your supplies and hers, you ought to be well stocked for quite some time."

"Jake's dead."

Scotland closes his eyes and folds his gloved hands across his abdomen. Takes a deep breath and tilts his head to the sky. "He's with the Lord now. No longer suffering this world and its heartaches."

"Or he's just dead."

He shakes his head. "No, Cooper. It's not like that. This world, it'll tear the guts right out of you. As you well know. But this isn't all there is." He clears his throat then tilts his head to the sky and begins to sing: "'Come Thou Fount of every blessing, Tune my heart to sing Thy grace . . .'"

Warm from the shoveling, I unzip my jacket. That haunting, smooth singing voice of his. How can it be so irritating and so heartbreaking, all at once?

"Just wish you could see it, that's all." He packs a snowball in his bare hands. "Does Marie know?"

I keep on shoveling the path. "Know what?"

"Oh, come now, Cooper. Don't be coy. I mean does she know who you are?"

"We met once, a long time ago. She knows Jake and I served in the Middle East together."

"And the rest of it?"

"Why do you care?"

He lobs the snowball at a tree nearby. "It's a simple question, Cooper."

"Jake told her I lost Cindy and I'm staying here until I get my footing."

"Get your footing." He grunts. "That's one way of putting it."

I toss a shovel of snow at Scotland's feet.

"You gonna tell her?" he asks.

"No, I'm not gonna tell her. I don't even know her."

"But you want to. Know her better."

"She'll be gone as soon as the snow melts."

"Secrets, secrets," he clucks, shaking his head.

Finch bounds out of the house, her jacket unzipped and flapping at her sides. Boots but no hat or gloves. "Scotland!" She runs to him, arms open. "We had a snowball fight. We rode the sled."

He kneels down and hugs her. "I saw that, little bird. It sure looked fun." He glances at me. "Your daddy sent me a hand signal."

"You should've come down."

"Well," he says, casting a meaningful look in my direction, "I wasn't invited. I didn't want to crash the party."

"You're never invited," Finch says. "But you're always welcome.

And you always know just the right time to come, somehow. You always know just when we need you."

Marie steps onto the porch, all bundled up. She trudges through the snow and extends her hand. "Hi there," she says. "I'm Marie."

"Scotland, your neighbor. I knew your family."

"I'm afraid I don't remember."

I refrain from explaining that when Scotland says he *knew* them, what he means is that he spied on them, watched their every move through a spotting scope.

"You were small," he says. "Anyway, you're back. Snowed in, it seems. And a wonderful place to be stuck for a while, if I do say so myself."

She doesn't answer, instead gesturing for Finch to come closer. She pulls the hat over Finch's head, then slides the pink gloves onto her hands.

Finch reaches out and takes Scotland's hand. "Come on," she says. "I want you to try out my sled."

He unstraps his snowshoes and follows her to the little hill at the edge of the yard. She plops into the sled and gestures for him to climb in. Which he does. Sits right down behind her and tucks his legs up onto hers and off they go, whooshing through the snow on one of the runs we pushed out earlier. They dip out of sight and I can hear them laughing.

"Are you all right?" Marie asks.

"What? Sure." The path is cleared but I keep on shoveling. "Why?"

She shrugs.

I gesture toward Scotland. "He sort of puts me on edge."

"He seems nice."

"Yes," I say, heaving a shovel load of snow. "He *is* nice."

She squints. "So what's the problem?"

"Nothing." Of course I can't tell her about the day he waltzed into the yard with a crow on his shoulder and an AK-47 strapped to his back and his stack of carefully selected newspapers, a litany of my many offenses. "It's just he shows up here, all the time."

"He's probably lonely."

"Maybe."

Finch and Scotland emerge, the tips of their hats, then their faces, shoulders, body.

"You're up, Marie!" Finch calls.

Marie tramps through the snow and climbs on the sled behind Finch. A different picture altogether, seeing her with Finch, instead of Scotland.

"Haven't been on a sled for decades," Scotland says. He wipes his eyes with his sleeve.

"You all right?"

"Cold." He reaches into his pocket and slides out a skull. "Give this to Finch, would you? Gotta get on home." He hands me a white skull, small enough that it fits in my palm. "Wood rat," he says. He slides back into his snowshoes, straps them down, and trundles off into the woods.

TWENTY-THREE

The snow has continued, three or four more inches that have arrived in waves, here and there, and meanwhile, Marie has met the chickens, gathered the eggs. She's chopped wood and kept the fire going. The second night, she made us grilled cheese for supper. Each evening, at dusk, we roll up a towel and press it against the door to keep the snow from sliding under. We lock the doors, I prop the shovel. And though I try and hold back, though I know it will almost certainly lead to disappointment, I feel myself slipping down a trail of *what if?*

After dinner on the third night, Marie asks if she can see Finch's notebook, and although I thought she'd be tickled by this request, she throws a sideways glance at me and says, "Only if we go up to the loft." She's still mad about not going to the valley, I guess.

"I'll do the dishes," I say. "You go have some girl time."

The two of them climb the ladder and as I pour hot water into the washbasin from the kettle, I can hear them settling in upstairs, sliding the plastic storage bins and crinkling the bags of items.

"Jake brought me a notebook every time he came. And he got me Prismacolor pencils, for drawing, which he said were the best, according to his research. So, this is a goldfinch from last spring. They get brighter and brighter yellow throughout the season. Well, the males do. The females aren't as colorful. This is a pileated woodpecker."

I scrub the sides of the Dutch oven, wanting to give them their space.

"This one's an indigo bunting. They're the most beautiful of birds we get. I didn't quite capture the color just right, but can you tell how pretty? This is a tree swallow, in the spring. They're like acrobats in the sky, diving and looping, and they make a sound like this"—she pauses to attempt it—"sort of like water gurgling. They're my favorites."

"And who's this gal with the long red hair?"

I pause, clenching the scouring pad in my palm. The sketch of the girl in the woods. I'd forgotten about it.

"That's my friend I told you about. At first I thought she was a princess who'd run away from a nearby kingdom, but then I realized that wasn't right. A princess wouldn't live in the woods."

"No?"

"Not the way she does. So that's when I realized she's actually a wood nymph."

"I see," Marie says.

The suds slowly slide from my arms.

"There's a butterfly called a wood nymph. It's brown, with two dark spots that look like eyes to confuse predators. But that's not the type of wood nymph she is. She's the kind in books. Do you know what I mean? They're beautiful maidens who live in the woods."

"And sometimes they have special powers," Marie adds. She's playing along, I realize with relief.

"Exactly. Like, they can transform themselves. They can *meta-morphose*." She says the word carefully.

"Like the butterfly."

"Yes."

"How long has she been here in your woods?"

"Oh, not long. A few days. She arrived just before you came."

I swirl the scouring pad around. The steam pours off.

"Do you know the story of Daphne and Apollo?" Finch asks. She doesn't wait for an answer. "It's from one of our books. Apollo was stricken with love for Daphne, a wood nymph and the daughter of the river god, but she wanted nothing to do with him. She just wanted to live in the woods. Because, well, she was a wood nymph. Anyway, Apollo chased her, and she ran and ran, but he was faster. He was closing in. But just as he was about to get her, she called out to her father for help, and poof! She turned into a tree."

"Is that what you call your friend? Daphne?"

"Sometimes."

I hear the rustle of a page turning. "And what's this?"

"That's where she lives. See all these big rocks? She hauled them up from the river for her fire ring. She's not very big, but she's strong."

"That seems fitting," Marie says. "A nymph would be robust and capable."

"This is her tent. Plus she has a chair that folds up."

"So colorful and imaginative. I like the blue kettle."

Finch's voice drops to a whisper. "You want to know a secret?"

Upstairs, Marie must nod. I picture her leaning close.

"You have to promise not to tell Cooper."

I clink a glass, making noise so it seems like I'm not paying attention. I hold my breath, wonder if I should cough or clear my throat—something to stop the conversation—but I also want to know what Finch is about to say.

"I promise," Marie says.

"I didn't imagine her. She's real. I go visit her sometimes."

I drop the forks into the Dutch oven, the metal clanging loudly. "Does anyone want some hot chocolate?"

Finch hollers and scoots down the ladder, and Marie follows.

After hot chocolate, I begin the long event of getting Finch to bed. We brush her teeth, wash her hands and face, read.

"Finch," I say, finally tucking her blanket beneath her chin, "I'd like you to quit talking about that girl."

She heaves, pulling the blanket up over her mouth. "You weren't supposed to be listening. You said when two people are talking and you secretly try to hear what they're saying, it's called eavesdropping, and it's rude."

"I know. But this is a little different—I'm your father, and it's my job to keep an eye on you." I place a hand on her knee. "Sugar, I'm asking you to quit obsessing."

"I'm not obsessing. She's my friend."

"I'd like you to put it from your mind," I say, sternly.

She wrinkles her nose. "I can't."

I take a deep breath. It's becoming a concern, the fantasizing. The way she blurs the line between reality and make-believe. I realize she's only eight, but I'm not sure she even knows the difference all the time, and it worries me. "You can, and you must."

I lean down and kiss her forehead, walk to the door and tell her good night.

Out in the main room, Marie has brewed two cups of tea. She sits on the couch, waiting. Outside the cabin, the temperature plummets and the wind howls, tugging old snow from trees. Come morning, I'll need to shovel everything out again. The truth is, Marie does most of the talking, and I'm content to sit and listen, to hear her voice, to watch the light from the candle flicker over her face, the wide brown eyes, the tiny nose and wide lips. Is it possible for a person to grow more attractive over the course of a couple of days? Because she has, to me. Earlier today, I found myself wanting night to come, wanting to open up. But Finch's conversations have reminded me that I can't afford to do that.

"I met him in Oxford. My husband. Ex. I was twenty and studying abroad," she says, sliding her slippered feet across the coffee table. "Twenty years old! So young. And unreasonably innocent, I suppose. I thought I had a grasp of myself. I thought I knew how I wanted my life to look. And then I met him. It was—it was like waking up."

I don't tell Marie that the same spring she was gallivanting around Oxford, Jake and me were fighting what was, at the time, our worst skirmish yet, pinned down for four days in between a speck-on-the-map town and a constellation of caves so befuddling that even my preternatural instinct for geography couldn't quite get a handle on them. Phillips, wounded the first day, was slowly bleeding out and brewing an infection that was beginning to smell. At night, we spooned, all four of us, unprepared and so very cold. By the end, we were drinking our own urine. Although of course what happened later on, the next tour, would make all of that seem like nothing.

"I say now that I hate him," Marie says. "After what he has done. The humiliation. But I don't. I loved him then and a part of me always will." She looks at me. "I don't know why I'm telling you all this. I guess there was no one else to tell. My parents are gone, and even if they weren't, I wouldn't have told them. Of course they disapproved of him from the start. He was an outspoken atheist. He and my father, they'd get into it. Not friendly father-in-law and son-in-law banter, mind you. War."

"What about your mom?"

"My mother never said a word about Thomas, good or bad." Marie sips her tea and seems to contemplate this. "And, I suppose in her silence, she was saying quite a bit."

"And Jake?"

"Jake wouldn't have voiced his disapproval, but I knew he didn't like him. I think back to family dinners, holidays. Jake would always have a reason to leave the room or the table. It was like he couldn't stand to be close to Thomas for too long. There was something poisonous about him, I see that now. Jake saw it. They all saw it, but I didn't." She plucks a chocolate from the box and skips the slicing, pops the whole thing in her mouth. "Anyway. That's my sad life story and how I ruined it by falling in love with the wrong guy. I'm sorry I've been talking so much. You probably think I'm pathetic."

I shake my head. "Not at all." I swallow hard, clear my throat.

I want to tell her something, some truth about us, but I can't. It's not safe, for her or for me.

"We finalized the divorce just before I came here. It's strange that somehow, that feels simultaneously like a great victory and a terrible failure. My parents were married for twenty-nine years before Mom got sick."

She picks up our mugs and walks them to the kitchen counter. It's late, so I stand and tell her good night. Marie walks over and stops right in front of me. She reaches up, places her hands behind my neck, her fingers warm and soft. She presses them into my skin. We stand there, like that, so close. "I see why Jake loved you," she says at last, holding my eyes and waiting for something, and then she rises up, standing on her tiptoes, and kisses my cheek before pulling away. "Good night, Cooper," she says.

I think I mutter good night but—hard to say. I stumble into the small bedroom, slip past Finch, who rolls over when I step on the wrong floorboard, and then I stub my toe on the bed. I slide out of my jeans and flannel shirt and crawl into bed, toe throbbing. Head spinning, too. What just transpired between Marie and me? Did I step back when she reached out to touch me? Did I flinch? I think maybe both. And was she going to kiss me? I mean for real, not a friendly kiss, not on the cheek.

This isn't new for me, this ungainliness around females. In high school, there were opportunities. Well, let me be clear. There were *two* opportunities, two times that I was with a girl and maybe something could've happened. They seemed willing and available, and I wanted it, whatever they were offering, but I was always afraid and nervous. Plus, there was the factor of me imagining that one day, Cindy and me would get together.

I pulled away from those girls, both times. Just like I did now, with Marie.

It's cold in the bedroom, and I pull the extra blanket from the foot of the bed and cover myself. The moonlight slides into the room through a small sliver of space between the curtains. I can't sleep. I still feel Marie's fingers at my neck, the softness of her body pressing into mine. It's different from those girls back in high school. Back then, I wanted it but I also didn't, and my desire for one thing was greater than the other. This time, there's no conflict that I can pinpoint, no clash of desires: only want. And yet.

I double back, replay the moment, doubt myself. It had been there, hadn't it? Something blooming between the two of us. A closeness. A possibility. And what had I done? Pulled away.

TWENTY-FOUR

The next morning, I open my eyes to see Finch standing at my bedside and leaning over, watching me, her face a few inches from mine. I squint in the sunlight, which is pouring through the windows and hitting her hair so that it appears to glow.

"Look!" she says, smiling, mouth wide.

I frown.

"It came out. My tooth!" She holds it out. "Look. Marie washed it off for me. It was bloody."

I nod and rub my eyes and sit up, the transition of waking more disorienting than usual. "Did it hurt?"

She shakes her head. "Well, maybe a little." She drops the tooth in my palm.

I look at the tooth, the pointy roots. I think about those months when Finch was teething, whining, flapping her arms, and drooling everywhere. I'd let her gnaw on my thumb, just to keep her happy.

Seven, eight years back and somehow it feels like yesterday. "You'll have to put this under your pillow tonight."

"I will. Come on, time to get up. I've been awake for almost an hour. Marie and I already ate breakfast. Pancakes again. And eggs. She said to let you sleep."

I shoo Finch out of the room and get dressed. I pause and pull the small handheld mirror from the top drawer of the dresser. First time in years I've taken a good look at myself, and here is what I will say: I don't recommend it, not using a mirror for all that time and then looking. You have a certain idea of what you look like, and of course you'll be different from when you last saw yourself, and there's something jarring about that. Plus, most likely, the changes will not be good. My hair, for starters, has patches of gray, and the beard is worse: gray, too, and long and tangled. *Cooper, you look like Jeremiah Johnson. Or Charles Manson.* Something in between the two but maybe more like the latter. I reach up and press the hair down, try to comb it, but no use. I pull on a baseball cap. Wonder if maybe I should reconsider the beard.

Out in the main room, the woodstove is clicking and the fan on top is whirring and the whole place smells like syrup. At the table, Marie is seated, back to me, and at the spot across from her, there's a plate and a cup. She turns and when our eyes meet, I have a sudden feeling that I'm walking on the surface of a wide river, in winter. Iced over, at least by the looks of things, but maybe not thick enough to hold your weight. "Morning," I say, my voice hoarse.

"Cooper."

I walk to the stove and grab the French press off the trivet. I pour myself some coffee and sit down across from her. Worry that whatever waved between us last night has now passed, that maybe it was just one of those times when the lateness in the day had dulled the senses: the moment, the possibility, gone. We're lonely, both of us. Sad. Fragile. And we're stuck here in this cabin and all of those factors are enough to pull two people together. I see that, I get it. But that doesn't mean this will inevitably end in more sadness, does it? Well.

For the first time in a long while, there's a spark of hope in my gut that maybe everything won't go wrong like it always does, and I sort of like it, that feeling.

Later that day, we trek out to cut down a Christmas tree. As we slog through the woods, the realization darts to me: it's warmer, today. The snow, it's getting soft, our feet sliding a bit. I tilt my head to the sky, squint at the sun that is pushing through the clouds. Typical of December. Noncommittal, the temperatures still up and down. The unpredictability—a cold stretch but then a day in the fifties, bright sun against a cloudless sky—I've always sort of relished it. The way December can surprise you. Not today, though. No. Today all I can think about is another snowstorm. That's what I want, down in my depths. Because that would mean she'd have to stay.

Finch leads the way, selecting a tree that's a little taller than she is. I let her use the saw to cut it down, and she's thrilled, and when the tree topples down and whooshes against the snow, she whoops and holds her arms high in the air. We drag it back to the cabin, fill a bucket with stones and water, and prop the tree inside. Heat popcorn in a pot on the woodstove, thread a needle and then string up the popped kernels in long streamers of white. Marie slices two apples into thin circles, and we hang those up, too. I pull out the Christmas lights I bought at Walmart and let Finch add the batteries.

We drape the string of lights back and forth across the tree, too, and Finch presses her hands together and steps back and sighs, her face twinkling in the light. All of this takes up the better half of the day, but when it's done, we make hot chocolate and sit and admire it, the popcorn and apples and most of all, the lights, and it's like it's the best accomplishment of our lives, that sight.

What I realize, sitting there by the tree, is how quickly my mind has shifted from contentment out here with just Finch and me to seeing there could be more for us, and wanting it. Wanting what, exactly? Days like this, I suppose. A wholeness that wasn't there before. I don't fully trust my instincts around relationships—never was good at it, plus I'm out of practice, Scotland and Finch and Jake being the only people I've interacted with for the better part of a decade now. But twice, I catch Marie looking at me from the other side of the tree, and I think maybe I'm not the only one who is sensing the pull of this, the possibility of a thing that could bud and bloom and grow.

Later that night, Finch is asleep, and Marie and I tiptoe into her room. I slide my hand under her pillow, feeling for the tooth, until at last my fingers settle on something sharp and hard. I tug it out and slide the feather of a scarlet tanager—red and fading to gray—in its place. I found the feather in the woods months ago, but I'd been waiting for the right moment to give it to her. Finch opens her eyes for a moment, and we freeze. She says something about Walt Whitman and rolls over. Marie and me creep back out into the living room, two giddy kids, sneaking around. I drop the tooth into a corner of the Raisinets tin and replace it on the shelf.

Marie cracks open a bottle of bourbon—it's Christmastime, she says—and we sip it from Fiestaware mugs, hers turquoise and mine red, both of us on the couch, knees touching. The woodstove purring, the Christmas tree glowing in the corner. She turns to me and moves closer, her hip to mine, and this time, no thought of Cindy, no holding back at all. I'm ready. Our lips touch. Tentative, at first. It has been so long. I place my hand on her neck. Pull her closer. I'm not sure I remember how to do this and meanwhile my body wants and is racing ahead and so there is a conflict of pace. We kiss again. My hand in her hair and her hands on my face and our mouths pressed and I'm ravenous and want all of it. Body, yes. But also the connection: the acceptance in the two of us coming together. The surrender.

She pulls away suddenly.

"What is it?"

"I'm sorry," she says, and then she's crying.

I lean back against the couch. Head spinning. I hadn't meant to upset her but meanwhile I'm also torn. Worked up now and trying to readjust and, well, confused. And it seems like maybe I'm the one who should be apologizing, though I can't say for sure what it is that went wrong. "I'm sorry."

She shakes her head. "No." She grabs my hand and wraps her fingers around mine. "He was the only one I ever . . . I was twenty and there was never anyone else." She squeezes my hand. "I want this. I do. I just can't rush into something again. I'm grieving and lonely and heartbroken right now and this would make things better temporarily, but in the end I would regret it. I would wonder whether it was real. And if there's one thing I don't need right now, it's more regret. More doubt." She looks at me. "Does that make any sense at all?"

It does and it doesn't, and she is still touching me, her fingers laced around my knuckles, and our legs are touching, too, knee thigh hip, and it's hard to shift gears from where things were headed to where things are now, so I just go ahead and tell her: "I need a minute." The best thing to do would be for me to peel away from her. Remove myself, get some physical space, cool down. But I don't want to hurt her feelings. I gently pull my hand from hers, lean forward, rest my head in my palms.

"I have to go home."

What I want to say is, Do you? And why? Come spring, the whole world will pull awake, open itself up, and we could be happy, here. The three of us, leaning on one another. We could have a life together, couldn't we? I swallow, trace the rim of my mug with my pointer finger, quiet.

"The snow seems to be melting, don't you think? I should probably leave as soon as it clears. If I wait until another storm blows through, I might be stuck here all winter."

"Would that be so terrible?"

"It sounds kind of lovely, actually. But my job," Marie says, smiling a little. "School will be starting up again. And my brother's house. Tempting as it is, I can't just leave those things behind." She twirls the fringe of the blanket around her finger.

I nod.

"But I could come back. Maybe in the summer. I mean if that'd be all right with you."

"You own the place," I say, nudging her but also thinking back to that first night, when she mentioned selling.

She presses her fingers into my palm. "About that. Cooper, this is your home. I see that now. I want you to know I would never take it away from you."

"Appreciate that. And like I said before, we can pay rent."

She shakes her head. "Don't worry about that. The place is paid for. And I like thinking that I'm honoring Jake. Carrying on his tradition. I like knowing you're here."

I slide closer. "I'd like it. I mean, if you'd come back."

"Good."

For a long time, we sit there, her shoulder pressed against mine. The candle burns way down and then out. Maybe I doze off, maybe not. Outside, the wind howls, pelting the windowpanes with clumps of snow, but we're warm here on the couch, and Finch is sleeping soundly in her bed. At peace, because this moment—it's just that. A moment, and it's good.

Well. I should've known that wouldn't last.

TWENTY-FIVE

On the sixth day of Marie, the weather continues its warming, and the snow begins a quick retreat. We make one last snowman in front of the house, Finch and Marie and me, and we fetch two black chunks of charred wood from the stove, let them cool, then press them to his face for eyes. We add a stick for his nose.

By late afternoon most of the snow in the yard has melted, and only the snowman remains, a five-foot white statue in a sea of slush and mud. We are finishing lunch, and Finch is reading her book to us aloud, a novel about people finding a spring that allows them to live forever, and I almost miss it, the noise.

A low hum. An engine, something coming. Someone driving up the road.

"Finch."

She ignores me and keeps reading.

"Finch!"

She stops and looks at me.

"Root beer."

Her fork clatters on the plate and she darts for the root cellar. As she lifts the trapdoor, I clear the plates and stack them on the counter and then grab the Gerber knife from the shelf above the woodstove. All of this in a matter of seconds.

"Cooper? What is it? What's going on?" Marie rises from the table, confused.

Finch clambers down the rickety steps to the cellar.

I grab Marie's hand. "Tell them you're alone. You own the place; you're spending some time here. Vacation or something. You got snowed in but you're fine. Just don't say a word about us, no matter what."

A glint of bewilderment in her eyes. But also fear. Maybe she is mad, too, and I don't blame her but I can't explain anything to her now. There's no time. I squeeze her palm in mine. "Please."

I ease onto the steps. Tug the trapdoor, and it whines as it closes overhead. When I'm in, I pull at the ropes that are connected to the bottom of the rug, two pieces that slide through knots in the floor, a contraption I set up long ago, and the rug slips back into place, hiding the door. Above, silence in the house but the engine grows louder, closer. Marie is still at the table, her feet twitching ever so slightly, I can see: a sliver of space between floorboards. Her slender ankles, navy-blue tights, the slippers she has worn all week, red moccasins with a little white bow.

She will tell them she's alone. She will she will she will. I pull Finch close, tuck her head beneath my chin. "It's okay," I whisper into her scalp. "It's gonna be okay." If she were looking at me, she'd know I was lying because she always knows, somehow. The way she knows I'm always troubled—"disconcerted," maybe, is a better word—on January 28th (my birthday). The way I'm always sad on the third of June (the day of the accident). That startling ability of hers to read people, that's from Cindy. Cindy could look at someone and see right into them, deep into the recesses of their heart, and just know things. Once, we were at dinner, and she leaned over and told me, "That man hurts his wife." She didn't know them, didn't even know their names. But a few weeks later, we read about an arrest in the paper, and there it was, a mug shot of his mean face on the first page. I recognized him right away.

Outside, the engine grows loud and then it's quiet. One door slams and then another. Two of them. Voices: deep, muffled. Men. West side of the house, next to Marie's car. Then footsteps, heavy on the porch. Stomp, stomp, kicking off the snow. Knocking at the door, knuckle to wood. Marie is still sitting at the table, her slippered feet in the same spot. From the root cellar I will her to move. *Come on, Marie. You can't just sit there. Get up!*

And she does. Slides the chair back, clears her throat, unlocks the door. I can't see but I imagine her peering out. "Yes?"

"Afternoon. I'm Sheriff Simmons, and this is Manny, my deputy. How are you doing today, ma'am?"

In the cellar, the heavy, pungent smell of dirt. Potatoes from the store, the stubby carrots from our garden. Butternuts from Scotland in the corner. A wooden crate of apples.

"Fine, thank you." She clears her throat again. "Is there something I can help you with?"

"You mind if we come in?"

"I'd rather you didn't." Pause. "With the mud. Your boots."

"It'll just take a minute."

Shuffling overhead, door moaning as it opens, cold air pouring into the house the way it does, and drifting right down through the floorboards to us. Finch shivers and tucks in closer.

"If you don't mind," Marie says, "I'd prefer that you stay on the rug there. I like to keep the place tidy."

"Sure, ma'am. No trouble at all. Nice place you got here. Never been back here but we have an emergency, and the gate was open. Hope that's all right."

The gate. I should've trekked out and closed it, that first day.

"My father built this place ages ago," Marie says.

"You live here year-round?"

I dip my head, hoping to catch a glimpse through one of the cracks in the floorboards. My throat tightens. No. Is it—Yes. The uniform, the military stiffness, those intense blue eyes. The sheriff from the gas station. Will he see the Bronco parked in the woods? Will he recognize it, the way the licorice-chewing attendant did?

"I'm just here for the holidays," Marie says. "Listen, what's this all about?"

"Right. Well, ma'am. Not sure if you're aware of this, but there's a girl who's gone missing. A local. Six days now and no sign of her at all."

Finch wraps her hand around mine and squeezes hard. I think back to that day in the woods, the girl and her camera. I squeeze back. Her nails dig into my palm.

"A girl?" Marie clears her throat. "How old?"

"Seventeen. Why?"

"Just curious."

Finch looks at me. Slowly, I press my pointer finger to my lips.

"How long have you been here, ma'am?"

"Five days. Six."

"You seen anything? Heard anything out of the ordinary?"

"No." Through the floorboards, I see her reaching for her cup. "Nothing. But I've been inside mostly, with the snow."

"You cut all that firewood? Quite a stash there." A different voice. The deputy. Manny.

"My husband, last trip. He didn't come this time."

"And the snowman? Did you make that yourself?" Footsteps overhead, heavy and careful, someone moving across the room but trying not to mess up the floor with the snow and mud.

"Yes. Hey," Marie says. "You said you'd stay on the rug."

"Come on, Manny."

"This book. *Tuck Everlasting.* It's a kids' book. My daughter read it last year."

Manny is standing over our heads, his thick boots covered in mud and dripping slush. A small piece of ice falls through the crack and lands on Finch's cheek, and I hold her arms tight to keep her from reaching up to move it. Manny opens the book, and Finch's bookmark, a one-inch-wide piece of cherished construction paper, decorated with pressed lavender from the summer before, falls to the floor, floats, flips over and over and lands just above us, right on the crack where a shaft of light spills through. If he sees us—

Finch clutches my hand tighter. The drip from Manny's boot slides down her face.

"I'm a librarian," Marie says. "I read all sorts of books. Adult books, children's books." Her voice shaking now. Hands, too. I can see them through the floor. She sounds defensive, guilty.

Steady, Marie. Calm down.

Manny kneels and picks up the bookmark and he is so close I can smell him: sweat, coffee, bacon. "Finch," he reads.

I press my hand over Finch's mouth.

"One of the library's patrons."

He slides the bookmark back into *Tuck Everlasting* and puts the book on the table, tiptoes back to the front door. "It's a good book, Carly said. Made her cry."

"Heck, Manny. Look at the floor. She asked us to stay on the rug."

"Just doing my job, boss."

"Yeah, yeah. We'll clean it up, ma'am," Sheriff says. "You got a towel? A rag or something?"

"No, no. Please: don't worry. It's all right. I'll get it."

"Well, let me show you this before we go. The parents, they're understandably beside themselves. Both of them, just a wreck. Anyway, they had a flyer made. It's posted all over town, but I'm assuming you haven't seen it. The girl's a senior in high school. Her name's Casey Winters."

A torrent of thoughts. The girl we saw—she's *missing*. Whatever that means. She isn't home, hasn't been to school. It seems unlikely, impossible, almost, that she has been in our woods all this time, but what if, for some unknowable reason and against all odds, she's still here?

Marie mutters and grips her skirt and then takes the paper the sheriff is holding. Finch and her notebook and the story of the girl with red hair in the woods—I can picture it, Marie connecting the dots, piecing together some semblance of truth.

"Anyway, the girl was a photographer," the sheriff says. "Good at it, apparently. Worked for the school newspaper but her parents say she wanted to work for *National Geographic* or one of those places someday, so she would go out in the woods sometimes. Sort of an *Into the Wild* type, apparently."

"But all the snow," Marie says. "Surely you don't think she's out in the woods now?"

"Hard to tell. You know kids. We found two SD cards from her camera in her room, so hopefully we'll get some answers from those."

I knew it, that day. I knew that girl was trouble but it was nice, living in this dreamscape with Marie and Finch and the snow. Chocolates and tea and companionship. Christmas lights strung on a white pine. Got swept right into it, let my guard down. I see it now, plain as day. Let myself believe maybe it was nothing, our crossing paths with her in the woods. Just a flicker of bad luck that had passed us by. I thought we were safe. But no.

Marie clears her throat. "Do you have any suspects?"

"Not really. But we just started looking through pictures this morning. Thousands of them, but something might turn up that could be of use to us."

It dawns on me that this is bad bad bad because we were there, and she was there, and even if she didn't see us when she paused, looked in our direction, if she clicked when we were in her viewfinder, if there are pictures of us—

Through the cracks in the floor, I can see the sheriff unbuttoning his pocket and pulling out a business card. "We'll get to the bottom of it, hopefully. But meanwhile, keep an eye out. You see something or hear something that seems a little fishy, get in your car and drive out to 86. I doubt you have cell coverage here, but you'll get reception once you're there. Here's my card." He turns to go but then stops. "Ma'am," he says, resting his hand on Marie's shoulder. "You sure everything's all right?"

All she would have to do, I realize, is point downward. Communicate with her eyes, gesture. Her back is to me; I wouldn't even see it.

"Yes," Marie says, but her voice is shaking. "Everything's fine. Just a little nervous now, that's all. It's so quiet here, and usually I don't see a soul, and then you two show up and tell me there's a girl missing and to keep an eye out. I'm just a bit ruffled, that's all. You understand."

"Well. No need to be nervous. We've got all hands on deck, I promise you that. You want us to come back out in a day or two? It'd be no problem."

"No. No, that won't be necessary. I'll be heading home soon. Later today, probably."

Finch fidgets, tries to turn and look at me. Upset about Marie leaving, I'm sure. I hold her still.

"All right. Give a ring if you need something."

"Of course."

The two men shuffle out, and we can hear them through the thin panes of the glass.

"What's the matter with you, stomping mud through the house like that?"

"You're just mad because you think she's cute."

Laughter, engine firing up.

They drive away, the motor fading until it is a low purr and then nothing at all. Finch is sitting on my lap, leaning against my chest, my chin resting on top of her head. My right leg has fallen asleep, and it stings and tingles when I try to stand, wants to give beneath the weight. "It's okay now, Finch. They're gone."

Her shoulders are shaking. From the cold, from nerves. "Coop," she whispers, her jaw chattering. "That thing you did to keep us together, a long time ago . . ."

"Yeah?"

"What was it?"

I press my cheek to her forehead. "I hurt someone."

"I'm scared."

"You don't have to be scared of those men. They're just doing their job."

"I'm not scared because of them. I'm scared because you're scared. Don't lie and say you're not because I know it: you are."

What is there to say to this? How do I explain to her that I have watched people step on mines and huddle as a building begins to crumble, that I have watched the only woman I've ever loved die of internal bleeding because a deer ran out on a dark road—how do I explain that I've seen just how frail the human body is, how everything can break, and will, and does, and that the one thing I have left, I cannot bear to see it break, cannot bear to lose it and so yes, I'm scared? "I just want to keep you with me. I want to keep you safe. That's all."

Finch leans her head against my chest. She points to the ladder. I need to go first to push the trapdoor open. "Marie's up there, remember?"

Yes, Marie. Marie will not be content with the simple answers that satisfy an eight-year-old. Marie will have question after question. Marie will want to know the truth, and maybe I owe her that, now that she's in on it, now that I've given her no choice but to be in on it. Heck, a part of me wants to tell her, wants her to know. It's just, well. Everyone has secrets. Things they've done that they regret. Some of them are bad enough that they could change the way a person perceives you. Of course I don't want that, but the real issue at hand is protection of the things dear to me. Survival. Safety. Not just ours. Hers.

TWENTY-SIX

After CPS took Grace Elizabeth and I realized I'd made a mistake in letting her go, getting her back didn't go well. That was to be expected, I suppose. Judge and Mrs. Judge wanted her, and they'd easily jumped through the legal hoops to get her. They'd geared up for a legal fight because they knew they could win. Which is exactly why I couldn't let the court be the place where the outcome for my daughter was determined.

I drove the Bronco, all packed up with supplies, and went to their place. Pulled up between the house and the little fountain and parked. I went to the door and rang the bell and said I wanted Grace Elizabeth. Judge came to the door and was holding her when I got there. Man, I hated that, the sight of her in his arms.

"Call the police," he called to Mrs. Judge.

She spun on her heel toward the kitchen.

"Stop," I said, and I hadn't planned on it, per se, but I pulled the Ruger, and when she turned back, she screamed.

Grace Elizabeth started crying. Judge handed her off to his wife.

"Kenny—"

"You set me up," I said. "You came to my house. You pretended you wanted to help."

"We do want to help, Kenny."

"You want to take her. And I won't let you. She's my daughter. My flesh and blood. You think you can just make a few phone calls and take her and that's that?"

"Put the gun away, Kenny. No need to be irrational here. We can work this out." Judge took a step closer. "Come on, son. Put it away."

"Don't." I thought of all the mean things he'd ever said to me and about me, then.

I pointed the gun right at him. Mrs. Judge screamed again, Grace Elizabeth wailing in her arms.

"Put the baby down," I told her, waving the gun toward the living room off to the right of the foyer. "Set her down on that blanket."

Mrs. Judge scuttled over, kissing Grace Elizabeth on the forehead before kneeling and placing her on the ground. She stood up, held her hands in the air.

"Both of you, downstairs." I knew there was a game room down there, a big space with a pool table and a leather couch and a wet bar.

They started down the steps, and I followed.

"Look at yourself, Kenny. Just take a step back from the situation and look. I should've let the police come for you like they wanted to, after your little incident at the diner."

I didn't know if that was true, whether he'd intervened on my behalf, but this was no time to get into it. I pressed the pistol into his back. "Move."

Downstairs, I pointed to a space between the table and bar. "Here. On the ground."

Mrs. Judge was close, and she shifted closer: a flash to my left and then her cold hand on my arm. I reacted. Swung the Ruger fast in her direction and made contact, the nose of the pistol grazing her cheek, just below the temple. Her head spun back and she stumbled, the blow knocking her off balance. She blinked, exhaled, looked lost.

Judge caught her. She was tall and thin, like Cindy, only not as strong, and she sort of buckled into his arms. He glared at me and his face was red and I could tell it took everything in him not to say something. Instead, he pressed his mouth to Mrs. Judge's ear. "Shhh," he whispered. "Shhh." He held her and eased her to the ground. She looked tired and she was bleeding: a slow dark trickle winding its way down her cheek.

I took the roll of duct tape I had on my wrist and pulled a piece off. Judge looked at me and called me a monster and then I covered his mouth. I taped his arms together behind his back and his feet as well. To my surprise, he didn't resist.

"Didn't intend for it to go like that," I said to Mrs. Judge, and I meant it. Then I taped her up, too. Mouth, hands, feet. I took my sleeve and dabbed the blood from her face. I couldn't look at her. I hated both of them, and I suspected she was the one who pushed for getting CPS to take the baby, but still, the sight of Cindy's mother bleeding and taped up, knowing I'd done that to her—it rattled something in me, deep in my gut, because even then I'd started convincing myself that I could be better.

I pulled the blinds shut and left the two of them there, on the ground in their basement. Upstairs, Grace Elizabeth was fussing, and I scooped her up. Smelled her, held her close. "Everything's all right now, sugar. Daddy made a mistake, letting you go, but I won't ever do that again," I whispered. She wrapped her hand around my finger and I kissed her forehead. Relieved but also aware that I needed to move. There was nowhere to go but forward now.

TWENTY-SEVEN

Finch and me climb the rickety ladder from the root cellar, the light from the windows bright and blinding after being in the dark. Marie is seated at the table, hands folded in her lap.

"Give us a minute, would you, Finch? Take your book to the back room."

She opens her mouth to argue but then looks at Marie, must see the tears, must see the look on her face, because she snatches the flyer from the table and darts to the back room, lips pressed tight, like she does when we're hunting, the words held in.

"Marie." I reach out and place a hand on her shoulder and she flinches.

"Don't." She shakes her head. "Don't touch me."

"I understand how it must look."

"You understand? I just lied. To officers of the law."

"I'm sorry about the lying. But if you hadn't left the gate open—"

She stands and looks me in the eye, her face close to mine. "Let's get this straight, Cooper. A girl is missing. The police are out there doing their job. You're hiding in the root cellar. Not just hiding, but you and Finch have a code word. You vanish in less than thirty seconds, like you've practiced it a thousand times. And you have the audacity to make this about *me*."

"I was just saying—"

She takes a deep, shaky breath. "Those pictures Finch drew. It's her, isn't it? The girl with red hair. Finch said—she said she didn't imagine her. She said she visits her sometimes."

"It's not how it seems."

She nods, faintly, then begins backing away from me.

At this point, I understand how things must appear from her point of view, and I realize, too, that if she went on home and decided to try and track me down by my old name, she might find some information that makes it look like something is wrong with me, something twisted and cruel. Six weeks after Finch and me came to the woods, thanks to Scotland's newspapers, I knew all the things Judge and Mrs. Judge and all the papers said about me. How they chose to spin things. How they could take something true and bend it just a tiny bit, word it just so, and I end up looking like a first-rate monster. And let's say Marie goes home and starts searching around and piecing things together. It might look something like this:

1. Kenny Morrison was a thriving Army Ranger who served three tours in Afghanistan, but when he came home, he was all screwed up in the head.

2. Eight years ago, Kenny Morrison kidnapped a little girl named Grace Elizabeth and disappeared. He kidnapped two other people, assaulted the woman with a deadly weapon, and tied both of them up in their basement.

3. Just this week, another girl disappeared, right where Kenny Morrison lives.

"We did see her," I say. "One time, that's all. But she has nothing to do with us, I promise."

Marie twists her skirt in her palms, wrings it tight. "I want to know. I want to know why you're really here. Why the two of you have to hide. Why you've changed your name. Why you have money but nowhere else to go. You didn't say that, but it's true. You're not just getting your footing like my brother said. I could tell by the look on your face, that first night when I mentioned selling the place. I want to know all of it. If you lie to me, Cooper, if you lie—" Her mouth twitches, lips red, cheeks flushed. "Swear to me you'll tell me the truth. Swear to me on my brother's grave. Everything. The whole truth."

I shake my head. The more she knows, the more trouble she's in. Aiding and abetting, harboring a fugitive. Who knows what way they might spin things, what kind of monster they might make her out to be, should all of this go south. Because they might. She could go to prison. Jake had gotten dragged into my mess, but I could convince myself he stepped into it of his own volition. But not her. Marie, school librarian, lover of dark chocolates with sea salt and caramel, drinker of tea. Marie, Jake's baby sister, making a simple delivery of supplies. No.

"I can't do that." I reach for her hand, but she pulls away. "I've put you in a predicament here, and I'm sorry for that. But I can keep you from getting wound up in it tighter. I can protect you from that. There are things you're better off not knowing about. I need you to leave it at that."

She drops her head, looks away. I want to pull her back. I want to apologize for all of it—for making her lie, for lying, for not telling her the truth about us—because I trust her. I want to, at least. But I can't. Something deep behind my breastbone pangs and sways. That hollow feeling that is always there but has somehow subsided since her arrival. Knowing that I've hurt someone, again, and realizing that this is how things go with me. I wound and destroy.

"This week." She shakes her head. "This week, I thought maybe something was happening. I thought maybe something was *there*. Something felt different in me. At least I thought it did. But the truth is, I'm a librarian whose husband has been cheating on her for years. I'm a person who's so lonely that I have no one to spend the holidays with, who's so desperate that I go and buy groceries for people I don't even know because honestly, I didn't have anything better to do. Really. It's the holidays and I literally have nothing on my calendar for the foreseeable future."

"Marie."

"You know the worst part? I actually started to picture myself here. You and me and Finch, the three of us together. The life my dad pictured." She wipes her eyes. "Me and my wild imagination. I think I'm out of my mind."

"You're not out of your mind." I take a step closer. "I thought it, too."

"But you can't tell me why you're really here, living in my

family's cabin, using a different name. Why my brother brought you supplies, all these years. Why Finch has never been inside a store. You can't tell me why the two of you have to hide."

"I want to. Believe me, I do. But I can't. It's for your own good. For your protection."

"I can't do it. Be with a person who lies. Who keeps secrets. I've spent the last decade of my life doing that, living with someone who lied to me, and I won't do it again."

"I understand," I tell her, and I do, but the whole thing is more complicated than that. "It's not the same, you know that. It's not the same, what your husband did and what's going on here. What he did, he knew it would hurt you, and he did it anyway. What I'm doing is different. What I'm doing is to keep you safe. I need you to trust me."

The bedroom door creaks open. "I need to talk to you, Coop."

"We need a few more minutes."

She ignores me. "It's urgent." She walks up to me and holds out the flyer. "Cooper, it's *her.*"

I look at Marie, who is standing there with her hand at her throat, biting her lip and sporting a look that makes me remember how once, a sparrow flew into Lincoln's shed, and fluttered about the window, trying to get out. I cornered it, and it was so worn out that when I scooped it into my hands, it didn't fight. I just held it there, and I could feel its tiny heart drumming against my fingertips, its body so light it felt like nothing. Those hollow bones.

"Look," Finch says.

I let it go, the sparrow. Carried it out of the shed and then kneeled down and slowly opened up my palms and the thing sort of tumbled out and onto the ground and stood there for a minute, stunned, and I'm telling you: it looked at me, with its small, darting eyes. It looked right at me as if to say thank you.

"Cooper, look." Finch holds out the flyer, and I take it.

The girl we saw, in one of those senior-portrait-style poses. Arms crossed, smiling, leaning against an old brick building. She looks confident, kind, happy. Just a picture and yet looking at it—at *her*—seems to knock something loose in me. I sink into the chair. "Tonight," I say at last, placing the flyer facedown on the table. "I'll tell you everything tonight."

TWENTY-EIGHT

Finch puts up a fight about going to bed, one excuse after another, anything to keep us from closing the bedroom door and continuing the night without her. When it's just me and her here, I read to her, or she reads to me, and I kiss her good night and pull her blanket up to her chin and that's it. She doesn't mind me going out into the main room because she knows she's not missing out on anything, just me sitting there with a book or working on her quilt. But with a guest here, and with the day's excitement, that's not the case. Her belly hurts, she thinks she may have sprained her ankle, she has a hangnail. Well, finally we get Finch settled, with Marie proffering a bribe about if Finch goes right to sleep, she'll make pancakes in the morning, and that's enough to motivate her to keep quiet and stay in the room.

Marie brews herself a cup of tea but doesn't offer any to me, which is all right because my stomach's in turmoil, like the first time in Ranger training when I slid out of an airplane. You're miles up in the air, and you have your parachute and you've been told how to do this, and a part of you is excited just to do it, but you're also scared out of your mind. There's something unnatural about it, humans, with our dense bones and heavy muscles, tumbling into the air like that. We weren't meant to fly, which means you're just surrendering yourself to the expanse and trusting everything will work right.

I take a sip of water and force it down. Where to begin? When Cindy and me finally got together? When we found out she was pregnant and Judge and Mrs. Judge tried to convince her to terminate? When she got so mad at them she moved out to Lincoln's to live with me? When, at the hospital, with her labor going on nineteen hours, she begged me to call her mother, and then it was Mrs. Judge there in the delivery room, her on one side of the hospital bed and me on the other, waiting for the baby to come, and somehow everything she'd said to Cindy, all those hurtful things about the both of us, was forgiven, abracadabra, gone?

Well. We have time. All night, and the way I see it, this will most likely be the last night I ever have company here in the cabin, so I start way back, at the beginning. My whole sad life story. How my mother woke up one morning when I was seven, kissed me on the forehead and said she'd be right back, but then loaded up two suitcases, climbed in the car, and drove off, never to be seen again. How she waved. How I waited and waited until night closed in and I put two waffles in the toaster and ate them with so much syrup it was like soup.

I tell Marie about growing up at Lincoln's farm, about meeting Cindy in the eleventh grade. Me joining the Army and meeting Jake and serving in Afghanistan. Cindy going off to college. I explain how

Cindy had been home for months by the time I got back, living at home and, in her own words, about to go crazy stuck there with her parents, who were constantly on her about what she intended to do with her life. For the time being, she was working at an art gallery and volunteering at the elementary school, and going back and forth about what to do next. Her parents felt strongly that she should pursue law school, but she was thinking about social work. Which her parents didn't like at all: no money in that line of work, no gratitude, either.

Anyhow. I tell Marie that yes, I have considered the possibility that maybe part of the reason why me and Cindy ended up getting together was because she'd been there at home, bored and lonely and treading water, all of her friends having moved on, and I was there, and I didn't care one bit about whether she became a lawyer. Believe me, I've considered all that, the chance that maybe we just got together because we happened to be in the same place at the same time, both of us available and Cindy finally not dating some loser. But there was something more, too. Something between us, where we could just look at each other and understand things.

By the time we got together, we'd been seeing each other every day, though technically we were still just friends. After work, we'd go to the river and I'd fish for bass, the water sleepy and slow that time of year, and Cindy would sit along the edge on a big rock and either read or sometimes just stretch out and watch me fish. And one day, she walked out to the middle of the river, stumbling a little over the round and algae-covered rocks. She wrapped her arms around my neck and kissed me, and well, I was done.

The following spring, I tell Marie, Cindy found out she was pregnant, and two weeks after that, she showed up at Lincoln's with two suitcases, and that started the happiest time of my life, her standing at my doorstep. I cooked for her, set up pillows beneath her legs to elevate her swollen feet when they bothered her. I rubbed cocoa butter across her growing abdomen, along the widening sides, the belly button that eventually bulged out. What a miracle it was, to watch her body transform as the weeks passed. Sometimes, I would press gently into Cindy's belly, and the baby would push back, like she felt me out there in the world, like she wanted me to know it.

I have to go quickly through the part where Cindy and Finch and me are driving home and the deer jumps into the passenger side and we roll and roll. The funeral, too, although I tell Marie what Mrs. Judge said about it being my fault Cindy was dead. And then I tell about the nightmares and what happened at the diner before me and Cindy got together, and also about Child Protective Services coming to the house with a police officer and hauling Finch out the door without so much as a warning.

"I got her back," I say, weaving my pointer finger through a loop in the crocheted blanket. "I went to the house and got her back."

Marie frowns. "They just let you take her?"

"No." I pick up a spool of thread from the bowl on the table and roll it in my palm. "Things got out of hand, and I regret that. I truly do. Anyhow, after that, they put a price on my head. Got the word out everywhere."

Marie shifts her weight on the couch. "When you say things got out of hand . . ."

"Someone got hurt. Not bad, but still. It wasn't my intention, going in there, but it happened."

It's the first time I've told the whole story aloud. I see the inconsistencies, I hear how it sounds, I remember the newspapers and the way they painted the picture. "We would've been in court, duking it out for months and months. Over a year, maybe. In the end I would've lost, anyhow. I would've lost her." I clear my throat. "So I handled it."

Marie doesn't say a word so I keep going.

"For six weeks we lived in a tent until I decided I owed your brother a call. I didn't want to bother him, but I was also feeling like a sneak out here, living on the property and not even telling him about it. Plus once Scotland showed up, I figured I better tell Jake. Finch and me drove out to the gas station and used the pay phone. The only thing Jake asked was whether we were all right. Whether we needed anything. Didn't tell me I'd screwed up. Didn't try to convince me to change my course."

Marie begins to quiver, her shoulders bobbing up and down.

"I'm sorry. Should I have skipped the part about Jake?"

She shakes her head. "No. No, I want to hear it."

"Finch loved him, you know. Broke her heart when I had to tell her he wasn't coming. Kids, they used to flock to him, over there, too. No matter where we were, they'd find him. Follow him around. Gathered around him like you see pictures of kids with Jesus. There was something about him."

"At the end, he had round-the-clock care," she whispers. "He couldn't even get to the bathroom on his own. Couldn't even feed himself." She tucks her chin into her shoulder and begins to shake hard.

I reach out and press my hand to hers. "It should've been me," I whisper. "I offered to go first because it was more dangerous. I went right through and missed it. I don't know how. I've replayed it over and over, and I don't know how or why it was him and not me."

"You saved his life. That's the way he saw it." A tear skims her cheek, skating back and forth. "I want you to know, Cooper: I understand why you came here."

"I couldn't lose her. Not after—I couldn't."

"I know." She sighs. "I understand what you're trying to protect. But Cooper, that girl. If you and Finch saw her in the woods, one way or another, you need to tell the authorities."

I shake my head, pull away from her. "I can't do that."

"I understand there's some risk for you, but you can't just keep that type of information to yourself. It's not right. Think of the girl's parents. Think about Finch. If she went missing and someone had seen her, you would want to know."

I stand up, walk to the sink. Her words strike a nerve and I don't like it. "I only saw her the one time." I don't mention the footprints, or the lens cap, like maybe the girl had been there before, because the bottom line is: we didn't do anything wrong. We didn't go looking for trouble—it came to us.

"But Finch said she lives here, in your woods."

"Finch also said she's a princess and a wood nymph. You know how she gets; you can see it. She attaches easily, she obsesses. She has a vivid imagination. You've heard her."

"Still," Marie says, "you're holding what may be a vital piece of the puzzle, and you're refusing to share it. She's a minor, Cooper. A kid. You have an obligation to share that information. A moral obligation." She follows me to the sink and wraps her fingers around my hand. "You see that, don't you?"

I stare out the kitchen window, the moonlight illuminating the ground, still speckled with snow. I see her point—I really do—but there are odds to be weighed here, losses to be calculated, and there's too much at stake. "I can't draw attention to us. I go to the police, Cindy's parents find out about us, it's over."

"It wouldn't be *over*, Cooper. You're her father."

I shake my head. "It's not that simple."

"You have ample evidence to prove that you're a loving, competent parent. Finch is obviously thriving. Yes, you'd have some court hearings. You'd likely be separated for a few months. But when it was all over, you could live out there in the world. You wouldn't have to hide."

I take a deep breath, lean against the sink. Aggravated assault, up to twenty years. Kidnapping, up to twenty years per person, and Judge and Mrs. Judge—they said I kidnapped them, too. Which I guess I did, technically. So eighty years. Maybe sixty if I got a good attorney and lucked out with a sympathetic jury. Either way, once I set foot in a prison, I'd never get out. I knew this from Scotland's stack of newspapers, the first day he rolled into the yard.

I screwed up. I accept that. The way I got her back. At the time I was so desperate, so scared: it felt like the only way. But now we're boxed in. There's no stepping out of this life, no going back. "Like I said, it's not that simple."

"I could do it," Marie says. "I could say I saw her in the woods. Just tell me where. Show me. I can call. I can take them there myself. But I cannot leave here in good conscience knowing that you intend to hold on to a vital piece of information about a young girl who's missing." She turns to look at me, and I can see Jake. Their striking similarity.

It could work, almost. But her calling the authorities would also mean more lying. More involvement. Not to mention things could get sticky, her getting her story mixed up on account of none of it being true. Meanwhile we'd be back to square one, people prowling around out here, trying to piece things together, only we'd be giving them a big lead to come closer. "You already told them you hadn't seen her. Which means you'll have to say you were lying, and then they'll try and figure out why you'd do that." I shake my head. "You're not getting tangled up in this any more than you already are. Jake wouldn't have that, and I won't allow it. I'll take care of it myself. I'll go out to the pay phone at the gas station, tomorrow. Leave that sheriff's number and I'll call."

She looks relieved, tears welling. "Promise?"

"Promise."

"I still need to go home. I have things I need to tend to. Jake's house, my job."

"I'm sorry things turned out like this. Sorry you got dragged into it."

She rests her hand on mine, then rises from the couch, pulling a pen and a notebook from her purse. "This is my phone number," she says, handing me a piece of paper. "In case you ever need something. In case Finch does." She presses the piece of paper into my palm.

In the morning, Marie makes pancakes and coffee and the house is, for the last time, filled with smells that I suspect will now forever remind me of her. She leaves Finch a box of cookies and hands me the French press and what remains of the coffee. We load the final items in her Prius and Finch gives her a long hug goodbye.

Then Marie steps toward me. She leans in close, resting her head against my chest. "You're a good man, Cooper," she whispers.

Well. I feel bad about that, her saying that and thinking it about me, because it's not true.

I feel bad, too, because there's a girl missing. A girl nine years older than Finch, with parents who care about her but have no way of reaching her. I know what it's like to have a child slip through your fingers. I do. Pains me to think about what they must be going through.

And the girl was here, just over a week ago. Did she get turned around after we saw her? Did something happen to her? The river with its deceitful ice, the sand that pulls and holds. One fall, one broken bone, one wrong step. So much could go wrong. But I have to remind myself that even if I wanted to step in, I've got my own daughter to think about. I don't have the liberty of being a good citizen or doing the right thing. That's the scrape my own choices have left me in, I see that. The bottom line is this: any inch toward that girl jeopardizes everything for us. And if there's one thing I'm absolutely sure of, it's that under no circumstances will I do anything that puts my own child at risk.

TWENTY-NINE

"Saw you had more visitors," Scotland says, sauntering toward the cabin, right there in the yard, a breeze, a ghost. He takes off his backpack, pulls a stack of newspapers out, and sets them on the porch, where Finch is set up with her slingshot. "Sheriff Simmons and his esteemed deputy, the illustrious Manny Porter."

"You know them?"

"Simmons, yes. Porter, no. I saw them driving up the road. Couldn't get here in time to warn you but I was keeping an eye out."

"I'm sure you were." The possibility that Scotland knows about the girl—that maybe he knew about her before even Finch and me did—flickers through my mind. The spotting scope, the meticulous tracking of our whereabouts. Did he know where Casey Winters was? And if so, what was his game plan? And what if he were to end up trying to be a hero and leading the police right to me, after all this time?

I sit next to Finch and pull her closer.

"Marie talked to them, and then she went home," she says. "We hid in the root cellar. The man was standing right over us. Snow dripped on us from his boot. They're looking for that girl we saw in the woods. Remember? I told you. Down by the river."

"I figured that's what they were after." Scotland wipes his brow with his shirt. "There's an article in the paper. Front page. Her boyfriend says she was planning to run off to California. Wanting to get out from under her parents, apparently." He shakes his head. "Kids."

Finch frowns at this, then grabs the stack of newspapers and slides them closer. She stretches out on her stomach, leafing through. Walt Whitman climbs onto her back and settles there.

"Looks like Walt's feeling at home here," Scotland says.

Finch, absorbed in her reading, doesn't even look up.

"Listen," Scotland says. "They still haven't found the girl. So you're not in the clear yet. California or not, they'll be looking for her, I bet. Place could get busy. I'd stick close to the cabin if I were you."

Finch spends the next few hours poring through the papers, circling lines and photographs, jotting notes in her journal. Agitated, quiet. Later, I'm getting ready to sew the final square onto her quilt, a piece from a shirt with a rainbow and a unicorn that, for a long period of time, she insisted on wearing every single day. I had to wash it each night, hang it next to the woodstove to dry. Scotland's warning on my mind, I step onto the porch, scanning the woods for movement, listening. It's not quite dark, the sky flourishing pink and orange, the silhouettes of the trees leaning into the light. Everything quiet and still. I head back inside and settle on the couch. Cut the fabric and thread the needle. Finch sits at the table, the papers and journal spread out in front of her.

"Coop, that sheriff who came here?" she says, setting down her pencil. "We need to call him."

"Sugar, we aren't calling anyone."

"But . . ." She rises. "They're looking for her."

"I know that." My voice has an edge now, sharp and hot.

"And we saw her."

"Once."

"*You* saw her once." She stares at her feet, voice quiet.

I wait.

"She was back, after that," she says. "I went down there. On my own, after we saw her."

I point to her, my hands shaking, and my voice, too. "Why would you do that?"

She balls the hem of her pajama top in her fist. "She's my friend."

"That girl is not your—" I pause, change my words. The sadness of it striking a nerve: for a person who has no friends, watching a girl in the woods—that would feel like friendship, maybe. "You don't even know her, Finch."

"I know her enough."

"Did she see you?"

"No. Well, I'm not sure. Maybe. Actually, I think yes. Because— the last time, something happened. Someone else was there."

"Someone else?" A menacing thought, a flash of terror: Scotland, snooping after all. Meddling, or something worse, and Finch as witness, and the trouble we are in if this is true because what are we gonna do about it? Report him? Avoid him?

Finch steps closer, holding out a newspaper. "Him." She points to a photograph of a young man with brown, curly hair, standing next to Casey Winters. The two of them dressed up, like for a school dance or something. "And he's lying."

"Finch, you don't know that." She's been wading into the Nancy Drews lately, and apparently they're rubbing off on her.

"It said in the papers that he told the police she was going to California. Why would he tell them that? He knows where she is."

She begins clenching the corner of the quilt, hand wrapped tight around an old onesie. There's more, I can tell.

"What else?"

"He was yelling at her. And then he pushed her."

I look at her, taking this in. Throat tight.

"I sent a rock at him," she says, "with my slingshot. I hit him square in the back." She juts out her chin and her eyes glimmer. "It hurt, too. I could tell. He started after me, but you know how I am in the woods. He would never catch me."

I slam my fist onto the trunk and rise, the needle and thread tumbling to the floor. "You got any idea how stupid that was, Finch? How dangerous? After all I've taught you." The spool of thread rolls away, stuttering across the floor.

She steps back, startled, but not deterred. "He was hurting her. What was I supposed to do, just stand by and watch?"

Yes. No.

A series of emotions scuttle through: anger, frustration, disappointment, pride. But also fear. Because someone is out there, maybe close, maybe not. Someone capable of violence, someone who saw Finch. Could he be looking for her, now? I walk to the window and peer out, hand on the Ruger.

I shake my head, scoop the needle and thread from the floor and dump them into the wooden bowl on the trunk. "Well, where?"

She bites her lip. "Close to where we saw her, but north a ways, up the valley. I meant to go back and check on her, but then Marie came, and the snow. I can show you where. If we leave now, we can get there before dark."

"We're not going anywhere near that place. You got that?"

"But I'm worried about her. What if something happened to her? What if he did something after I left? We need to check on her."

This whole time as a parent, there were two things I wanted. The first and most important was to be with Finch, to take care of her. But close behind that goal was the second, which was to raise her right. To help her grow up to be a person with good values and compassion. A person who did the right thing, no matter what. Which is what she was doing, really. Standing up for someone. All these years, the choice I made to come here, the risk that choice entailed and the so-called rules that I broke in order to do it—all this time I've been justifying it by telling myself that at least we're together and at least my daughter is growing up with a sense of right and wrong.

But now here we are, Finch and me at an impasse and my own two desires in direct opposition. Where, no matter what, one of those things must be let go.

"We can't afford to get involved in this. I'm sorry but that's how it is." I look out the window again, scanning the woods. "There are things you don't know, Finch. About us."

"I don't understand what anything about you and me has to do with this."

"We aren't going down there, Finch, and that's that." I lean down close and look her in the eye. "You knew the rules and you didn't stick to them. You broke my trust. For that, you're grounded."

"What does that mean?"

"It means you've lost your privileges for a while. Till this thing blows over, you're not leaving my sight. No trapping, no scouting. Nothing."

"But—"

I return to my sewing. "I don't want to hear another word about it. You got that? Not a word."

Her face crumples and she squints her eyes and pushes her lips out. "'All faults may be forgiven of him who has perfect candor.' That's Whitman and I know you remember." She points to the couch. "We were sitting right there when you read it to me. I asked you what it meant and you said no matter what happens in life, you should be honest. Be a person of honor."

Whitman with his hat and his fat white beard, staring into the sky and making up pretty lines. He wasn't a soldier. He never had people show up at the house with a clipboard to write down everything that was wrong about his life and then haul his kid off. "It's easy for a person who sits around and writes poems all day to have certain philosophies on life."

"The Bible says it, too," Finch says, her voice a whisper. "I read it myself."

"Finch, enough."

She's crying now: tears pouring down her cheeks. She spins on her heels and stomps to the bedroom, then returns with her pillow and blankets. "I'm sleeping in the loft," she says, picking up the cat and tucking him under her arm. She climbs the ladder, blankets draping behind her. She begins sliding the boxes around to make a space for herself.

I finish my quilt square, and then lean over and blow out the candle. "Night, Finch," I call up to her. Her flashlight is still on.

"You should be ashamed of yourself," she says, so quiet I can barely hear.

It's the first mean thing she's ever said to me. My whole life, people have said such things, but coming from Finch, it hurts. A pang of sadness ricochets through my chest.

I am, I want to tell her. I am ashamed of myself.

THIRTY

The next morning, I wake with a heaviness, the weight of the previous night's conversation with Finch a burden that has swelled into something physical: dull pain pulling at the shoulders. Sadness, fear. I sit up in bed, then stand. My feet resisting the weight. I get dressed slowly, stumble into the kitchen. I pour the water in the kettle to heat and then slide into my coat to go out and get the eggs. At the door I freeze, jacket half on.

The shovel isn't propped against the door handle, nor are any of the locks locked.

"Finch?"

Fast as I can, I climb the ladder. Blanket, pillow, Walt Whitman curled up in the thick of it and purring loudly. But Finch isn't there.

I shuffle back down the ladder and slide into my boots. Dart to the bedroom to get the Ruger, tug a beanie over my ears. The kettle begins to sing, loud and piercing, steam spewing from the spout and dancing across the stove. I grab the kettle and place it on a trivet. I step outside.

"Finch!"

I know she doesn't hear me. And if she did, would she answer, anyway?

You should be ashamed of yourself.

My heart pounds, pulse drumming at the ears. Panic: a freight train, thundering down the track, closer closer closer because she is out there, Finch, and if the guy she saw in the woods has come back scouring the place to clean up after some dark deed—if he's looking for her, and finds her—God, who knows what might happen. Who he is, what he might do.

Slow down, Cooper. Think. She didn't just run away, she's not lost. She's checking on her. What did Finch say? Near where we saw her but higher up the valley. The ground is still patched with snow, a collage of brown and white. Not enough snow that I can easily pick up a trail. I head west, moving fast, up the slope behind the cabin, through pines that sigh and whisper. Feet sliding on the lingering ice. It's not quite light, the woods just coming awake with bird songs. Cardinal, wood thrush. Northern flicker, stuttering at a tree. But mostly, silence. Funny how what is usually so calming and reassuring can become so terrifying. I run past the big rocks, descend. Cross the stream, which is now bloated with ice. Clamber my way up the other side.

At the top of the next hollow I pause, leaning, listening: the rush of the river below. The valley is choked with fog. Dense and glaring and I can barely see ten feet in front of myself. I circle around the side of the hill and head into the mist, so thick I can feel it hitting my skin, dense and palpable.

"Finch!" I yell, fully aware that if by chance someone is close by, every noise I make could pull them closer.

Nothing.

The forest floor grows soft, my feet sinking in. All the snow melted and the ground saturated in this place that is, even at dry times of the year, wet enough to grow cattails. I push through the alder, red and looming and catching my jacket. The ground heavy and pulling with each step, my feet covered in mud.

It's getting light, fast. The valley brightening.

It's hard to see but ahead, a flash of color that's out of place—pink. Thirty, forty yards. I take off, fighting the sand and mud, almost quicksand but not quite. Finch's new glove, snared in greenbrier. I tug the glove free from the thorns. On the ground, her notebook. I pick it up and tuck it in my jacket. Pull the Ruger from my pocket. Then, hair. Red, long and spread out but clumped with sand and mud. The upper half of the body visible, arms, neck, head. The lower half sunk into the mud. With the snow melting, the river swells this time of year, moving dirt and even shifting its course sometimes. The land, it's taking back the body. The cold weather has kept it from decaying, the face swollen and white, the lips purple and wide and cracked. Still, the girl we saw, that picture the police officer left with Marie, the long red hair—she has changed significantly but it's her. Casey Winters.

With a quick scan I see that she has done some work here. Straight ahead is a fire ring: stones stacked in a circle, charred wood in the middle, a metal grate for cooking. A tent, brown and tan, with a large camouflage tarp draped over the top and staked down a few feet beyond the tent, like an awning. A piece of rope tied between two trees with a shirt draped over it. But also a green camp chair, turned over, its top deep in mud. Strewn about the campsite, a blue enamel kettle, a fork and knife. Beneath the awning, a cast-iron skillet, blood caked along the rim. I swear under my breath and walk back to the body. Kneel down, force myself to look at her. I didn't notice before, but now I see it: the bruise at the left eye, the delicate skin cracked at the cheekbone. I grab a sycamore leaf, dry and dead, wrap it around my hand, and lift the girl's head. Blood caked on the broom sedge beneath her, blood at the back of the head. A wound that gapes.

"Finch!" I yell, turning around, scanning the willows and cattails. She was here last night or this morning, I know, but when? And whoever did this—were they here, too?

I spin, thinking about that day in the woods when we first saw Casey Winters from our hunting spot, high in the King of Trees, and I can't say what it is but I start walking in that direction, south, pulled there, hoping. I shield my eyes, the sun rising, setting the valley ablaze. The King of Trees, its wide, white branches, stretched out and up. The small treestand we built and dragged across the valley together. Empty. She isn't there.

A ruffed grouse darts from the brush, startled and startling me, its wings thundering into the trees.

I head closer, shimmy up the tree for a better look across the valley. The sun now blinding as it burns through the fog. The river murmurs, wide and white and resisting its banks, treacherously full from the snowmelt. Another unbearable thought: what if she fell in? I picture it—a small foot rushing and slipping, the river taking her. Cold. She wouldn't stand a chance. Nobody would. I should've listened to her. We should've come down here together because if something happened, if it's my fault, I couldn't live with myself.

A muskrat scuttles into the water, lithe and quick.

I keep looking hard, focused, scanning the landscape: cattails, alder, swamp oak, all of it beginning to blur from the panic. I'm not sure I believe in God, but I pray, then. A muttered something. A beg. *Please.*

"Finch!"

For hours I walk the swamp, slogging back and forth, looking. No sign of her. At last I head home, sliding back down the ravine, my legs weak. The tiniest hope that maybe Finch came to the valley, found the body and the campsite, and turned home right away. Maybe she took a different route. I step across the ice-thick stream. As I climb the steep hill back toward the cabin, my eyes scan the rocks, like always. A habit. There. A tiny flash of pink. I take off running, scrambling up the slope, tired and out of breath and all those dens and their potential inhabitants and what if something or someone got her—

She's there, head to toe in her camouflage with her one pink glove, huddled in a cave, balled up tight and not even looking at me. Rocking. I run to her, scoop her into my arms, and she is cold and wet, her bottom half covered in mud.

"I was too late," she sobs into my shoulder, shaking bad. "We were too late."

THIRTY-ONE

I carry her home, heavy and wet and limp. Shuffle through the pines as fast as I can. She's probably dehydrated, almost certainly hypothermic—as close to death's door as she has ever been—and strangely enough, I don't panic. All that military training, it kicks in, and there is simply an emergent situation that needs attention, and I have the training and skills to handle it. I put the kettle on, open the draft. I help Finch out of her wet clothes and wrap her in a blanket and set her right in front of the woodstove, which by that point is already humming and cracking. Finch's teeth chatter, her body shakes. I wrap my arms around her, rubbing her back. Friction, heat. But not too much, too fast.

The water's warm. I dump a heaping scoop of hot-chocolate mix into a mug, fill it with water. I hand it to her but her hands are shaking too bad and she can't hold it. I press it to her lips then set the mug next to her. I pour water into the stainless-steel bowl and dip a dishcloth in, wring it out. I kneel down next to Finch, pressing the cloth to her forehead, wiping away the mud that has caked to her face. Her cheeks are scratched from thorns: thin red lines, puckered in the middle. I dab gently, she winces and pulls away.

"You're gonna be all right, sugar. You're gonna be just fine."

And she is, after a while. Physically, at least. I carry her to the couch, wrapped tight in her blanket, dry now, and warming. She sleeps and sleeps. I wake her every half hour to give her sips of hot chocolate, some broth made from a bouillon cube. The day trundles on; darkness sweeps in. I wedge myself onto the couch, prop her head in my lap.

As she sleeps, I leaf through her notebook. In the past, I've only done this by invitation. An effort to respect her privacy. But I decide recent events warrant an unauthorized look.

December 19th. We saw a beautiful girl in the woods with long, red hair. Cooper had a panic attack and had to rest. I was scared but I recited poems to myself. I saw a flock of turkeys. They came in close. Do you know how still you have to be for a turkey not to see you? Very, because of their excellent eyesight. I also saw a pileated woodpecker.

December 20th. I couldn't stop thinking about the girl we saw in the woods. Who is she? What's her name? Why was she there with her camera? I tried to get Cooper to play along and imagine, but he wouldn't. (He is sorely lacking when it comes to imagination.) Anyway, I decided to go back to the valley where we saw her. So that's what I did.

She was back! She has set up a tent and fire pit. Sometimes she sings. I hope she will be our neighbor. I hope we can be friends. I saw three deer and four squirrels, as well as a red-shouldered hawk.

December 21st. There was a boy at the girl's campsite. He had wavy, brown hair and is very big next to her. He yelled at her and pushed her. She seemed scared so I shot my slingshot at him because Cooper says you should step in when someone needs help. The guy stopped and looked in my direction and then started toward me so I slipped into the woods. He would never catch me, and if he got close I would hide. I'm an excellent hider. I want to tell Cooper, but he would be livid if he found out I went down there and the two of them saw me. Livid = very mad.

December 22nd. I should've mentioned yesterday that I have another new friend. She came last night in a blue car. My whole life, my only friends have been Jake and Scotland, and Cooper, but he's my dad, so I don't know if he counts. And then, over the course of three days, two new friends?!? And just in time for Christmas. My newest friend is Jake's sister and her name is Marie. She brought supplies because Jake asked her to before he died. Marie has soft, brown hair and eyes like a doe. I love her. I tried to get Cooper to go back to the river, but he wouldn't. It snowed, and we went sledding! I hope my other friend is okay.

Late at night, Finch wakes, pushing herself up. The dull glow of the coals in the woodstove illuminating her face. I reach out, tuck her hair behind her ear. "You feeling better? Need something?"

She looks at me. Hears me, I know she does. Those eyes—they're not distressed, not confused. Her lip trembles, and she holds my eyes.

"Finch?"

She blinks. A tear slips and slides down her cheek.

"Sugar."

She just keeps on looking at me. A blankness, there. A spark that's gone out.

The next day we stay close to home. I sit on the porch, keeping an eye on the woods, watching for movement, listening for the slightest sound. A twig snapping beneath weight, leaves crunching. Every hour on the hour, I circle the cabin, checking for any sign that some-one has infringed.

Finch doesn't even leave the porch, and she still hasn't spoken. Not a single word.

I will admit: the silent treatment, when it's just two of you out there in the middle of nowhere—it's a powerful way to exert your wrath. All that chatter, the nonstop questions about who made the world and have I ever noticed that insects have barbed legs and which Whitman poem is my favorite: I miss it.

And moreover, the silence gives me space to start thinking. Which feels like a dangerous thing to do. Ever since the day I got Finch back from Judge and Mrs. Judge, I've been getting along by not overthinking because that's when things get dicey, when you let yourself contemplate the choices you've made. Better to just do what needs to be done, and deal with the aftermath. But Finch's silence is throwing me off: no constant stream of conversation and I'm thinking about everything, and soon I'm buzzing with guilt and doubt and fear. Just keeps gurgling up, one thing after another.

Casey Winters with her red hair.

The promise I made to Marie, and broke.

A killer who knows that Finch saw him hurting Casey Winters. According to the papers, he hasn't run, which means he'll be back. The body, the destroyed campsite, maybe even the murder weapon. All of it just sitting there, all those clues, waiting to be discovered. Not to mention a witness. Maybe immediately, maybe not, but at some point, he'll have the urge to tie up loose ends. Which means that this place that has been our home, our sanctuary—it's no longer safe. It may never feel safe again. And it's not just because of what I did.

Well, it *is* because of what I did, deep at the heart of it all, which is hard to stomach.

But somehow just as troubling as the rest of it is the change in the way Finch looks at me. There's no longer that wonder and regard. Something magical about the way your kid looks at you and even if they don't say it, you know that they think you're the smartest, strongest, most interesting person on the face of the planet. That they trust you. That your existence offers a sense of meaning and security. Maybe I'm being sentimental about this, but I'm telling you: something has shifted in her. Whereas before, she possessed a sort of confidence in her limbs and countenance, now there's doubt, and it flickers and looms and radiates out. Like she has somehow gotten smaller, like she has grown less sure of the world.

That shift in Finch just about breaks my heart. Because if your own child, the person for whom you've sacrificed everything, for whom you've broken laws as well as your own personal sense of boundaries, has lost confidence in you, and in turn, in themselves and the world at large, then what's the point of any of it?

Later on, Scotland appears. Shows up in the yard, sweating and out of breath. For the first time since I've known him, he looks old, squinting in the sunlight. Troubled. His jaw clenching, his angular face, which at this moment looks gaunt, somehow. "Got some bad news," he says, running his hand through his hair. "Come on over here, Cooper. Have a seat."

I've never seen him disturbed. Ruffled. Sweat beading on his brow and it's cold out here. "Cooper, it's bad." He pulls a newspaper, folded in thirds, from his back pocket. Part of a newspaper. "Look."

I reach out and take the paper. Open it up, and there, on the front page— No.

It's a picture of Finch and me, up in the treestand in the King of Trees.

Just below the picture, the headline: a single line, in large, bold, capital lettering.

WHO ARE THEY?

Knees weak, I slump onto the porch. Panic swelling, roaring at my ears: a thunderstorm, a train. Finch darts over, squeezes beneath my arm, reading, too.

Among the 2,381 images found from the missing Casey Winters' camera, investigators found one to be of particular interest: this photograph of a man and a girl. Winters' family confirms that they do not recognize either one, and now investigators are doubling down on their efforts and shifting their focus. . . .

I lean back against the post while Finch finishes the article. Close my eyes because everything is spinning and burning white. The sheriff. If he missed the Bronco—and I'm not sure that he did—he now has a second clue. He'll almost certainly recall that right around when Casey Winters disappeared, he had a run-in with us at the gas station.

"They've called in the FBI," Scotland says. "Cooper, the technology they have now." He begins pacing back and forth. "Twenty-four hours. That's what you have, max. Paper printed this morning. By tomorrow, they'll know—they'll know who you are. That you're here, close. They'll find you. Cooper, you have to do something, quick. No time to sit around."

I pull my knees to my chest.

"Facial recognition. They'll figure it out. You, Finch."

"What do you want me to say, Scotland?"

"I don't know. You got some kind of contingency plan?"

"A contingency plan for what? A girl wanders onto our land, takes our picture, then dies. Yes, *dies*." We hadn't seen him or told him yet. "Found her down in the valley. Yesterday. And—" I flash a glance at Finch, then motion for him to follow me to the side of the house. "It wasn't an accident. Someone did it. Killed her."

"Does Finch know?"

I nod. "She went down there looking for her."

He shakes his head. "Is she all right? I mean after seeing that."

"She's shook up."

"You need to talk to her. Help her sort it out."

"That's the least of my concerns." It shouldn't be, I see that, but for the moment there's no time. I tell him about the boyfriend, Finch seeing him hurt Casey Winters. "He saw her. Finch. Came after her." The words are spilling fast.

He shakes his head, takes in a sharp breath. Anger ripples across his face, the scar above his eyebrow glinting. He turns to the woods, looking. "Want me to stay? Help you keep watch here? Whatever you need. Just say the word."

Overhead, the December sky: an endless, swallowing blue.

Tired, that's what I am. Wore out. I've never wanted to be a person who gives up. A quitter. But there are times when a man has to assess a situation and call it. Fall back. Fold. "Naw. Appreciate the offer, though. And the heads-up."

"Well, if you're sure then I'll head home. Got my CB radio, and I'll be listening. Watching, too. If anyone's coming this way, I'll be here." He lumbers off across the yard and into the woods.

A twinge of guilt, for suspecting he might've been tangled up in Casey Winters's disappearance, for thinking he might betray us. "Thanks," I call after him, and he raises a hand.

A plan is swimming to me, piece by piece, and I hate it but once I've come to it—looked it in the face—I can see there is no other way. Which allows me some resolve. Some clarity. I'm well aware I'll need both.

THIRTY-TWO

There is a moment, in parachuting, when you must yield yourself to the pull of the earth. You're twenty, sometimes thirty thousand feet in the air. You've been breathing straight oxygen, trying to get all the nitrogen out of your system. You've got your pack and your parachutes; you've done everything you can to keep yourself alive. With HALO jumping, you step out of the airplane and you're sailing through the air, flying, but not really, because flight has a certain element of control. A certain beauty to it. Not so with HALO. You're dropping. You don't open the parachute until you've gone down thousands of feet and meanwhile you're going a hundred miles an hour through open sky.

The first few times, my instinct was to panic. I would think about what if the parachute didn't open, what if I got tangled up, couldn't open my arms and legs wide, what if I died. But after a while, I learned to like it. That feeling of letting go. Surrendering.

* * *

I tell Finch to climb in the Bronco.

"Are you going to the police station?"

"Yes, but not yet. We'll be back—there's just a quick thing I need to do."

"Can I take Walt Whitman?"

"Sure."

"Where are we going?" she asks as she scrambles into the back seat, Walt tucked beneath her arm.

"Need to make a phone call. Get a few things in order."

We drive to the gate. Unlock it, close it back up. Trundle over the dirt road, soft and rutted from the recent snowmelt: the ground, saturated and soft. On the paved road, Finch asks if we can listen to the radio, so I click on the music. We pull into the gas station, and I grab a handful of coins from my pocket and dial the number Marie wrote on a scrap of paper for me.

I explain to her, best I can, what has transpired, and ask her if she can come. To her credit, she doesn't ask a bunch of questions, doesn't tell me I should've reported seeing the girl days ago, like I promised. She just says she'll gather up a few things and be at the cabin by morning, and I think back to that first time Finch and me drove out to the very same pay phone and called Jake to tell him we were staying at the cabin. How he came right away. I hang up the phone and climb back into the Bronco.

"You know when I go in to tell them about the girl," I say to Finch as we head back home, "I won't be back."

In the back seat, she wrinkles her nose. "Well, you *might* be."

"No, Finch. I won't." Am I ready to tell her? If I go through with this, there won't be another chance. The world, all the secrets I've kept, this strange and precarious and beautiful life we've built, it's crumbling. Fast. I take a deep breath. "There's something you should know. Something I need to tell you. That thing I did, to keep us together? Well, there's more to it than that. People took you. And I had to get you back. But in order to do that, I hurt someone. And I tied the people up and left them and brought you here, to the woods. Which means I broke the law. And like I've told you, there are consequences for what I did. Serious ones. Years of prison."

"You did what you had to do." A line, memorized years ago.

I clear my throat. "There's more. The people who took you away—the people I tied up and left—they were your mother's parents. Your grandparents."

"I have *grandparents*?"

"You do."

"You never told me."

"Well. We didn't get along, exactly."

"I wouldn't get along with them either, then." She crosses her arms across her chest. There's reassurance in that gesture of defiance. Her spark: it's back.

"Nah. Me, they didn't like. They would've treated you different, though. They would've loved you, in their way."

"Still. It was wrong of them to want to take me away from you."

Was it? I look back now with a degree of clarity that my grief blinded me to, back then. I reach into the back seat and squeeze her knee. "Anyhow. I made choices and there's no going back on them now. The thing is, there are consequences for those choices, and going to the police means I need to face them. Which I'm ready to do."

Here's what I've come to realize. If this is the end, if I'm gonna lose Finch, I'd rather it be on my own terms. If that boy is left to his own devices, who knows what kind of madness might unfold.

But also, we run, we hide, the authorities find us: it'd be ugly. I'd be arrested, right in front of her. Maybe someone would get hurt. And that will be her final memory of me: fighting, getting carted off, handcuffed. This way, at least I have some control over the situation. Some dignity. At least I can say goodbye.

Finch pats my hand. "I think, Cooper, if you do the right thing, you'll be back. Everything will be all right."

"Finch, this isn't a storybook, where things turn out happy. That's not how things work out there. So when I tell you I'm not coming back, I need you to get that through your head. I need to know you won't be here waiting on me." At first, I told myself that there was a chance that I could go in there and inform them about the body, about the boyfriend, and they'd write stuff down and send me on my way. But of course that's not how it will go, not with our picture out there in the world. Not once they see me.

I won't be back. There's no returning to this life in the woods, and I need Finch to come to terms with that, to the degree that she can. The thought of her looking out the window, waiting, like she did for Jake, for the sound of my truck rounding the bend—

"Marie will be here in the morning," I tell her. "Once I'm gone, you'll pack up your things. Marie will drive you to your grandparents'. You'll be all right. Marie will make sure. And sugar, I want you to know that getting to live here in this place, getting to raise you—I wouldn't trade that for the world. All the things I've done in my life." The words catch in my throat. "Getting to be your dad, that is my greatest accomplishment."

I realize: I need to find Finch a poem. Something beautiful. Something she can lean into, once I'm gone. That's what she would pick: a poem. And so I look. Once she's tucked in—and tonight, it's a short process, though I want it to last. I want her to beg me to tell her a story of Cindy, or read a long time, but she's spent, and she kisses me on the cheek and turns over in her bed, back to me. I sit there awhile and take her in. The curvature of her spine, the small shoulders, the tangled blond hair. Can I really leave her? Is it really the right thing to do? Because at the moment, it sure as heck doesn't feel right.

I sneak out to the main room, leave the door cracked and secretly hope that she calls me back in for some reason, needs me. I add a fat piece of oak and stoke the fire. I open the cupboards and trace the rims of the plates and then run my hands along the red countertop. I start leafing through the books on the shelf in the main room. Page after page. Nothing is right. Nothing is perfect. And in this case, it has to be. It has to be precisely right. It can't be depressing. It can't be about the wrong type of love. It has to offer some kind of advice, even if it's not overt. It has to be about me, somehow. It has to be about Finch. It has to create a world. *"Oh, little girl, my stringbean."* No Anne Sexton. Sylvia Plath, I set to the side as well.

From the top shelf I pull a small book with a simple cover. *New and Selected Poems* by Mary Oliver and somehow in my eight years here I've never read it. I crack the spine. Jake's name on the inside cover. I begin leafing through the pages. Then, "The Summer Day."

Finch tumbling into the grass and stooping and soaking in the world. All her questions, all our days. This wild and precious life. I know it right away: this is the poem I will write in my crooked lettering and leave for my daughter before I get in my truck and drive to the end of myself.

THIRTY-THREE

For a while I lie on my bed, listening to Finch breathe, shuffle through the sheets. I crawl out and kneel next to her, stroke her blond hair, rest my palm on her back. The thought that this will be the last time I see her here in our home. That she will grow and shift. That every muscle and bone will expand and her looks will change and she will become someone I won't know. Maybe not even recognize. And that I will change, too. Not grow but be different all the same.

I can't go through with this. Can't. Won't.

I sit up. Crying hard now and shaking bad. I sneak out to the main room and slump into the couch and wipe my eyes with Finch's quilt, finished now: all those squares, all those pieces of things she wore. The blue and white dress from the summer she learned to walk. The yellow sweatshirt she wore all last winter. The pink onesie with an elephant. Cindy had picked that one out before Finch was born.

"It's not safe here anymore," I say aloud, to Cindy. The weight of her absence like a stone in my gut.

And even if it were safe, that's beside the point. Knowing that girl died a terrible death. Knowing her parents are out there, hoping she'll come home. Waiting. I wipe my face with my sleeve. "I can't just sit on it, what happened to her. It's not who I am. Who I want to be. For Finch and also for myself."

I rise from the couch, grab a box of matches and the flare, from the first time Scotland showed up in the yard, all those years ago. I unlock the front door, move the shovel at the handle, and step out into the night. For some reason the story in the Bible where Jesus is in the Garden of Gethsemane keeps roiling through my mind: Jesus asking God whether there is some other way. Not that I'm comparing myself to Jesus, mind you. But the wanting there to be an alternative. A different path. Some way to avoid the heartache that looms just ahead. Terrible feeling, to know that though it's not here yet, something bad is aiming toward you, lumbering its way closer. And to know that you do indeed have a choice: it's on you. You could decide not to. You could back out. You could run.

I step off the porch and lie down on the grass, stretch myself out and look up. The yard is bright, the moon almost full and the sky without clouds. The stars endless out here, visible and distinct. Orion, Taurus. Some assurance in the fact that the sky will stay unchanged. I don't look, but I know the hens are roosting, quiet and defenseless.

I set off the flare, the blaze shooting through the night. Which hopefully he is watching, this late. I grab some kindling and a few pieces of firewood from the porch and get a fire going in the ring. A final luxury, a campfire, just for the sheer pleasure of it. The warmth against the cold night air. I sit on a boulder and watch the embers lick the tinder. The sparks sail into the dark. No good to think about how this is the last time, but I do. Think about it.

How small my world has become, here. How simple and good. *Eight years of that, Coop. Peace and quiet and happiness. More than a lot of people get, really. You should be grateful.*

In a while, he is there, his figure moving toward me, illuminated by the light of the fire, his body casting a long shadow across the yard.

"Cooper?"

I think of the first time he showed up, right here, with the AK and the flare and the dead rabbit in his backpack and a crow hovering at his shoulder. "Thanks for coming," I say.

"You all right?"

"I got a favor to ask."

He settles onto a boulder across from me. His forehead damp with sweat, huffing a little. Must've hightailed it down here. "Sure. Anything."

"I'm heading to town, in the morning. Gonna tell them about the girl. Take them to her. Marie is on her way. She'll take Finch to her grandparents'." Funny how saying something out loud can bring such grief. It rises up, settles in my throat. "What I'd like from you is some help with the chickens. Can't leave them here. Don't want to set them loose in the woods, either. They won't last a single night."

He blinks, his face lit by the fire. Pain in his eyes, distress. "I could hide you. I know places. Let me help."

"Appreciate that, Scotland. More than you know." And I do. All these years of his spying and meddling—for the first time, I wonder if maybe all along what he wanted was to help us, in his own strange way. "With our picture out there, that changes everything for Finch and me. Like you said, FBI's probably already figured out who we are. Cindy's parents, if they think we're alive, they'll be looking. They'll relaunch the search, get our faces out, all over again. Every-where, just like before."

"You could go somewhere. Move. Start over."

"Nowhere to go, this time." I let the end of the stick catch fire. "We're backed into a corner. I did that to us, I know that. Time to face the music."

Scotland sits in silence, watching the fire. "Your mind's made up?"

I nod.

"You got pen and paper? I'd like to write Finch a little note if that's all right."

"Sure." I stand up, go into the cabin, and get a notebook and pen from the drawer.

I return to the fire, and he settles onto the porch and begins writing, his back propped against the front of the house. He's there a long time, staring into the night and writing, until at last he rises. "I'll set this on the table," he says, disappearing into the house.

He comes back. "Tell Finch—" His scar twitches, his face a constellation of grief.

"I'll tell her."

"I'll come by and get your chickens tomorrow."

"Wait till the afternoon, if you don't mind. Give Marie and Finch a chance to clear out of here. It's just—if she sees you."

"I understand. Tomorrow afternoon, then."

I surprise myself. Reach out and place my hand on his shoulder and wish for a moment that I hadn't chosen to hate him all these years. "Thanks."

"You take care now, neighbor."

And then he is gone.

I fall asleep for a while, and when I wake up, my back and neck are stiff, and the fire has died down to a heap of coals and it's cold. I drag myself up and stretch. Open the chicken coop and peer in. "You girls keep on with what you're doing. You'll be in a new home, but you'll be all right." I reach in and pat each one of them on the head, which they don't duck away because it's dark and they can't really see. "Bye now," I say.

Coop, you crazy old bird. Talking to chickens again and maybe even crying a little bit.

Marie arrives at first light. Finch is still asleep, but I'm on the porch, waiting. Drinking a hot cup of coffee, French pressed, because this is the last time. Last sunrise at the cabin, the woods turning red and then pink and then all of it yellowing, bright. Last time pumping water from the pump. Last scooping of coffee. Last everything.

She parks the Prius and steps out, and seeing me, runs. Wraps tight around me, body pressed close. I rest my chin on her forehead and breathe her in.

"I'm sorry," she says. "I'm sorry if I brought this on you."

"It wasn't you. Bad luck, that's all. And some bad decisions, years ago. But I'm gonna settle things. Make things right."

We stand there, the two of us, and I consider what might have been. How close we'd come to something like happiness, here, that week of Christmas. Its wings had brushed against us: an almost.

I press the piece of paper with the name and address for Finch's grandparents into her palm. "Judge is a piece of work. Mrs. Judge is worse." I kick at the gravel. "Tell them you found us here. That she's been cared for. Loved. All that. And also—tell them I'm sorry. If there's anything you can do. If you can help me have a chance to see her—"

Marie wraps her fingers around my hand. "Of course."

At eight, I say my goodbyes. Kneel down and fold my arms around Finch. She holds the note Scotland left on the table, pressed tight in her hand, but she won't look at me, just flat-out refuses. Stares straight ahead. I climb in the truck. Pull the door closed, roll the window down. Marie wipes her eyes with her sleeve and waves, and Finch stands there with her face buried in Marie's skirt. I gather my courage. Turn the key.

I drive away, slowly. Take a mental picture of the whole place in my mind. The cabin, clothesline, well pump, orchard, brambles. This place where I have grieved and toiled and also grown whole again. Marie and Finch in the yard: my second chance at happiness and I have no choice but to drive away from it. I watch it grow smaller in the rearview mirror and then Finch—Finch is chasing after me, all arms and legs. I step on the brake and pull the shifter into park and climb out.

She throws herself into my arms and wraps herself around me, squeezing hard. She nuzzles her face against my neck. Crying hard. "I changed my mind," she sobs. "I don't want you to go."

"Sugar, don't do this."

"Don't go. Please! I'm sorry. I'm sorry I said you should be ashamed of yourself. I didn't mean it. I was wrong, I take it back."

"You weren't wrong, sugar. Casey's parents. They deserve to know she's not alive. They deserve to know the truth. And Casey deserves justice. I have to do this, Finch. Not just for them. For you. And me."

"Marie could go."

"Even if she did, people will be looking for us. That picture. Finch—there's no other way." I try to pull away from her, but she clings tighter. I stand up and she doesn't budge. Wraps her legs tight, like a clamp.

"Daddy, please."

She has never called me that, and the way she says it—a plea, deep and desperate, barely a whisper. Makes me pause. Question everything.

Marie walks toward us. She places a hand on Finch's back. "Finch."

Finch shrugs her off. "Get away from me," she hisses.

"Let go now, Finch," I say gently, trying to keep my resolve. "Be a good girl."

She is crying so hard.

"Give me a hand," I say to Marie, and the two of us work together to pry Finch from me and she is screaming screaming screaming. I pull free and Marie has her. Sits down in the gravel and wraps her arms and legs around Finch, restraining her, and she's fighting hard, bucking and kicking and flailing, every ounce of her. A wild animal, vicious with rage.

I dash to the Bronco, climb in. Drive off and once I'm a hundred yards down the road, just about to curve out of sight, I look in the rearview mirror once more. Finch has fought free and is chasing me, and Marie is running after her and even above the roar of the engine I can hear Finch screaming, *Cooper, don't leave me! Cooper, don't!* and that's the last memory I'll have of my daughter out here: begging me to stay and me driving off and I think maybe I have never hated myself more.

THIRTY-FOUR

The night Jake and me were pinned down and he was dying and I killed the two people, darkness rolled in. After it was quiet for a bit, I slung Jake over my shoulder and started walking, tucked in close among the shadows of buildings and thinking we'd never make it but since we were out of water and had no means of contacting anyone, we had no choice but to try. That night, I was sure we would die, sure of it. Though I wasn't the religious type, I'd always believed there was an *after*. Answers you had to give, maybe. Explanations. I'm not saying heaven or hell per se, but a time of reckoning. My ugly soul would face what it had coming and there was no way to explain my way out of what I'd done, but even then I suspected there was a worse alternative, too: that living with the weight of my own actions would be its own sort of hell. Which it was. Is. We survived and I have relived what I did that day ten thousand times over, and I assure you, it has worsened now that I'm a father myself because becoming a parent—it makes something inside of you bloom and deepen. You love as you haven't loved before.

Once, months later when Jake was recovering and I was on leave, he said to me that he had a dream sometimes, that he was on that table dying, and two people brought him a cake with dates and nuts and it was so good that he thought he was at the entrance to heaven. "Probably all this morphine," he said as he lay on the hospital bed, hooked up to various machines. I didn't tell him that it wasn't a dream, not quite. I didn't tell him that there were terrible things from that day that he was lucky not to know about. That part of my saving his life was a deed that would haunt me the rest of my own miserable days. He was worth it: that's what I've told myself, all these years since. Better than me from the start and full of goodness and worth it.

I think about all of this as I head toward town. Twelve miles of woods, the gas station, a handful of country houses, more miles. Then town. Which, "town" seems too big a word for the place, tiny as it is. The card the sheriff gave Marie had a phone number and an address, 401 Main Street.

I pull into the only empty spot on Main Street, park the Bronco, and look for numbers on the buildings so I know which way to head. Nice little place, really. No stoplights. And every hundred yards or so, a metal bench beneath two Japanese maples. I walk past a brick building with wide steps and fancy columns: the library.

Just up the street, there's a commotion. Lots of people on the sidewalk, plus a van from a television station parked out front. A man leans against a building, smoking a cigarette.

"What's going on?" I ask him, motioning with my head.

"That girl who went missing before Christmas. They may have found her." He takes a drag from his cigarette.

"Yeah?" I try to sound nonchalant. I think back to the newspaper articles.

The man shakes his head. "Strangest thing. Early this morning, a guy shows up at the police station and says the girl's dead and he knows where the body is. Says he didn't do it but he'll take them right to her." Cigarette smoke shoots from his lips. Haven't smelled that for years and though I've never been a smoker, something about it feels good, then. "They're out there now," he says. "Sheriff and the deputy and a few other folks." He points toward the people up the street. "Everyone is waiting for them to come back."

"What?"

He gestures toward the building. "Guy has them out there now. In the woods."

How to process this. How to make sense. And is this man telling the truth. And who has reported the body and how did they find it. And are all those people out in our woods, stomping around and closing in on Finch and Marie. "Did the guy say where the body was?"

The man with the cigarette shrugs. "Close to national forest land, I think." He slides his sunglasses off and squints at me with his light blue eyes. "That's not all of it, though. Those people from the missing girl's camera. The man and little girl. Do you know what I'm talking about? It was in the paper. A photograph, bunch of fuss over who they were."

I adjust my sunglasses, grateful he doesn't recognize me.

He takes one last drag from his cigarette and then drops it to the sidewalk and twists his foot over it. "The guy says they were squatting on his land so he killed them. He brought evidence. Dog tags from the man. A tooth, from the little girl." He spits to the side. "Says he saved them as a memento. Makes me sick to even say that out loud. Local guy. Psychopath, right here in our midst. Of all the places."

I can feel it coming, barreling hard: a panic attack. The sun is too bright, the sidewalk, too. The buildings and cars begin to sway back and forth; they blur and shift. I lean against the building and grip the bricks. "You got another smoke, man?"

He looks at me, seems to think about it, then reaches into the pocket of his shirt and pulls out a cigarette and a lighter. "You all right?" he asks, handing them to me.

I nod. Light up and take a small puff. "The bodies," I say. "What did he do with the bodies?"

"Says he had these bugs that eat the flesh off things. Let them have at it, then dumped the bones in the river. At least that's his story."

"Who was it?" I say, when I finally catch my breath.

"Taxidermist. Lives north of here. Long time ago, he was a preacher. Then he lost his wife and daughter. Car accident, he was driving. Tattooed their pictures on his arms and then went off to live in the woods. Been a little strange ever since, I guess. Never went anywhere. Local lady took him his groceries. Left them on his porch. But nobody thought much of it. I mean, who wouldn't be a little strange after that, right? Everyone assumed he was harmless." He shrugs his shoulders. "Did a buck for me, one year. Ten-point, nicest one I ever got." He slides another cigarette out and lights it. "He always did good work. I mean as a taxidermist."

"What was his name?" I ask, taking a deeper drag. My hands are shaking hard, the cigarette trembling at my lips.

"Marcus Barnes was his name," the guy says, "but I only ever heard people call him Scotland."

THIRTY-FIVE

Finch. I stumble back to the truck, the sun dizzying and my mind trying to sort it all out but maybe it can't. Because it's too much, this. If it's true. If he did. What it means. And at the center of it all: why?

But before any of that, Finch.

Finch and Marie are packing up the cabin or maybe already packed up and on their way to Judge and Mrs. Judge and I will never catch them and then what. I go back to the cabin and live there by myself for the rest of my life? Or steal Finch back? Again?

I shouldn't have left her. Crying and begging me to stay and then chasing after me. What kind of father does that to his only child, love of his life, center of his world. I should've packed up, like Scotland said. Moved. Hid. Gone to the caves, camped until next winter. I shouldn't have left her and now maybe I've lost her forever.

I drive fast, the old Bronco roaring, its engine pushing harder than it should. Hot, the thermostat climbing and it might burn up the engine, but it doesn't matter. Nothing matters but Finch. Past the little houses. I slow at the gas station, the parking lot full. Never noticed on my first pass through. Two white vans with the names of television stations painted on their sides. Three police vehicles. People standing around the parking lot. I try not to look.

I pull onto the dirt road, still miles from home, and slow a bit. The shale loud beneath the tires, dust sailing behind me. Watching for Marie's car coming toward me. Hoping I'm not too late.

At last I come to the gate. It's closed. Locked. Which could mean they haven't left. Slow packing, maybe. Finch pitching a fit or dragging her feet. Both possible. Or it could mean that they scuttled out of there quickly. That they've already left and closed the gate behind them and they are long gone. Panic swells, but I force myself to stay focused. Get home. Breathe in, breathe out. I breathe her name. In, out: Finch, Finch.

I round the final bend and the cabin comes into sight and Finch is sitting on the steps of the porch, wrapping twine around the handle of one of her bone knives. When she sees me, she rises, dashing toward the truck. I turn off the ignition and run toward her and lift her and press her tight to my chest.

"You came back," she says, snuggling close, squeezing hard. A tear spills and twirls its way down her cheek. "I knew you'd come back." Her lip quivers.

"It wasn't supposed to be like this." The words catching. "Something changed."

She pulls back and tilts her head to the side. "Are you all right?"

Marie runs toward us from the porch. Confused, concerned. "What happened?"

I set Finch down. "I think Scotland told them about the girl. I think he took them to her."

Finch bites her lip. "Are people still looking for you and me?"

"I don't know."

She glances at Marie. "But I thought since the girl took our picture, we weren't safe. That people would be looking for us."

How to put it, how to explain. "I think he took care of that, too."

Finch kicks at a stone. "How?"

I stand up. "It's a long story, but I think he figured out a way to protect us. To let us be together. Sacrificed himself in the process. Listen, there's something I need to check on." I head for the house. If it's true, what the man said about Scotland bringing in evidence, my dog tags and Finch's tooth will be missing from the Raisinets tin.

I push open the door, stride to the stove, reach for the tin on the shelf. I pry off the lid, and a folded piece of paper tumbles out onto the floor. I reach down and pick it up. A letter.

Dear Cooper,

If you are reading this, you've come back, which means you've gone to town to report finding Casey Winters and you've learned about my decision to go to the police. I suspect you're now contemplating whether to come in and set the record straight and rescue me, because, though you can't seem to see it yourself, you are a good man, deep down, Cooper.

With the campsite and the body, they will sort through what happened to Casey Winters, I'm confident of that. And with my "confession," combined with the evidence I supplied, they should have sufficient reason to close the books on you and Finch. In other words, no more dashing to the root cellar. No more hiding.

I know that right now, you feel it's unjust for me to carry this burden on your behalf. But Cooper, there is a word for such unmerited favor. That word is "grace." The thing about grace is that you don't deserve it. You can't earn it. You can only accept it. Or not.

This was my decision. I know the consequences, and I have no regrets. Doing this for you and Finch—it is my great honor and my final wish, and I hope and pray that you will choose to accept.

Your neighbor and friend,
Marcus Scotland Barnes

P.S. "Greater love hath no man than this, that a man lay down his life for his friends." John 15:13.

P.P.S. Sorry for taking Finch's tooth. It was the only way.

Well.

I fold the letter back up. Tuck it in my pocket. Look for the dog tags and tooth. Of course they aren't there. And then I start walking. Into the jack pines, my feet quiet on the soft, brown needles. West, up and over the hill behind the house, moving fast and not knowing where, exactly, not having a plan, but on the way there I realize I'm heading toward the valley.

Scotland. All those times he appeared in the yard. All the gifts for Finch. The bones and skulls, gleaming and white. The flesh-eating bugs. The tattoos on his arms. The Bible verses, too. All of it. All the things I'd imagined him to be. All the things I'd said and thought and wanted to do to him. Wrong, wrong, wrong. Had I really misread him for so many years?

I arrive at the overlook, hunker down. Down in the valley, a whole gang of people at work. Parked where the ground is solid are two pickup trucks and a Jeep, which I recognize as the vehicle of the sheriff who was at the gas station when Finch and me did our supply run, who also gave Marie his card that day we hid in the root cellar. There's yellow caution tape strung around the area where the body was. My eyes scan the gathering, searching for Scotland. At last, in the back seat of one of the pickups, I see the profile of someone sitting, the window open just enough to let in some fresh air. It has to be him.

I slump to the ground. Pull the letter from my pocket, unfold it, and start reading again, wanting to make sense of it. Wanting, too, to take back the years where I looked at him sideways and called him names and got so bent out of shape about him sneaking up on us in the yard.

Rustling in the leaves close by. My heart shoots into my throat. *Whip-poor-will.*

Finch emerges from the trees, sweaty and out of breath. She collapses next to me. "I couldn't keep up," she says.

"How'd you know where to find me?"

She shrugs. "Where else would you go?"

I sling my arm around her shoulder and pull her closer, and we sit in silence, our backs against a rock. A breeze pushes in, bending the trees overhead.

I think back to what I observed at the campsite. The bloody skillet, the wound. Most likely, the boyfriend's DNA was all over that place, and Scotland would be cleared when it came to Casey Winters. Down in the valley, where the old logging road ends, an ambulance is parked, and two men are loading a stretcher with a body bag.

"Is he down there?" Finch asks, finally.

"I saw someone sitting in the back of a vehicle. I think it's him."

"Cooper?"

"Yeah?"

"I like the poem you picked for me."

I nod. "I'm glad."

For a long time, we sit in silence. Then Finch stands up and brushes her pants off, pine needles sticking to them. "You ready to go back?" she asks, reaching out her hand. "Marie's waiting."

I've always believed that if something was meant to happen, you'd have a second chance at it. But never have I been so bold as to believe in a third or even a fourth chance. Almost like the world was trying to hand you something good after all it had dealt you your whole life was heartache, like it had changed its position on who you were and what you could have. Call it what you will: karma or good luck or maybe something more. Grace.

I pull myself up and take one last glance over the cliff to where, just over a week ago, a young girl showed up and veered into our lives. The ambulance carrying her body is pulling away, disappearing into the pines, the flashing lights and white fading behind the trees. The truck with Scotland remains parked, and I can still see his profile in the back seat. "Thank you," I mutter, and though I know he can't hear me, I hope that somehow he can feel it, my acceptance. My gratitude.

Finch holds out her hand, and I wrap my large palm around her smaller one. Days and days and more days. That's what I thought I didn't have, and now I do, again. We walk quietly, hand in hand,

Finch and me, back through the beds of pine. As we come to where the trees end, Finch stops, gasps. She points ahead, to our yard, to Marie on the steps of the porch, arm stretched out and calling softly to a black bird with a red band on its leg, hovering close and considering a landing: a crow.

EPILOGUE

I'm nearly there now, the car my grandparents bought me as a graduation present growling over the long, gravel road that leads to home. I'm getting close and I can feel it—the pull of the woods. The murmur of the river, the pines swaying overhead, the oaks tossing their leaves. The birds and their familiar songs. All of it, beckoning. Even after the year with my grandparents, the first year of college, too, it is still here, in the woods where I have crawled and walked and run and climbed, that I can find respite from the noise of the world. It is the place where, as Jake apparently once told Marie about my father and as my father later relayed to me, I can get my footing.

Cooper will be waiting. Marie, too. The year I turned eleven, she sat Cooper and me down at the little table and said that, with our blessing, she'd like to sell Jake's house and move in with us. A month later, she arrived with her belongings and three crates of books. She and Cooper exchanged vows and the three of us had a wedding.

It was Marie, mostly, who paved the way for my entry into the world beyond the cabin. I was fourteen when she initially broached the topic. Specifically, she pointed out that there were significant benefits to be had from my connecting with my grandparents. My father didn't budge on this until I turned sixteen, which, knowing Marie's wisdom in such matters, may have been her goal all along.

Perhaps the sixteen years that had passed since they'd lost my mother as well as me had softened them. Alternatively, maybe my grandparents were never quite as cruel and impenetrable as my father had perceived them to be. There was the initial shock, of course. For all of us. But the truth is that by the time I was sixteen, I was growing more and more restless for answers, for connection with the outside world, and I was willing to face whatever awkwardness might ensue. As Cooper predicted, it didn't take long for them to accept me. They were good to me. They are good to me still. We've come to an agreement not to speak of my father at all, and that has helped.

The same year I met my grandparents, I enrolled at the local high school, where Marie had been working as a librarian since I was thirteen. I entered as a junior. I loved learning, but I have to confess: I hated that place. Academically, I thrived. Socially, not so much. Despite my grandmother's provision of stylish attire, makeup, and a haircut, I never managed to fit in there. College has been better. People are much more forgiving than in high school, much less judgmental. They're interested in my unique upbringing, and my friends understand that sometimes certain places are too loud, too full for me, and that I must slip away.

There are days when I find my mind drifting to the girl in the woods. Not often, but sometimes. It has been over a decade now, and what I wonder is this: what life, in the woods or elsewhere, might she have lived? Would we have become friends? How long would she have stayed? Sometimes, even now, I envision her as Ovid's Daphne, who, just as Apollo was about to overtake her, slipped from those forceful hands and metamorphosed into a laurel tree.

I think, more often, of Scotland, the neighbor from my childhood, a man whose face has grown vague to me over the years, as much as I try to hold on to it. When I was twelve and could still remember him vividly, my father told me the truth about what he'd done. I took the news hard. I never got to say goodbye, I never got to say thank you, and knowing what had happened to him hung heavily on me. For a long time that knowledge burdened me, but over time, Cooper and Marie helped me understand that Scotland never would've wanted that for me. That, rather, if we accepted his gift, if we lived life as he must've pictured it for us, then we honored not only his final wish but the sacrifice itself. Marie pointed me to the words of Scotland himself: *The thing about grace is that you don't deserve it. You can't earn it. You can only accept it. Or not.*

Lately I've been pondering my father's decisions to get me from my grandparents and head to the woods. Would I have done the same thing? I like to think that I'm not so instinctive, but perhaps if I were about to lose the one and only thing I considered dear in this life, I might surprise myself. I've thought, too, about the childhood I might've had at my grandparents' sprawling home—the people who might've buzzed in and out of my world, the abundance of toys and clothes and opportunities that would've been at my fingertips—all of it punctuated by occasional visits with my father.

I never wish for that life.

I pull into the front yard and turn off the engine. Cooper is waiting on the porch, whittling, and he sets the knife to his side and rises. Starlings have gathered in the yard between us, pecking at seed or maybe crumbs that Marie has tossed for them. I step out of the car and for a moment I watch. I step closer and then—I can't say why, and I know I am nineteen and too old for it, but the impulse takes hold and I let it—I dart ahead, rushing into them. They take flight, the sound of their wings like a thousand heartbeats, whirling at first in chaos but then they are overhead, a hundred black spots lifting into a broad, blue sky: separate but also together, in some kind of magical union, soaring higher and higher and then out of sight.

ACKNOWLEDGMENTS

Writing this book was a spiritual endeavor for me. I spent count-less hours praying, walking in the woods, and sorting out the sto-ries that these characters were meant to live. Eventually, the time came to bring other readers into the fold, and by the point it is in its published state, this work will have passed through many generous hands. My heartfelt gratitude goes out to all those who've helped make this book into what it is today:

To my dear friend and always-first-reader, Bethany Spicher Schonberg, who, long before anyone else set eyes on this story, read it and told me that it was good. I'm deeply grateful for your literary guidance and friendship, and for all the delicious vegetables as well.

To Beth Loretto and Lauren Salinas, thank you for your will-ingness to read a very unpolished manuscript early on and offer feedback. I'm thankful for your time and support.

To Heather Holleman, for reading and planting the idea that the story shouldn't end where it did. You are always such a beacon of encouragement and wisdom.

To later readers, Megan Bridgwater and Corrie Passavant, who, despite their many commitments, said *yes* to reading a late draft very quickly. More importantly, thank you for your longtime love and friendship.

To my agent, Amy Cloughley, who read and read and read again. You offer patience and wisdom at every turn, and I'm so grateful to have you on my team.

To Sarah Grill, editor extraordinaire, whose indefatigable efforts made this a better book, and whose high standards made me a better writer. Thank you for believing in me and for embracing this book with such vigor.

Thank you to Terry McGarry, whose incredible attention to detail helped me iron out my oversights and errors.

Thanks, too, to the rest of the team at Minotaur—Kelley Ragland, Andrew Martin, Paul Hochman, Allison Ziegler, Hector DeJean, David Rotstein, Lisa Davis, and Cathy Turiano—who welcomed this novel with such enthusiasm and warmth.

To my friend who reviewed sections on serving in the War on Terror: thank you for helping me to render that experience more accurately. Thank you, even more, for your many years of service and for the endless sacrifices you made along the way.

To my parents, who always believed in me, and who never once told me I should consider pursuing some other more reliable or useful occupation.

To my husband, Chris, for believing in this book from the get-go, but more importantly, for tolerating the fact that my being a writer means I often choose to spend time with made-up people instead of with you. Thank you for loving me and supporting what I do.

To Hudson and Holt, who inspired so many of the scenes and lines in this book. You will always be my favorite and most brilliant creations.

Soli deo gloria.